THE GEMS OF DESTINY

LUCY KHAN

All correspondence to the author:
khanlucy2016@gmail.com

© Copyright Lucy Khan

First Printed in Australia, 2024

Cover artwork by Miblart.

Reference:
The Holy Bible, New International Version® NIV®
Copyright © 1973, 1978, 1984, 2011 by Biblica, Inc.®
Used by Permission of Biblica, Inc.® All rights reserved worldwide.

The right of Lucy Khan to be identified as the author of this work
has been asserted by her in accordance with the Copyright,
Designs and Patents act. All rights reserved.

ISBN: 978-9-694-49208-7

Proudly produced by

TheBookStudio

www.thebookstudio.com.au

To Kelly, Larissa, Luana, Cat, Isis, Jendy and Phil.
Thanks for your support, advice and help
with the creation of this book.

And to God, for everything he has done in my life.
Thank you.

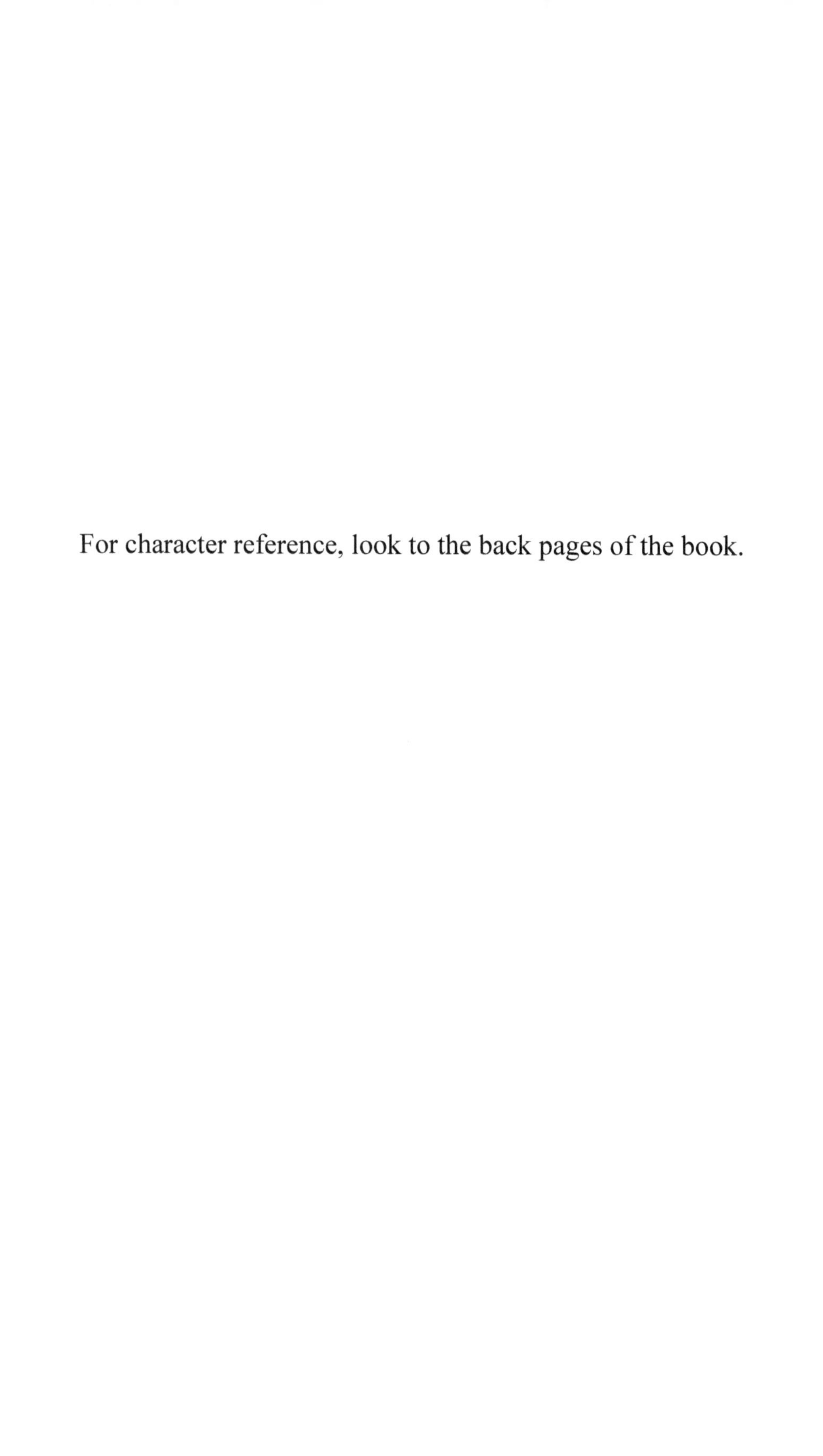

For character reference, look to the back pages of the book.

PROLOGUE

As the sun sets over the horizon, deep in the jungle just west of the Kingdom of Elaxon, a cave is unknown to man's eyes. Only when one is looking for it, will he find it. Deep in the cave lies a dark secret that will affect the four kingdoms. By working together, they will conquer evil; alone, they will fail. Crows caw at their mistress's arrival as she walks confidently over to the fire, book in hand, speaking just above a whisper to the contents of the book. The flames turn a dark red with a hint of black. She smiles as she watches the flames rise. Capturing the fire in her hands, she turns towards the back of the cave. In the cave's darkness, the fire captures a lone figure, hands bound, sitting by the cave walls. She slowly lifts the prisoner's face to meet hers. Their eyes meet briefly before she places the flames into his chest. The prisoner grimaces for a moment before opening his eyes again to reveal the blackness in them.

CHAPTER ONE

*"For it is by grace you have been saved, through faith
and this is not from yourselves, it is the gift of God."*

Ephesians 2:8

"Medical team, evacuate the injured now," yelled Captain Issac.

"Quick, everyone, gather as many people as possible," Juliet told her medical team.

They all cautiously scattered around the battlefield, trying to escape the fight and find people to save. Juliet looked around and saw her medics dragging people away from the battlefront. The sky was black with smoke, as a storm of arrows buzzed and hissed through the air from the front lines. Men hollered and wailed as arrows penetrated their skin, while others who were not affected ran to the front line to engage the enemy. Swords clashed as though it were thundering. The sound of the injured grew as the battle wore on. Juliet spotted one of her soldiers near the front line who had an injured leg. Blood gushed from his wound as he tried to crawl away from the battlefront. Juliet was about to go and help him when someone grabbed her arm.

"Where do you think you're going, Princess Juliet? It's dangerous," Captain Issac said.

"Dangerous! What about my medical team? It's dangerous for them as well," Juliet protested. "These are my people, and I want to help them."

The Captain looked at the Princess, debating whether to let her help. He sighed.

"Fine, but you'll go with protection; otherwise, the Queen will have my head," he said.

"Thank you," Juliet smiled, relieved to be able to help.

The Captain gestured for two men to follow and protect Juliet on the battlefield. Juliet followed the two soldiers into the battlefield with their swords drawn and her medic bag in her hands. Sadness and grief overwhelmed her, as she witnessed so many people suffering. Blood covered the ground, as well as the bodies of those who had fallen. Juliet quickly scanned the area for the fallen soldier she had seen before. But her eyes were wet from crying, so she had trouble finding his location.

"Help," Juliet heard a faint cry. "Over here."

Juliet turned at the sound from behind her, and ran to where she thought she had heard it from. She found the injured soldier trying to drag himself to safety. The wound on his leg looked worse. The blood was a strong odour to which she felt nauseated. She immediately dropped to her knees and removed her supplies from her medical bag.

"Princess, why are you here?" the solider asked worried.

"I'm here to help you, but you have to be quiet," Juliet said, and he nodded in acknowledgement.

While attending to his wounded leg, the two guards stood ready to fight and protect the Princess. All around them, soldiers were fighting to the death. Blood filled the earth, and the smell of death had worsened with every kill. Juliet suddenly heard arrows fly through the wind, then soldiers hollering, and a thud as the arrow heads found their mark. Hoping it wasn't near them, she quickly finished bandaging the soldier's wound.

"I need you to help me get this man up?" Juliet asked her two guards, to which none of them replied. Juliet turned around to find them both on the ground, their blood-soaked shirts marking where the arrows had hit. Their eyes were wide, and their last expression was that of shock. Juliet looked up to see their killer. The King of Zolatta's son, Prince Nikolai, stood only meters away from her with his bow and arrow aimed at her. He was ready to shoot. His black hair was dirty and covered with sweat, and his white shirt was stained with blood. Whether it was his or someone else's, she didn't know. Her heart caught in her throat; she could barely breathe. She was terrified this was going to be her end. Her mother would be devastated, but she could see something as she looked into the Prince's eyes. Was it sadness or fear? Surely, not the enemy. He stood there staring at her, then lowered his bow and arrow. He did not move from his position.

Why didn't he shoot me? To him, I am the enemy Juliet thought. Nikolai saw something to his left from the corner of his eye and ran over to Juliet. She screamed as she tried to shield herself, but nothing came. Slowly looking up, Juliet saw the arrows that were intended for her, were protruding from Nikolai's leg and shoulder. Juliet looked up into his green eyes as he knelt in front of her. She saw him grimacing in pain. Before Juliet could say anything, he stood up quickly and backed away, but not before she heard him whisper something to her.

"Run."

Juliet watched Nikolai run off into the battlefield, despite the arrows protruding out of him. She looked down towards the soldier she was trying to help, and realised he had fallen unconscious. Juliet felt the side of his neck for a pulse, and was relieved he was still alive. But he wouldn't be for long if she couldn't get him out of here soon. She heard Captain Issac calling her name.

"Princess," Captain Issac yelled, running up to her.

Juliet turned to see him with two of his soldiers running not far behind. She turned back and quickly packed up her medic bag before they arrived. Once Captain Issac arrived, his men carried the injured soldier back to safety while Captain Issac stayed beside Juliet, armed and ready to protect her. Suddenly she heard screams coming from behind her.

"Run and don't stop until you're back at the palace," Captain Issac ordered, returning to the battlefield.

Juliet turned back to the battlefield to find an enormous beast attacking the men. Its claws ripped through the men as if they were rag dolls. Its ears twitched continuously, as it tried to find its prey through sound. Its mouth dripped with saliva as it growled at its target. Its fur, white as snow, was mixed with red as it killed more of her soldiers. This creature was indeed a monster from a nightmare. She couldn't believe her eyes, all those stories she heard the men tell in the infirmary were true. She didn't want to consider it; her enemy had control over a Fox spirit.

CHAPTER TWO

"Do not fear, I will help you."

Isaiah 41:13

10 years ago.

"My sweet child." Juliet opened her eyes to see her mother, Julia, staring down at her.

"Mum," she yawned.

"Follow me, my child; I would like to show you something," Queen Julia said, leaving the room. Juliet quickly and quietly got her dressing gown on, and followed her mother into the castle library. Her mother picked up a book from the table and gestured to her daughter to sit. She looked up at her mother who looked worried.

"What's wrong, mother?" Juliet asked.

Queen Julia turned to the table, retrieved a small box, and gave it to her daughter.

"Happy birthday, Juliet," her mother smiled. Juliet opened the box to see a beautiful sparkling blue sapphire Gem inside, shaped like a teardrop. It sparkled in the morning sun, as she held it up for

11

a proper look. It was attached to a necklace, as was her mother's. It was beautiful, and before Juliet could thank her mother, she spoke.

"My child," she said, sitting beside her daughter. "Every firstborn child in my family receives their sapphire Gem on their 10th birthday."

"Why us?" Juliet asked with curiosity.

"To help people," she replied as she took the Gem from her daughter's hand, and placed it around her neck. "This Gem gives us the power to heal others."

Juliet looked at her mother with amazement. "Really!"

"Yes, and if you choose to, you can start learning how to heal others," Queen Julia said, smiling at her daughter.

"Yes, please," Juliet replied, nodding happily. "Why don't other kingdoms have any?" she asked curiously.

"They do, but not our Gem. They have their special Gem which is passed down from their own families," her mother explained.

"Huh," Juliet sat thinking, "Who made the Gem's for us to use."

Queen Julia smiled at her daughter. "He has many names, but we call him the God of Light."

✦ ✦ ✦ ✦ ✦

"Princess Juliet," a voice echoed.

Juliet snapped back into the present; her hands clasped around her Gem. Looking around the infirmary, the smell of blood and sweat filled the room. Hundreds of wounded soldiers lay in small cots, while the nurses attended to their wounds.

"Princess Juliet," someone called again. Juliet looked around the room to find one of her students calling for her. She walked over to him and looked down at the wounded soldier he was attending to.

"This is beyond me; he'll need your healing gift," he whispered.

Juliet nodded and moved toward the wounded soldier.

"Your Highness," the man spoke up. "Thank you for what you did on the battlefield." She looked down to see that it was the man she had saved with the wounded leg.

"I'm happy to help," she replied.

Juliet moved towards his wounded leg to get a closer look; the wound was much bigger than she had thought. She hovered her hands just above his leg, which needed healing and concentrated on the power of her sapphire Gem. The bright blue light radiated from her hands to his wound. It would take longer for her to heal and more concentration, as the injury had worsened. But that was okay as she had gotten much better at healing since the war started, and her mother constantly taught her every day, so she could get stronger.

As time passed, Juliet started to feel tired. That was the downside of healing someone; it took away your energy. But it didn't bother her because she loved to help others.

"Still can't get used to that," the wounded soldier laughed. Juliet smiled and looked down to check the wound; it had healed completely and without complications.

"All done, get some rest and food, and you'll be fine," she said.

"Thanks, Princess," he said.

"You're welcome," she replied smiling.

There was silence as Captain Issac walked into the infirmary. He stood at the front with his hands clasped behind his back; he looked worn down and tired.

"The enemy is retreating for the night," he addressed everyone.

There were cheers around the infirmary, but silence soon followed as they realized that the war was far from over, and they had lost too many good soldiers.

"Princess Juliet, your mother wishes to see you," Captain Issac said, approaching her.

"Thank you, Captain Isaac," Juliet said. Night had fallen when Juliet exited the infirmary. There were still people around helping the wounded. Women and children gathered on the streets, to mourn the loss of their fallen partner, brother, or friend. It saddened her to see so much pain caused by the war.

When will this end? How did it start? Juliet thought. She will have to ask her mother another day when she has a clear head, but she was happy with food and rest for now. As Juliet entered the castle, one of her maids approached her.

"Your mother is waiting in the dining area," she informed, bowing and gesturing for Juliet to follow her. Once Juliet entered the dining area, Queen Julia embraced her with tears.

"I was so worried. I heard about what happened on the battlefield," she cried.

"I'm okay. Captain Issac was there," she stated.

"Oh, bless him," sighed Queen Julia. Juliet looked at her mother, and for a moment, she saw admiration in her eyes. Her smile grew, and Juliet suddenly realized what was happening.

"Have you told him how you feel, Mother?" Juliet asked her.

Her mother blushed and looked away, sighing as if remembering a distant memory.

Since her father died when she was young, Juliet has no memories of him. She does have memories of Issac before he became The Captain of the Royal Guard. He always taught Juliet new things. He taught her horse riding, archery, and even knife throwing. But she always remembers how her mother and Issac admired each other from after. And when they spoke, they never spoke casually; it was always formal.

"I fear it may be too late, my dear," Queen Julia said, wiping a tear away.

"Mother, it's never too late for love," she replied.

There was a knock at the door, and Juliet and Queen Julia both turned to see Captain Issac coming through the door.

"Your Highness," he bowed to both. "I've come to report."

Queen Julia gestured her hand to the table. "Come, join us for dinner Captain, and we can talk."

"As you wish, Your Highness," Captain Issac said bowing, before moving to a vacant chair. As Queen Julia and Captain Issac talked about the war's progress, Juliet sat across from them, looking at them curiously. Her mother had her brunette hair braided, with flowers embedded throughout. She noticed she only wore them when she wanted to look her best.

Juliet smiled to herself.

Her mother was beautiful even as she reached her late thirties. She watched Captain Issac speak gently to her mother; he was always very calm with her, even with the most frustrating topics. He was like a father to Juliet, and she would not have minded him marrying her mother.

Captain Issac became The Captain of the Royal Guard at twenty-five. He had shown promise during his training, and was chosen to be the next Captain after the previous Captain had passed. He was well built and muscular, and had brunette hair and eyes. He always looked after his men, and never left anyone behind.

"I don't know how much more this kingdom can take," Captain Issac sighed, rubbing his chin, his stubble showing, he hadn't shaven for days.

"I know," Queen Julia sighed. "I'm not sure what else to do."

"There is a way," Captain Issac placed his hands onto Queen Julia's. "A marriage alliance."

Queen Julia's hands pulled away quickly as if she had burnt herself. "No," she said, tears forming in her eyes.

Captain Issac sighed. "It may be the only way."

Queen Julia exited her chair and left the room in a heartbeat. Once the doors were closed, Captain Issac turned to Juliet.

"She loves you, you know," Juliet told him.

"I know," he said. "But I'm just a soldier, not a royal; I can't bring anything to this Kingdom."

Juliet thought for a moment before talking again.

"Back when I was young, you told me you were a wanderer. Travelling worldwide, experiencing things others could only dream of, but you stopped here and settled. Maybe the reason why you haven't left just walked out of the room." Juliet said, standing up and walking out the door, smiling to herself.

✦ ✦ ✦ ✦ ✦

Juliet walked back to her bed chambers to sit by the fire. It was a cold evening, and her maid had just tended to it. She smiled, wrapping her arms across her chest as the heat surrounded her. Juliet thought of all her people without a roof over their heads due to the war and shivered. She couldn't sit here warm while her people were freezing. She needed to move and think of something to do for her people. As the future Queen, it was her duty. She thought about the palace Chapel and stood up. She grabbed a jumper and walked out of her room. It was just after seven in the evening, and the corridors were empty. Wrapping her jumper around her, she started towards the palace Chapel.

The Chapel was a small space at the castle's edge, surrounded by a beautiful garden that the priest and his helpers looked after. Juliet walked up the steps, looking towards the brick arch that welcomed the people and smiled. Flowers had grown over and around the archway and down the sides. They had bloomed pink and white roses. Juliet had always loved the Chapel. The details done by the builders, made this a special place, and it was astounding. She had always dreamed of having her wedding here, with the flowers in bloom and decorations inside and out, making it an extraordinary day. She sighed as she walked through the arch and into the building. Row upon rows of chairs faced the front, and further back there stood a high table where the priest would put his books and notes for the week's service. The Chapel was built for everyone; the people in the palace and the people in town. They all use this Chapel to thank and pray to their Creator, the God of Light.

The God of Light made and gave different types of Gems to each kingdom royalties, to protect and help others. The Gem is then passed down through generations, ensuring that the King and Queen will continue to defend their Kingdom and their people. Each royalty goes through unique training by their predecessors, to ensure they can control the Gem's power, as each Gem can protect their own Kingdom or destroy it.

"Princess Juliet," Priest John greeted bowing.

Juliet smiled and gave him a bow in return. She then walked over to one of the chairs and sat. She needed to be alone to think, and this was the one place that calmed her.

"God of Light, what can I do?" Juliet prayed silently.

Juliet felt upset that she couldn't do anything. Fear and anxiety crept into her mind at the thought of losing this war.

She sighed.

"Anything I can help with, Princess Juliet?" Priest John asked. Juliet looked up to see Priest John standing at the end of the row of chairs, with a book in his hand.

Juliet smiled. "Just trying to figure out how to stop this war. As future Queen, I feel it's my responsibility. I keep praying and waiting for a sign, but I'm having trouble concentrating," Juliet replied.

"Would you like me to pray for you?" he asked.

"That would be nice," she said smiling.

Juliet closed her eyes as she listened to the words Priest John declared to their Creator. His faith was strong; she could tell by how he spoke and prayed. She envied him. She loved the Creator but had doubts now and then.

"Creator, listen to your daughter as she speaks from her heart to you. Guide her to do what is right and according to your will. We pray for all those suffering from this war and ask you to show us a way to end it. Amen," Priest John finished.

"Amen. That was beautiful," Juliet praised. "I wish my faith were strong like yours."

He looked at her silently, hoping to hear why she thought that.

Juliet sighed. "I love our Creator, but I have been having doubts lately."

"It's perfectly normal to have doubts," Priest John said. "We are human after all. It's also good to ask questions about our Creator, as it deepens our faith."

Juliet suddenly had a thought. She's had this thought over the past few days but was too preoccupied to listen. It suddenly dawned on her how she could help her people.

"By the look on your face, I'm guessing your prayer has been answered," Priest John laughed.

"This thought came to me days ago, but I was too preoccupied to listen," Juliet explained standing up. "Thank you, priest John, I know how to help my people." She quickly bowed to him and rushed out of the Chapel.

Juliet ran down the steps and through the palace corridors until she reached her mother's bed chambers. She knocked on the door quickly and waited eagerly to be let in. One of her mother's maids greeted her.

"Princess Juliet," she greeted bowing.

"I need to speak to my mother, please," Juliet stated.

She nodded to her and opened the door. Juliet walked through the door and into her mother's bedroom. She saw her sitting on the bed, wiping away unwanted tears. Juliet sat down next to her mother and took her hands.

"I will do the marriage alliance," Juliet whispered to her mother.

Her mother looked at her daughter in shock.

"I want this war to end, and I know you do too," Juliet said smiling.

"Oh, my darling daughter," she cried holding her hands. "Do not give up your happiness to save mine."

Juliet smiled at her mother and sighed.

"As the princess, and future queen, I want to do this for my people and my family," Juliet told her mother. "We must put our trust in our Creator; he knows what is best."

Queen Julia looked at Juliet for the longest moment before giving a sigh and a nod.

"Thank you, Mother, I shall send a letter," Juliet told her.

"Give the letter to Issac; he knows someone who can deliver it," her mother said smiling. "Juliet, I'm so proud of you."

Juliet hugged her mother tightly and whispered, "Thank you. Trust in the God of Light."

Juliet left her mother's bed chambers, and walked back to her own with a purpose. Before bed, she got a piece of paper and her ink, and started constructing a letter to the Kingdom of Zolatta.

After what felt like hours, she put her ink down and re-read her letter. Satisfied with how it sounded, she put it on her dresser, ready to give it to Captain Issac first thing in the morning, before her mother changed her mind.

She was nervous about the marriage alliance. She had only seen Prince Nikolai a few times before the war, during their parents' alliance meetings when they were young. He was tall for a person, and she would remember him teasing her about how small she was compared to him. But the one thing she remembered most of all was his smile; it was a kind smile. That night, when Juliet's head hit the pillow, she finally slept well for the first time in many nights.

✦ ✦ ✦ ✦ ✦

As Captain Issac exited the castle, the sun was just rising over the mountains. He made his way over to the village to deliver an important letter that would change the future of the kingdom. It was entrusted to him by Princess Juliet.

Once Captain Issac entered the village, he headed straight for the blacksmith's forge and knocked on the door.

"Comin'," the blacksmith shouted. The door opened just a tiny fraction, and a man in his late thirties peaked through.

"Captain," he gasped, opening it further. "Sorry, I thought you were the enemy, being here so early in the morning. What brings you here at this hour."

"Something I wish to discuss with you in private," Captain Issac said, looking around hesitantly.

"Of course," the blacksmith said, opening the door to let him in.

"Coffee?" he asked as Captain Issac walked in.

"No thank you Matthew, I'm here on an urgent matter," he said, taking out the letter.

Matthew gave Captain Issac his full attention.

"Do you still have contact with your cousin Fitzwilliam in Zolatta?" Captain Issac asked him.

Matthew hesitated and looked worried.

"You're not in trouble, we just want this letter delivered to the

Zolatta palace," he reassured, holding up the letter the Princess had given him. "If Fitzwilliam delivers it to Prince Nikolai, it may be our only hope in stopping the war. But the Prince must receive this letter."

He placed the letter in the blacksmith's hand.

"You have my word. This letter will get to him within a day. I will have my messenger bird deliver it right away," Matthew replied nodding.

Captain Issac nodded and left the house, hoping it would get to Prince Nikolai before it was too late.

CHAPTER THREE

*"Now faith is confidence in what we hope for
and assurance about what we do not see."*

Hebrews 11:1

Nikolai woke up to his bedroom door being barged into. He shot up out of bed, still half asleep.

"Today's the day, my son," King Harold declared, walking over to his son's bed. "Today, we will win this war."

Nikolai looked to his father, who was already dressed for today's battle and sighed.

"Come to the conference room; I have things to discuss with you," King Harold ordered, leaving the room before his son could say anything.

Nikolai dragged himself out of bed, and was just about to shower when he heard a knock at his door. Before he could open it, his best friend and advisor, Theo, walked in with a smile.

"Why the hell do you look so dam happy, especially so early in the morning," Nikolai said, rubbing the sleep out of his eyes.

Theo walked over to his friend and handed him a letter.

"Because of this."

Nikolai looked at his friend and then at the letter. He was too tired to care.

"I'll look at it later; my father wants to speak with me," Nikolai told him, putting it on his bed.

"It's from Princess Juliet, the Princess from the Kingdom of Elaxon," Theo said smugly.

Nikolai looked at his friend, then back at the letter on his bed. He was too shocked to speak. He quickly opened the letter and read the contents inside. His heart pounded in his chest, as he sat back on his bed.

"So?" Theo questioned, walking over to sit on the bed next to his friend.

"She's asking for a marriage alliance to stop this war," Nikolai responded, still looking at the letter.

"That's great news," Theo exclaimed.

"Yes, it is," Nikolai whispered.

Nikolai was reminded of her kindness all those years ago, when they used to meet for the alliance meetings that their parents held. He had always liked her and thought she was beautiful and kind.

"Earth to Nikolai," Theo said, grinning at his friend. Nikolai snapped out of his thoughts, laughed at Theo, then looked at the letter again.

"I'm surprised it was Juliet that asked you and not the other way round," Theo said confused.

"What do you mean?" Nikolai asked.

"You've had a crush on her since you were little. I remember you telling me stories when both of your families gathered for meetings. You were pretty smitten," Theo laughed.

Nikolai laughed along with his friend, stopping when he realized why he hadn't asked for the marriage alliance first.

His curse got in the way.

"Nikolai, are you ok?" Theo asked.

"Just worried about my curse and how it will affect her," Nikolai sighed. "Maybe it would be best if we found another option to stop this war instead of a marriage alliance. I don't want to be a burden to her."

Theo sighed and started to pace around the room. Before he could say anything to his friend, a knock at the door interrupted his thoughts, and a servant came in and bowed.

"Your father wishes to see you in the conference room," the servant informed, bowing before he left the room.

"Nikolai, I think you should agree to the marriage alliance. I don't think there's another way. We are running out of time, and your father plans to win this war today," Theo advised.

Nikolai thought for a moment, hesitated, then sighed in agreement. "Ok, but we have to convince my father first."

An hour later, Nikolai was knocking on the conference room doors. One of the servants opened it to let him in. His father was sitting at the head of the table. His sharp green eyes found Nikolai, as he entered the room and smiled. His black hair and beard were long and messy, indicating he did not care much about his appearance. Looking into his sharp eyes, Nikolai felt small, as he quickly sat facing his father at the opposite end of the table.

"Glad you could join us, son," King Harold said gruffly.

Nikolai nodded to him as he didn't know what else to say. He hated these war meetings, and didn't want to be here listening to his father boasting about his latest victory. But when his father insisted on something, it was wise not to question him.

There were others present in the room. Sitting to the King's right was the Captain of the Royal Guard, Oberon. Oberon was in his early forties but could still defeat an enemy with his bare hands. Though, he chose to wield a broadsword as his weapon. A large scar covered his right cheek, and although many have asked how he got it, he keeps them guessing. Oberon was tall and bulky, a result of always lifting weights in his free time.

Next to him sat Finnick, his first lieutenant. Finnick was a joker, always carefree and pranking people. He knew the Captain better than anyone else, as they both trained together back in the day. He also goes by the name of Lord Hain, but refuses to use it until his father is dead in the grave. His blonde hair and blue eyes made him younger than he looked, and he always attracted the ladies' attention throughout the palace. His weapon of choice was a large axe and a small dagger.

Next to Finnick was Jarreth, the second lieutenant. Jarreth never spoke. A result of being attacked as a child and losing his vocal cords. But that didn't make him weak. He is most skilled in archery, and is the stealthiest among the men. His jet-black hair made him even more mysterious, and his blue eyes were always observing. His weapon of choice was a bow and arrow, and multiple tiny daggers hidden within his clothing.

"First, I would like to say, after yesterday's efforts, I can happily say that I'm confident we can end the war today. Especially with the help of my son and his abilities," King Harold said triumphantly.

"I agree," Oberon nodded.

Nikolai's abilities, which his father was so proud of, were a curse to him. Some days Nikolai could control it; other days he could not. He hated hurting people. He would sometimes lose control, and wake up somewhere without knowing how or why he got there. His curse was that he could transform into a fox spirit. His mother always said that if he used these abilities for good, it wouldn't seem like such a curse; he loved her for that. She also told him that when he was born, a rouge Gem user, and follower of the Prince of Darkness, cursed him. Both his parents were worried for him, but nothing happened. Not until he had turned sixteen. His curse started to show, and his mother spent the last remaining years of her life in search of a way to break it, so Nikolai could have an ordinary life. She discovered that if the person who cursed him died, the curse would be broken, and he could have a normal life again.

He hasn't stopped looking for that person, and never will.

Thanks to his mother, he now has a chance at an ordinary life. He still mourns for her even though she's been gone for years. On the other hand, his father mourned her for a week, went riding one day to clear his head and came back two days later a different man. Nobody knew for sure what happened in those two days, but it changed the King.

And not in a good way.

"Son," King Harold interrupted his thoughts.

Nikolai looked up and noticed that all eyes were on him.

"Sorry," Nikolai apologized, feeling guilty that he wasn't paying attention.

"Do you have anything you'd like to say?" King Harold asked him.

"Actually, yes. I would like to propose a marriage alliance, with the Princess of Elaxon to end this war," Nikolai said confidently.

Everyone stared at him, and when Nikolai looked at his father, his expression scared him. His eyes were cold and filled with hatred.

"I need to have a word alone with my son," the King ordered. "Leave."

The others all left the room as quickly as possible.

"What brought this on, son?" his father asked him.

"I'm sick of this war, father," Nikolai told him.

"Son," his father came to him and touched his shoulder. "We have come so far; our victory will be today. Why waste your time with our enemy? You can have the whole kingdom if it makes you happy. And with your power, we can take the other kingdoms and rule them all."

His father's eyes went black for a minute before returning to its usual green shade.

Nikolai took a step back from his father. Something wasn't right.

"Son?" King Harold questioned.

"No," Nikolai said, raising his voice. "What you are doing is not right. I want the marriage alliance and peace. Aren't you sick and tired of the war, the killing? We have lost so many good men and women."

"Son," his father yelled. "You will listen to me, and you will obey my instructions; we are going to win this war, no matter what."

"No," Nikolai said, backing away. "I'm done."

At that moment, his father scared him more than usual; something was not right. It hadn't been right for a long time. He wished he had said something earlier, but he didn't, as his father terrified him. He needed to get away now.

"You will obey my instructions," King Harold said, taking out the moonstone Gem.

It was too late.

Nikolai was transfixed, ready to carry out anything his father instructed. That was the power of the moonstone Gem. Nikolai feared it because his father would use it against him, forcing him to transform into the fox spirit and kill people to win this war.

"You will transform into the fox spirit, now," the King demanded.

Almost immediately, Nikolai started to feel the change in him. Bones expanded and broke within him, making him more fox than human. The pain was excruciating, like having hot lava thrown upon you. Nikolai screamed in pain as he looked down at his hands, which were now claws. His nose could pick up scents from miles away. His long tail stretched out before dividing into six, and his teeth were as sharp as a sword.

He was the perfect killing machine. Nikolai was indeed cursed.

His father stood not far from him, smirking at his son's transformation.

"Well done," he said, looking at the complete change. "To get this silly marriage idea out of your head, I want you…." King Harold stopped and laughed. "NO, I demand that you kill Princess Juliet."

Nikolai's heart broke at what his father had just demanded of him. He tried to fight it but could not control his body.

"No," he screamed, but no words came out, only a loud and defining roar.

Nikolai jumped out of the palace windows, landing at the front gate. He sniffed around to get Juliet's scent. Once Nikolai found it, he started running in that direction. He tried to control his movements but failed. The power of the moonstone Gem was too strong. But he wouldn't give up; he had two days of running before he reached Juliet's Kingdom, as his speed was faster than a cheetah's.

He still had time.

When night fell, he hunted for food and devoured it before returning to his mission. He tried repeatedly to break free from his father's control, but with no luck. He was devastated and scared. He hadn't felt like this since his mother's passing.

His mother had supported him and his curse, always finding the positives instead of the negatives in everything. Nikolai missed her so much it hurt.

Remember who you are, a tiny voice whispered.

Who am I?, Nikolai thought to himself, trying desperately to think.

You are a child of our God the Creator, a tiny voice whispered.

Nikolai remembered his mother's words.

Remember, everything happens for a reason.

Nikolai found his mother's words always comforting. She was a wise woman, loved and certainly missed by all.

Nikolai's heart pounded as he realized he was running over the border and into the Kingdom of Elaxon.

It was a couple of hours after dawn, as he ran through the village. People screamed at the sight of him. Men gathered, with their weapons ready to attack him, but his mind was not on them, so he continued past them and up towards the palace.

The closer he got to the palace, the more he fought for control. But the power of the moonstone Gem was too strong. He still would not give up; he had to try and break free.

The guards blocked the gate leading into the palace. He swiped at them with his claws, injuring some. Others came from behind him with weapons, so he turned and ran through the gate as quickly as he could. Arrows pierced his body from all over. He yanked them out using his multiple tails, but pulling out the arrows caused his body to bleed. Dripping with blood, he continued with his mission. He stopped at the palace entrance and sniffed the air, trying to find the princess's scent. Once found, he sprinted down the side of the castle, around the back and into the garden and stopped, panting for air. She was sitting on a bench with a book in her hand. She suddenly looked up and gasped. Nikolai slowly made his way over to her and growled, bearing his sharp teeth at her. Saliva dripped from his mouth as he reached a claw out towards her.

"Stop," Nikolai cried to himself. "Stop."

The look on her face saddened him; she looked terrified. He

managed to stop his claws just inches from her face. He stared at her, gazing upon her beauty. He managed to have enough control to stop his claws from touching her face, but could not pull them back. He stared at her, and she stared back. A sudden wave of embarrassment overwhelmed him.

Can she see the real me?

She couldn't as he was still in the form of the fox spirit. But the way she looked at him wasn't that of someone who was frightened, but of someone curious. She lifted her hand to touch his fur, but he moved away quickly as he did not want to hurt her. He looked at her once again.

"Your eyes," Juliet whispered, then she realized. "I know you."

Nikolai looked away from her feeling ashamed and howled. She reached up and touched his white fur. This time he lowered his head as she scratched his nose, feeling relaxed at her touch.

Kill her, he heard his father's voice in his head.

Nikolai needed to leave before he lost control. He was about to turn and run when he felt a sharp pain in his shoulder. He roared in pain, turning to growl furiously at his attacker, and saw fifty soldiers armed with their bow and arrows, and swords ready to attack him.

"Protect the Princess," one of the soldiers yelled.

"Wait, stop," Nikolai heard the princess yell. "Wait."

But the soldiers weren't listening to her; they were focused on Nikolai.

Nikolai let out a furious roar as he ran to the soldiers who blocked his path, swiping at them with his claws and tails so he could get past. Once he saw an opening, he fled as he began to feel his consciousness slipping away. Nikolai had to get away from the princess before he lost control again; he had to.

Sprinting out of the palace gardens and through the town,

more men came after him and attacked. He let out a roar, hoping to scare them away so he could escape. The pain in his shoulder was burning now. His mind was going fuzzy and he was getting weaker as he ran on. Passing the village was easy. Women and children hid in their houses in fear, as the men ran after him. No one could match his speed. He was beginning to think the arrow in his arm was poisoned, because the further he ran the slower he became. Nikolai felt like he would collapse, but had to return home otherwise, he would end up dead.

After running non-stop for two days, Nikolai arrived at the border of Zolatta; his home. He slowed to a walk and panted; blood dripped from his open wounds and onto the ground with each step. Nikolai eventually stopped and collapsed onto the dirt, unable to move anymore. Nikolai could feel himself transforming back into a human, but the pain of change wasn't as bad as the pain in his arm. He looked up at the sky; falling asleep and never waking up would be so peaceful. He closed his eyes and let the darkness take him, hoping he would see his mother again soon.

◆ ◆ ◆ ◆ ◆

"What have I done?" King Harold said staring at himself in the mirror.

The person he was looking at was not him; not the real him. Every second of every day, he tried to fight the control that women had over him. His biggest regret was leaving the palace for solitude after his wife's passing. Instead, he found something worse: loneliness. He knew his son could see the change in him. It saddened him because he could not do anything about it. He tried breaking her control on him, but his efforts proved useless.

King Harold held the moonstone Gem in his hands. He could tell that the demand he made to his son, hurt him. It hurt him as well, to see that he was wounding his son. Deep down, he approved of the marriage alliance. It was a wise and logical idea, and he was proud of his son. But the control the women had over him made things almost impossible. King Harold looked at the Gem in his hand and had a thought. He ran out of his bed chambers, down the palace stairs, and headed into town. There was still time to protect the princess and his son. He just hoped he could stay conscious long enough to complete the task.

The townspeople looked at him with curiosity, and bowed to him as he passed by, but he ignored them and continued to the blacksmith.

The blacksmith looked up and bowed when King Harold entered his workshop. "Your Highness."

"Fitzwilliam, do you have a steel hammer in this shop?" the King asked him eagerly.

Fitzwilliam nodded and turned around, searching his workshop for the hammer. King Harold began to panic as he felt his consciousness slip away. He was afraid that his time would run out, and he wouldn't be able to help his son the only way he knew how. Once found, Fitzwilliam held out the hammer to him. King Harold looked at it, willing for his hand to take it, but he couldn't. He was seconds away from losing consciousness, so he quickly removed the moonstone Gem from his pocket, and placed it on the workbench.

"Smash it," King Harold ordered, his words strained.

Fitzwilliam looked at him with curiosity, then shrugged. As he lifted the hammer ready to smash the Gem, King Harold had to fight the impulse not to reach out and grab it. The hammer came down and the Gem shattered into tiny pieces. The King gasped, realizing he was holding his breath. He just hoped it wasn't too late for his son or the princess.

"Thank you," King Harold said nodding to Fitzwilliam.

Before leaving, King Harold handed Fitzwilliam an envelope. "For my son," he managed to say.

Fitzwilliam nodded back, taking the envelope from King Harold, and placing it on his workbench. As the King turned to leave, he saw Fitzwilliam scraping up the tiny bits left from the Gem, and discarding them into the trash. Relieved, he turned and headed back to the palace. Dark storm clouds began forming in the sky, and he was certain that the women knew what he had done. But he felt peace for the first time since his wife died.

While walking up the steps to the palace, one of his footmen stopped him and bowed.

"You have a visitor, Your Highness. I have sent them to your office," he notified.

King Harold nodded to the footman. "Thank you."

Dread filled him as he made his way up to his office. He knew who the visitor was, and knew it was his time. He had faith that his son would be a great King. He stood outside his office door with his hand on the doorknob and hesitated.

"Your Highness," Theo greeted bowing as he walked past.

"Wait, Theo," King Harold called.

Theo stopped and turned towards him with curiosity and fear.

Have I been that cruel to people for them to fear me, the King thought.

"Tell my son that I love him, and that I'm sorry," he said turning towards the door, and walking through for the last time.

King Harold closed the door behind him and stared at the women sitting in his office chair. She was beautiful, but that was a lie. She hid her true face and age from others. Only a few people knew what she looked like, before she made a deal with the Prince of Darkness, for eternal youth and beauty. Her crimson-red hair was braided and hanging over her shoulder. Her eyes were bright green, and she stared at him wickedly. She wore a long green robe, which made her blend in with the crowd effortlessly. She was an expert in hiding, and it was impossible to locate her when you wanted to find her. She would be the one to locate you. She smiled, stood up and walked around his desk. She held her scepter in her hand. It was just as tall as she was, and was made from branches and twigs fused together. The scepter was a dark green; matching the robe she was wearing. The branches were infused with black, as if the branch had been poisoned. Nestled at the top, inside the staff's center, was a big green emerald Gem.

"Well, well, well, what do we have here?" her long fingernails snaked around her scepter.

"Mildred, it's, it's good to see you," King Harold stuttered.

She stared at him with intensity and fury.

"Why have you broken the moonstone Gem?" she demanded. "I gave you everything you wanted."

"No! All I wanted was my beloved wife. But you took advantage of my grief, promising me that I would see her again. You controlled me, made me do unspeakable things, and turned me against my son. I never wanted that," King Harold yelled.

Mildred sneered at him, slowly walking towards him until she was just inches away from his face.

"Your right," she exclaimed. "I did promise you that you could see your wife again."

King Harold suddenly gasped as he felt a burning sensation in his stomach. He looked down and saw Mildred with a knife embedded in his stomach. He looked up and saw the hatred in her eyes. She pulled out the blade quickly and stashed it back in her robe. He fell to his knees, coughing up blood as the pain engulfed him. Mildred lifted her hood over her head and walked out the door. Laying on the floor of his office, unable to move, King Harold wanted to tell his son so many things. That he loved him, was proud of him, and that he would make a fine King and father one day, but that would never happen. King Harold knew he was dying, and it was his own fault. In his grief, he felt guilty for turning away from The God of Light.

"I'm sorry," he whispered, as his breath left him for the last time.

CHAPTER FOUR

"Love is patient, love is kind.
It does not envy, it does not boast, it is not proud."

1 Corinthians 13:4

Nikolai could barely move; the pain was so intense his breathing was ragged and shallow. The heat he felt was unbearable, like being in hot water for too long. Nikolai felt the soft sheets beneath his hands, and was relieved to be home again in his bed. He tried opening his eyes but found that he couldn't, but he could hear people in the room around him.

"How is he doing?" Theo asked, worried for his friend.

"Not good," replied a woman's voice. "He needs the antidote for whatever has poisoned him."

Theo sighed in frustration.

"Do you know where he went before he got shot?" asked the woman.

"No, I don't," Theo replied, getting agitated.

Nikolai tried to speak, but only mumbling came out.

"Wait," Theo told her, hearing his friend try to speak.

Nikolai felt someone next to him.

"Nikolai, if you can hear me, give us a clue," Theo encouraged.

"Juliet," Nikolai croaked.

"On it," Theo replied, running out of the room.

Nikolai heard the door slam and drifted back to sleep.

✦ ✦ ✦ ✦ ✦

Nikolai was woken again by the slamming of a door. He tried again to open his eyes, but only managed a little. It was nighttime, but he wasn't sure what time. He heard multiple voices in his room. He tried to move, but someone grabbed his hand.

"Try not to move, Prince Nikolai," a soft female voice directed. "We're trying to extract the poison."

Nikolai knew that voice immediately. It was Juliet.

How was she here? Where is my father? Is Juliet safe? Nikolai thought.

He tried talking to her, but only mumbling came out. The pain and fever was still quite high, and he was still weak from the poison.

"Is he going to be okay?" Theo asked.

"Yes, but he'll need plenty of bed rest," Juliet replied.

At that moment, Nikolai felt a cold sensation over the shoulder that had gotten shot. He used his uninjured hand to try and touch it, but Juliet's hand found his.

"Don't move," her voice was calm and soothing. "I'm healing your shoulder."

At that moment, he remembered what his mother had said about the Kingdom of Elaxon, and their amazing abilities to heal people with the power of their Gem. He thought his mother was telling a tale, but now he was experiencing it, and finally believed it. The intense pain turned into a dull ache, and he immediately started to feel much better, though he still could not move. He opened his eyes and saw Juliet standing beside him. Her hands were hovering over his wounded shoulder, as she concentrated on healing him.

She is beautiful, Nikolai thought to himself.

Her long brunette hair ran down her back and ended in a braid. Her brunette eyes found him, and a warm smile lit up on her face.

"Hi," she whispered to him.

Nikolai tried to say something but could not, so he just smiled at her, and she smiled back. His heart fluttered at the sight of her smile, then he was overcome with dread.

Where is my father? Does he know that Juliet is here? If so, she would be in danger.

He did not want to lose control and transform again, only to be forced to hurt her. He would never forgive himself.

"Hey Nikolai," he turned to his left and saw Theo. "You need to calm down, man, otherwise the wound won't heal properly."

"Fath-," Nikolai tried to say, but his words couldn't form.

But Theo already knew what he was worried about.

"The Princess, Captain Issac and Queen Julia are safe," Theo reassured. "I'll explain everything once you're fully healed, but they're all safe."

Nikolai immediately felt reassured, but was not surprised that Juliet came with an escort. After all, he was still a threat.

He closed his eyes and drifted back to sleep.

✦ ✦ ✦ ✦ ✦

Juliet sighed as she removed her hands from Nikolai's shoulder. She had successfully healed him, after a long hour of concentration with her Gem's power.

"How is he, Princess Juliet?" Theo asked.

"He is fully healed; he just needs rest," she replied.

"Thank you, Princess," Theo said. "Allow me to show you to the sitting room, where refreshments have been prepared for you. You will be able to rest there."

Theo left the room with Juliet, and Queen Julia and Captain Isaac followed along. They walked down the corridor, and into another room, where the servants laid out drinks and food for them.

"Please have a seat," Theo said, gesturing to them as he sat on the opposite couch.

Juliet and Queen Julia sat on the couch opposite him, while Captain Issac stood near them against the wall. Juliet went to pick up a sandwich, but her mother nudged her and shook her head. She still did not trust them, even though the King, who was the main reason for this war, was found dead yesterday in his office.

"Of course, you still don't trust us," Theo said clearing his throat. "Don't worry, I completely understand. Allow me to put your fears to rest." Theo picked up every dish that was on the table and placed them into his mouth one by one, as if to show them they were not poisoned. Then to wash it all down he filled his cup with some wine and gulped that down.

"See," he said wiping his mouth with a napkin. "Safe."

Juliet hid her laugh as she took a plate from one of the servants. She looked down at the table at the many options before her. The servants filled the table with caramel slices, chocolate tarts, apple slices, strawberries, and wine. She put one of each on her plate to try, and her mother did the same.

"Captain, please help yourself," Theo said gesturing to the table.

He grunted, began filling his plate, and stood in the corner watching the whole room.

"My condolences for the late King's death, and the attack on his son," consoled Queen Julia.

"Thank you." Theo looked at Juliet and nodded. "I'm assuming the marriage alliance still stands."

Juliet's mother looked over at her daughter and sighed.

"Only if you tell us the truth," replied Queen Julia.

"The truth?" Theo questioned.

"My sources tell me your kingdom has control over a fox spirit," Queen Julia questioned him.

"Fox spirit?" Theo asked with dread.

"Don't play dumb with me. I know it attacked my daughter only a week ago," Queen Julia demanded.

"He didn't attack me, mother. He just startled me," Princess Juliet told her mother, for what felt like the hundredth time.

"HE!" Queen Julia almost yelled. "This fox spirit is a human."

Theo sighed and nodded. "Yes, Prince Nikolai can transform into the fox spirit, but I can assure you that the late King forced him. You see, the late King had in his possession a moonstone Gem."

Queen Julia gasped.

"What's a moonstone Gem?" Juliet asked her mother with concern.

"It is one of the very few Gems that can control people, and make them do unspeakable things against their will," her mother explained.

"Oh," Juliet said sadly. "How horrible. What made the late King do such a horrible thing."

"He wasn't always like that," Theo sighed. "His wife died a few years ago, and he left the palace one day to clear his thoughts, to mourn for her. He was gone for two days. The whole kingdom was in an uproar. You can imagine what Prince Nikolai went through; he was only a teenager."

Theo sighed, taking another sip of wine.

"When he came back, he was a changed man. All the King talked about was power and war," Theo explained. "And that was the first time we saw the moonstone Gem. He used it that night on Prince Nikolai, making him transform into the Fox spirit against his will. Their relationship was destroyed that day. Prince Nikolai never trusted his father after that."

"Poor child," Queen Julia cried, wiping her eyes. "How did he come to have the power of the fox spirit?"

"He was cursed as a child by a rouge Gem user, who follows the Prince of Darkness. She cast a spell on him which was made by the Prince of Darkness, hoping to control the power once he had matured," Theo answered.

"Oh my," Queen Julia gasped.

"You must understand that we all want peace. Prince Nikolai hated this war and still does. I am begging you to stand by your decision about this marriage alliance," Theo insisted. "For both our kingdom's sake."

They all sat silently for a few minutes, thinking about what Theo had just shared. Then Queen Julia spoke.

"I will leave this decision to my daughter. She initiated the marriage alliance to begin with," Queen Julia said, looking at her daughter. "It is your future. I won't force you."

"I'll do it," Juliet replied not hesitating.

Theo laughed in excitement and relief. "Thank you, thank you."

There was a knock at the door.

"Come in," Theo called.

A young man came through the door and bowed to everyone in the room.

"Adviser Theo, Princess, Queen," he hesitated, looking at Captain Issac. "Uh, Sir."

"What news have you brought?" Theo asked.

"Uh, I," he began, looking nervously around the room.

"Prince Nikolai and Princess Juliet," Theo said gesturing to Juliet, "are entering into a marriage alliance; whatever you have to say to me, you can say to them as well."

The young man nodded nervously, then continued.

"Before the, um, late King died, um, someone came to see him. A woman. I, um, escorted her to the King's office, and informed the King himself that she was there," he said nervously.

"Did you get a good look at what this woman looked like?" Theo asked.

"Only that she had red hair. I thought it was peculiar, seeing as we don't have anyone here with that sort of color, sir," he said.

"Not in our Kingdom either," Queen Julia added, thinking.

"Perhaps one of the other kingdoms?" Juliet questioned.

"Hmmm, perhaps. I'll have someone investigate. Perhaps we can ask for the assistance of the other kingdoms," Theo thought out loud. "Thank you, steward, you can go."

The steward bowed and left the room.

Theo turned to face his guests.

"What do you know of the other kingdoms?" Theo questioned.

"We trade with both other kingdoms," Queen Julia explained. "The Kingdom of Neylon is ruled by King Jabari and Queen Nala. They have a son, Prince Omari. We trade our metal and silk for their stone and cotton. Their kingdom is a seven-day carriage ride from here. The Kingdom of Kudzu is ruled by King Eros and Queen Athena, with their daughter Princess Iris. Their trade includes spices and wine, and they are a ten-day journey by carriage from here."

"Have you met them?" asked Theo.

"A long time ago, when we signed an alliance between both kingdoms," Queen Julia replied. "I can send word about your situation, and ask them if they know anything."

"Thank you, that would be great," Theo said.

There was another knock at the door, and a servant came in and bowed.

"Advisor Theo, you are needed urgently. The kingdom is in an uproar since the late King's death, and Prince Nikolai's accident." The servant bowed and left the room.

"I should go," Theo advised, getting up.

"Don't worry about us," Queen Julia insisted. "I would like to rest in my room before dinner."

"I want to check on Prince Nikolai again," Juliet said, getting up.

"Thank you. Call one of the servants if you need me," Theo told them, walking out of the room.

"I'll see you at dinner, Mother, Issac," Juliet said before leaving the room.

As Juliet walked down the palace hallway, she smiled at the maids and manservants as they passed. They were too busy with their work to stop and chat, as the kingdom had just lost their King, and the prince was currently out of action.

"Good evening miss, can I help you?" a maid asked, stopping, and bowing to Juliet.

"How is Prince Nikolai doing?" Juliet asked.

"He looks like he's doing well, Your Highness," the maid replied, looking past Juliet and bowing again.

Juliet turned to find Prince Nikolai in the hallway smiling at her.

"Asking about me?" he smiled.

"Just seeing if you need any more healing," Juliet blushed, stumbling on her words.

He smiled at her. "Thanks for your help, Princess."

Juliet smiled and bowed. "Anytime Your Highness."

"How long since….," Nikolai paused looking around, then

whispered. "Before, uh, the,"

"Since you came and startled me," Juliet whispered back.

"Princess," Nikolai sighed.

"Juliet," she stated. "And you startled me about a week ago."

"A week!" he gasped, looking at her in shock. "Thank you for healing me."

"You're welcome, how are you feeling?" she asked.

"Better, ashamed, hurt, scared, relieved," Nikolai began. "Better thanks to your healing powers, ashamed of you knowing my curse, hurt because of my father, scared because I almost hurt you and relieved to see you are unharmed."

"Prince Nikolai, don't beat yourself up. Nothing happened. You just gave me a fright, that's all. Once I realized who you were, I knew you wouldn't hurt me," Juliet explained.

"Call me Nikolai, please," he insisted.

"Okay, Nikolai, but you never hurt me," Juliet assured.

"Juliet," Nikolai sighed. "Do you know what a moonstone Gem is?"

"I do," Juliet said, knowing where this conversation was going.

"That day I came to you," he paused. "I was ordered to kill you."

He closed his eyes and rubbed his temple while leaning on the wall.

"I know, Theo told us. But you did not hurt me. You overcame the moonstone's control. In my opinion, it takes someone powerful to do that," Juliet told him.

"Thanks, Princess, but I haven't forgiven myself or my father," he said as he started to walk away.

"Wait, you need to rest," Juliet urged, walking after him.

"My father is still out there. The longer you're here, the more danger you're in," he explained, stopping in the middle of the hallway.

"I'm not in any danger," she insisted, standing before him with her hands on her hips.

He stopped, looked at her and smiled. His hand came up to caress her face, but he quickly pulled back as he thought he would hurt her.

"I got your letter but had no time to respond since the incident, but my answer is yes," he smiled.

Juliet smiled back. "Thank you."

He cleared his throat and nodded. "No, I should be thanking you. I better go find my father and persuade him to see reason."

He took her hand gently and kissed it, then turned, and continued down the hallway to his father's office. As Juliet watched him leave, she thought it was for the best that he heard about his father's death from a close friend. Not from someone he had barely known for a day, and with whom she agreed to form a marriage alliance with.

CHAPTER FIVE

"Blessed are those who mourn, for they will be comforted."

Matthew 5:4

Nikolai left in a hurry to try and find his father. He needed to talk to him, and help him see reason. He walked up to his office and opened the door, only to find Theo sitting down sorting through papers. Theo looked up and grinned.

"Had a good sleep, Your Highness?"

"I would have," Nikolai said smiling at his friend, "if I weren't so paranoid about what my father would do."

Theo sighed. "Take a seat, Nikolai," he sighed gesturing towards the late King's chair.

Nikolai walked over to his father's desk and sat behind it. Confusion and dread filled him; something was wrong.

"Nikolai, after your incident in the Kingdom of Elaxon, your father was found deceased the following morning in his office. He was found with a stab wound to his stomach," Theo explained, then paused, giving Nikolai time to process. "I have spoken with the palace staff, asking if they've seen anything. Only a few have come forward, and with very little information." Theo stopped and looked at his friend, then went on.

"The steward informed me that a red-haired woman came to see him before his death. She requested an audience with the King, so the steward led her to his office, then immediately informed the King," Theo told him. "Also, I was just returning from the markets when I found your father staring at his office door strangely. As I walked past, he told me to give you a message. He said to tell you I'm sorry, and that he loves you. After that he closed his office door so quickly, I didn't have a chance to reply."

Nikolai stared at his father's desk, sorting through all the information Theo had given him. He was sad, angry, and confused. Nikolai had questions that he wanted to ask his father, but could not anymore. Now that his father was gone, he was to be King. But he had no idea how to run a kingdom, because his father never taught him. Nikolai felt frustrated, helpless, and sad. He stood up and left his father's office. He needed some fresh air, so he went to the palace gardens. It was only a tiny garden, but he loved it. It reminded him of his mother. He sat on the bench, put his head in his hands, and wept. He mourned for his father. Despite the pain he caused, he loved the early years and had good memories of them. But his mother's death changed his father, and he became cold and distant.

Some time passed, and Nikolai began to feel better. After wiping his eyes, he walked out of the gardens and up to the church.

"Your Highness," the Priest greeted, shaking Nikolai's hand. "My condolences."

"Thank you, Priest Phil," Nikolai replied, returning the handshake.

"Follow me," Priest Phil gestured into the church.

Nikolai followed Priest Phil into the church and towards the back room, which was only meant for Priests, Sisters, and staff.

"I've appointed two male clergymen to prepare the late King's body for burial. We will hold a funeral for him tomorrow at midday," Priest Phil explained.

"Thank you for all that you have done. I know my father wasn't his best after my mother's passing," Nikolai said sadly.

"He was devastated by her death, yes. Never the same after," Priest Phil agreed. "Something troubled your father this past couple of weeks. He would come here regularly, asking for forgiveness," Priest Phil questioned.

"Really!" Nikolai said, shocked. "I had no idea he still visited the church."

"Oh yes, at least a couple of times a week," Priest Phil replied. "Here he is."

Priest Phil led Nikolai to where his father's body lay. The clergymen had already washed and wrapped him in fine cloth for his burial. He looked peaceful. Nikolai's heart ached, and tears began to form again. Priest Phil touched his shoulder in comfort.

"Oh, Heavenly Creator, please help Prince Nikolai get through this tough time. Please let him know you and so many others love him. I pray for peace and strength," Priest Phil prayed.

"Amen," they both said together.

"Thank you, Priest Phil. I will see you at the funeral," Nikolai said, wiping his eyes.

Nikolai walked out of the church and headed back to the palace. He went back to his father's office, hoping Theo would still be there. He was.

"Sorry," Nikolai apologized, sitting back down.

"Hey, you have been through a lot. I would not be surprised if I didn't see you till breakfast tomorrow. I also want you to know that I am here for you, if you need to talk," Theo said with a stack of papers in his hand.

"Thanks," Nikolai said. "I'll need your help to get the kingdom running smoothly again."

"Happy to help," Theo said, handing him a letter.

"What's this?" Nikolai asked.

"The speech you're giving the people, to tell them the war is over and of your marriage alliance as well," Theo replied, sorting through other bits of paper.

"Thanks. I haven't even thought about that," Nikolai said, reading the letter.

A knock sounded at the door.

"Come in," Nikolai called, looking up from the letter.

A servant came in and bowed.

"Your Highness, Advisor Theo, dinner will be ready shortly," the servant said bowing, then leaving the room.

"It can't be that time already," Theo exclaimed, looking at the clock.

"I guess so," Nikolai sighed, standing up to stretch.

Theo and Nikolai made their way over to the dining area. The others were already there waiting for them.

"My apologies, everyone," Nikolai said, sitting at the table's head.

"It's quite alright. You have been through a great ordeal," Queen Julia assured.

"Thank you," Nikolai replied.

The servants came around and placed various dishes on the table, along with drinks.

"I hope you don't mind, but I'd like to pray before we eat," Nikolai said, looking around the table.

"Of course," Juliet said smiling.

Nikolai smiled back.

"Heavenly Creator, please bless this food before us. I pray for wisdom for the future, my father, and the new friends that I have made. Amen," Nikolai prayed.

"Amen," they all replied.

"I wanted to mention," Nikolai hesitated for a moment, "we're holding a funeral for my father tomorrow at midday. You're welcome to come if you like, but do not feel obliged. I know he wasn't the best person in his later years."

"Of course, we will come to pay our respects," Queen Julia said. "But I'm afraid we will have to head back home after the funeral tomorrow. I fear we may have been away from my kingdom for too long."

"Of course," Nikolai replied, understandingly. "Also, I will announce the marriage alliance to my kingdom the day after tomorrow, after my father's funeral. I will speak to the Priest about the wedding, as well as both mine and Juliet's coronation. I think it will be easier to do them both at the same time, so you are not away from your kingdom for too long."

"Thank you. I think that is perfect. Let us know what date you set, and we will prepare things on our end," Queen Julia beamed.

"Thank you," Nikolai replied.

✦ ✦ ✦ ✦ ✦

Later that night after everyone went to bed, Nikolai walked over to his father's chambers. The servants had left the room unlocked, after clearing out his late father's things. He went inside and looked around. The bedroom was huge, with lots of space. The maids had left some pictures hanging on the wall, of him and his father when he was younger. Nikolai looked at all the photos his father had of him and smiled. He was still loved, despite the hardships in the last few years. He smiled at one of the photos and took it down from the wall to have a proper look. It was his first-time hunting with his father. In the picture, they both had big smiles as they each held a pheasant. Nikolai smiled at the thought of that day. He wanted to keep this photo with him constantly, so he opened the back up and took the picture out. To his surprise something else came out and fell to the floor. He bent over to pick it up and saw that it was an envelope addressed to him. Curious, he opened it and began to read the contents inside. Nikolai was filled with shock as he read the letter. He had to re-read it to ensure he was reading it correctly. Three things stood out to him. One, his father had been controlled by a rouge Gem user named Mildred, to do unspeakable things. Two, the Prince of Darkness was forming an army to take control of the world. And three, only with the Gems from each of the four kingdoms, working together, they could stop the coming darkness. If not, then the whole world would suffer.

CHAPTER SIX

"Be devoted to one another in love.
Honor one another above yourselves."

Romans 12:10

It was dusk when Emily entered the cave; the humidity was higher inside, and she could smell a dead animal somewhere. But it was better than dealing with the constant rain and thunder outside. Emily sighed, wishing she had stopped at the inn for the night instead of pressing on. But she was eager to get home. She stopped a few meters inside the cave and sat down; she was wet and cold. Hugging herself tighter, she buried her head into her knees.

Clank.

Emily startled awake; she could not believe she dozed off. She was obviously exhausted from the journey. She looked around the cave to find the source of the noise, but all she could see was darkness. She hugged herself again, wishing she were back home.

Clank.

She stood up quickly this time; dread creeping up on her. There was something else in the cave with her. She searched the darkness until she saw floating lamps. She stared curiously at the lights hanging within the cave, unsure why they would be there. The lamps suddenly went out, then back on again almost immediately. Emily started panicking as the lights came closer, and realized they were not lamps but eyes. It was a wolf, but not your ordinary wolf; this was much bigger. The wolf growled at her, showing its teeth; saliva dripping from its mouth as it crept closer. Emily began to back away slowly towards the cave opening. She was almost at the entrance when all her hopes shattered. She tripped over a loose rock and landed on her back. The wolf came upon her, instantly biting into her shoulder blade. She screamed in pain. The wolf kept biting harder, hoping to release more blood so she would become a weaker prey. The wolf backed away from her and waited. Pain spread throughout her arm as she tried to stop the bleeding. Emily's hand was covered in blood as she applied pressure to her bleeding shoulder. She began to slowly feel weaker and weaker until she could not move anymore. She tried to get up, but couldn't as she was too weak from blood loss. Instead, she collapsed onto the ground, unable to move. When the wolf was satisfied that she couldn't move, it bit Emily in the arm again and dragged her back into the cave's darkness.

"Well done, Selina," echoed a cold, dark voice. "Bring her closer so I can feast on her soul."

✦ ✦ ✦ ✦ ✦

Mildred walked confidently into the cave of Akuma. The smell of decay was pungent, and the humidity got worse the deeper she went inside. Darkness surrounded her as she tried to find her way through. After a few minutes, she spotted a light and walked towards it. The room got bigger the closer she got to the light. The light was placed on a stone table that sat to the left side of the cave. Surrounding the stone table were followers of the Master, waiting patiently for their orders. To her right was a wolf sitting on its hind legs, waiting for instructions from the Master. The wolf was massive and black, and its piercing eyes made her nervous. Mildred walked towards the middle of the cave to where the Master sat on his knees, with his hands and ankles chained to the wall. The Master closed his eyes, and Mildred knew he wasn't asleep, but planning. She walked closer to him and bowed.

"Master, I've returned," she said.

"And what have you brought?" his voice came out husky.

"I……" she began.

"Nothing, that's what. You let the King of Zolatta break the moonstone Gem, therefore losing our control over him," his voice was cold.

Mildred hesitated before speaking. Choosing her words wisely she spoke again.

"I did end his life," she spoke calmly.

The Prince of Darkness glared at her with hatred in his eyes.

"Did you not think, that after all this time, I could use him," his voice was terrifyingly calm.

Mildred shuddered, suddenly feeling very frightened.

"I am bound by these chains by the God of Light. I cannot escape them without my full power, and in doing so, I need to feast on human souls," the Prince of Darkness yelled.

Mildred tensed as she felt her Master's long, bony fingers reach the side of her face. He drew her nearer to himself and whispered, "Do not fail me again."

Juliet woke up to the sunlight hitting her eyes; it looked like a beautiful day. She climbed out of bed and headed to the bathroom.

"Morning, Ruth, morning, Grace," she greeted, walking past her maids.

"Morning Princess Juliet," they both greeted, bowing to her.

Today was the late King's funeral, and Juliet wanted to be there for Nikolai. She wanted to help him as much as possible, and hopefully make things a bit easier for him today. She couldn't imagine the pressure he must have felt over the past few days. She hoped Nikolai would let her help.

Juliet came out of the bathroom and saw that her maids had already made her bed, and were waiting for her in front of the vanity. She walked over and sat down at the chair provided, while one maid did her hair and the other did her make-up.

"Nothing too fancy; I like it simple," Juliet explained.

"How about enhancing your beauty using a natural look, and a loose braid with flowers?" Grace asked.

"That sounds wonderful, thank you," Juliet smiled.

"But do promise us that when your wedding comes, we can do something more elegant," Ruth pleaded.

"Of course," Juliet promised smiling, as the two maids giggled behind her.

"Now, about your dress?" Ruth questioned, running to the closet. "We have this A-line lavender dress with a V-neck top, to show off your stunning jewels. We'll then tie a beautiful white laced ribbon around your waist, and finish it off with these beautiful amethyst and silver earrings, silver bangles, and a beautiful beaded amethyst necklace."

"That sounds lovely," Juliet exclaimed, staring at the dress in amazement. "It's a very beautiful dress."

"Ruth made it," Grace blurted out.

"Grace," Ruth hushed.

"I'm honored Ruth. Thank you," Juliet replied, beaming as her maid brought the dress over.

"I've also prepared a black dress for the funeral. It will be finished with a black lace ribbon around the middle, pearl earrings, a necklace, and bracelets to match," Ruth explained.

"Thank you, ladies. For looking after me," Juliet replied smiling.

Juliet took the lavender dress that Ruth had given her, and went behind the wooden room divider to change. She came out and stood in front of the mirror, as Ruth tied the white laced ribbon around her middle, and Grace adorned her with jewelry. Once they had finished, they stood back to look at their masterpiece.

"You look stunning, Princess," Ruth exclaimed.

"Wait until the Prince sees you," Grace giggled.

Juliet beamed with delight at how beautiful she looked, and suddenly felt incredibly nervous about seeing Nikolai today.

"Come, let us get you to breakfast," the ladies said, almost dragging Juliet out of her room.

Juliet walked along the corridor and smiled, as she greeted the staff that passed by. Most of them curtsied or bowed as they walked past her, but a few gave her grunts or ignored her.

"Don't mind them," Ruth said, seeing Juliet's face.

"Instead of blaming the late King for the war, they're blaming you. It is not fair," Grace said to Juliet.

"Please don't take it to heart, Your Highness," Ruth pleaded.

"I won't," Juliet promised.

Grace and Ruth lead Juliet to the dining area, where her mother, Captain Issac and Nikolai were already talking at the table.

"I'm so sorry I'm late," Juliet apologized.

"You are not late, my dear. We are simply early risers," her mother replied.

Juliet looked over at Nikolai, who was at the head of the table and blushed. He was staring at her in adoration.

"I think I've had enough breakfast. What about you, Captain?" Queen Julia grinned.

"Shall we take a turn about the gardens, my Queen?" Captain Issac asked, offering his arm to her, clearly in on whatever she was planning.

As Queen Julia and Captain Issac exited the room, Juliet sat down next to Nikolai.

"You look stunning," Nikolai complimented.

"Thank you, Your Highness," Juliet blushed and looked away embarrassed.

"Juliet," he whispered.

She looked at him.

"Please call me Nikolai," he said.

She nodded and smiled. "Okay."

Juliet helped herself to some toast and condiments, that the servants presented beautifully on the table for her. As she ate, she saw Nikolai staring at her.

"Is everything alright?" she asked him.

"Sorry, I didn't mean to stare," he blushed. "You just look stunning."

"Thank you," she said smiling. "How did you sleep?"

"It took me a while, but eventually I got there," he replied.

"Oh, I'm so sorry. If I can do anything to help, please ask. I don't mind," she said, concerned.

He looked at her and smiled. "Thank you. How did you sleep?"

"Very good, thank you," she replied. "Your kingdom is magnificent."

"Thank you. How are your maids? Are they kind to you? If not, I can find others," he asked, concerned.

"My maids are wonderful. They are very kind to me, thank you," she assured.

"That's a relief. A few people here are unhappy with the

marriage alliance. If you have any concerns or inconveniences, you must let me know," he pleaded.

"Of course," she promised.

There was a knock at the door, and Theo barged in abruptly.

"Theo, good morning," Nikolai greeted his friend.

Theo rushed in. "I got your message. Is everything okay?"

Theo paused when he saw Princess Juliet. "I'm sorry. I didn't mean to interrupt."

"It's okay," Juliet said, getting up. "I'll leave you men to talk."

"Wait, Juliet," Nikolai said, reaching for her hand.

She turned and faced him. "It's okay, you talk with Theo. I've finished eating, so I'm going to head to the library."

"I'll see you later?" he asked.

"Yes," Juliet nodded.

CHAPTER SEVEN

"If a King judges the poor with fairness,
his throne will be established forever."

Proverbs 29:14

"Wow, she looks beautiful," Theo said, taking fruit from the table.

"Yes, she does," Nikolai said.

"I'm sorry I barged in and ruined your moment," Theo apologized, stuffing his face with food. "But after the note you left me, I knew it must be serious."

"It is," Nikolai sighed, leaning back into his chair.

"Oh man, you don't look so good," Theo observed.

"My father left me a letter. He hid it in one of my favorite photos in his bed chambers. I'm guessing he knew I would find it," Nikolai said, rubbing his temples as they started to ache.

"I'm guessing the letter's contents are bad?" Theo asked.

Nikolai nodded. "We may have stopped the war between two countries, but this," he said, holding up the letter, "will be mankind at war. A war with the Prince of Darkness and his army of creatures and followers."

"Oh no," Theo said with dread. "Does anyone else know?"

Nikolai shook his head. "I only found the letter late last night. I plan on contacting the other two kingdoms, and requesting a meeting. Once everyone is gathered here, then I'll reveal the contents of the situation all at once."

"Yes, it will be a lot easier to tell everyone once we are all gathered. That way, we can plan a course of action," Theo agreed.

"I will need your counsel," Nikolai told him.

"Of course," Theo replied.

"Thanks," Nikolai said, getting up. "Now to get some work done."

"Right, about that," Theo started, following behind. "The townspeople should be arriving shortly for you to hear their petitions. It will be held in the throne room."

"Thanks," Nikolai said as they both headed in that direction.

As they walked through the corridor heading to the throne room, maids and servants went about their daily jobs. Nikolai nodded to a few servants and exchanged greetings. He then saw Juliet exiting the library with a book in her hand. She looked beautiful, and her smile was contagious. He felt his heart flutter at the sight of her. She looked his way, and Nikolai smiled and waved at her. She smiled back at him. After reading his father's letter, Nikolai wanted Juliet close to him.

"Juliet," Nikolai called walking up to her, "I'm just about to hear the townspeople's petition. Would you like to join me?"

"I would love to," she replied.

"Great," Nikolai said happily.

He extended his arm to Juliet, and she took it. Together, they walked to the throne room. Once they arrived, the stewards opened the doors, and they made their way inside. About fifty townspeople stood in the room waiting to speak to the Prince. Nikolai directed Juliet to the Queen's throne, where she sat down.

Nikolai sat beside her in his father's chair.

"Let the petition hearing begin," Theo announced.

An older man came forward and bowed.

"Your Highness, I'm sorry for your loss," he said.

"Thank you," Nikolai replied.

The man fidgeted with his hat nervously.

"Don't be afraid to speak up," Nikolai said to him, clearly seeing how nervous the old man was.

The old man nodded.

"I own a farm near town. With the taxes so high, I am unable to provide for my family."

"How much tax are you paying?" Nikolai asked the man.

"Half of what I make, Your Highness," replied the man.

"What!" Nikolai said, shocked. "Half."

"Yes, Your Highness. The late King made the change a year ago, and most of us are struggling to live," the man said, followed by murmurs in the crowd.

Nikolai turned towards Theo. "Take note, all townspeople and nobles are required to pay one-tenth of their income, as tax to the kingdom."

Relief filled the room, along with murmurs of thanks from the crowd.

"Thank you, Your Highness," the old man cried. "Thank you."

Nikolai nodded and smiled. He tried to hide his anguish at what his father was forced to do, by Mildred, who controlled him. As the old man left the room, many followed chatting in relief, leaving only a few behind.

The next person to speak was a woman. She came up and bowed before speaking.

"Your Highness," she greeted, bowing to Princess Juliet and Prince Nikolai. "I work alongside others here today for Lord Blackstone of Ashmore. We want to petition for better working conditions. Lord Blackstone expects us to work from early morning to late evening, without having a break to eat and rest. He has also decreased our wages, and most of us are struggling to live."

Nikolai sighed as he rubbed his forehead. His head was starting to throb now.

"I'm so sorry, Your Highness," she said worriedly.

Nikolai felt Juliet's soft hands on his arm and looked up.

"No, don't apologize," Nikolai said, rubbing his forehead again. "It's been a tough year for all of us. I'm just sorry I didn't see it sooner. Please forgive me. I will have a word to Lord Blackstone. I will be passing through there in a few days."

"Thank you," she replied, and the rest of the people followed her out the door.

"You need to rest. You are going to overdo it. How about you go lay down before the funeral," Juliet suggested worriedly.

Nikolai picked up Juliet's hand, and kissed them gently.

"Thank you, but I have a lot to do before then," Nikolai said, standing up.

He offered his arm to Juliet, and she took it. Together they walked out of the throne room, and down the hallway to his father's office.

"I have work to do. Feel free to rest until the funeral," Nikolai told her.

"I can help," she said, looking hopeful.

Nikolai smiled and took her hand, caressing his thumb over her fingers. He looked at her and she blushed and smiled. His heart thundered in his chest. He fixed a loose strand of hair behind her ear and smiled at her, letting his hand linger on her cheek.

"I'm afraid it's just sorting through my father's stuff, and tossing whatever is unimportant," Nikolai said softly.

Juliet looked a little disappointed; which made him smile.

"I'm sorry, Juliet. I'll come find you after I'm finished," Nikolai said.

"Ok," she nodded. "Promise me you'll let me know if I can be of any use."

"Of course," Nikolai replied, smiling as he watched her leave down the corridor.

Chapter Eight

"Do not be overcome by evil but overcome evil with good"

Romans 12:21

Juliet strolled around the gardens while thinking of Nikolai, and how well he handled himself with the townspeople and their concerns.

He will make a great King, she thought.

Heat rushed through her face, as she remembered how Nikolai kissed her hand, and she smiled. She really liked him a lot. He was so caring and kindhearted, always thinking of others before himself. It made her want to help him and be close to him.

Juliet's hands came up to her face, as she felt her cheeks going red.

She heard her mother humming a tune to herself from behind her, and turned around.

"Are you ok, my child?" her mother asked embracing her.

"I am," Juliet replied smiling.

"I know that look," her mother said smiling.

Juliet smiled and chuckled at her mother.

"You seem delighted today as well, Mother. Anything I should know about?" Juliet asked, turning the subject onto her.

"It seems we have both found love," her mother beamed.

"About time, Mother," Juliet laughed. "Was it you or Issac who confessed first?"

"Oh, hush," her mother said.

"I'm afraid I am the culprit," Captain Issac said, coming up behind them.

"I'm happy for both of you," Juliet said, hugging her mother again.

"Princess, would you like to have lunch brought out here today?" Grace suggested.

"Oh, that would be lovely. It's such a nice day," Juliet said, looking at her mother.

"I think that's a splendid idea," her mother replied.

"Perfect, I shall let the kitchen know," Grace said, bowing before heading back inside.

"So?" Queen Julia asked, "How are you finding Prince Nikolai?"

Juliet smiled. "He's very kindhearted and caring, and is always thinking of others before himself."

"I think he'll make a great King, husband and father," her mother replied. "I haven't seen you smile this much in a very long time."

The servants brought out a small table and chair set, placing it in the middle of the garden. Others followed and set up lunch, which consisted of a variety of small sandwiches and tea. They made their way over and sat down to eat.

"Will the Prince be joining us?" Queen Julia asked.

"Not today. Prince Nikolai is not feeling too well. He has gone to rest before the funeral," one of the servants replied, before leaving them to eat.

"He's overdoing it, especially after his injury," Juliet said worriedly.

"Why don't you see if Prince Nikolai needs any more healing, while bringing him some food," her mother suggested.

"You don't mind?" Juliet asked her mother.

"No, it's fine. We will see you at the funeral," her mother said, giving her daughter a plate.

"Ok, thank you Mother," Juliet said.

Juliet stood up and took the plate her mother had given her, which was filled with different kinds of sandwiches, and got some water. She then followed one of the servants who led her to Nikolai. The servant took her to a seating room where he was asleep on the couch, with his arm over his eyes. Juliet placed the plate of food on the table, and knelt beside him, shaking him gently. He opened his eyes and smiled at her.

"Where's your pain?" she asked.

"My head," he replied tiredly.

Juliet nodded and went to stand at his head. She placed both hands on each side of his head, and concentrated on healing his headache. Her Gem started to glow, and Juliet knew her healing abilities were taking effect. She then closed her eyes to focus.

A few minutes passed and she could feel her energy draining, but she kept on healing. After healing Nikolai for another couple of minutes, she stopped.

"How is your head?" she asked.

"My headache is gone, thank you," Nikolai said, sitting up. "You are amazing."

Juliet blushed as she took a seat next to Nikolai. She pointed to the plate of sandwiches and water on the table.

"Have something to eat; you'll feel better," she encouraged him.

He picked up the plate and put it in front of her.

"Ladies first," he said smiling.

"Thank you," Juliet said, taking one. "How are the preparations for your father's funeral coming along."

"They're all done," Nikolai replied. "Priest Phil helped with the arrangements."

"How are you feeling?" she asked.

"Mixed emotions," he chuckled. "I mourned for my father a long time ago when he had changed, but it still hurts."

Juliet placed her hands on his. "I'm sorry. If there's anything I can do to help, please let me know."

"Your company is valuable to me, and your healing abilities," he replied smiling at her.

Juliet smiled back shyly.

"How long have you been practicing your healing abilities?" Nikolai asked.

"Since I was ten," Juliet told him.

"Do you know much about Gems?" Nikolai asked.

"A little," Juliet replied, putting her water back on the table. "Why do you ask?"

"Just curious," he said. "I'm still yet to find my kingdom's Gem. Apparently, each kingdom has one."

"I heard that," Juliet said trying to think. "Did your father mention anything about a Gem? Did he have anything in his possession before he passed."

"No, not unless whoever killed him found it and took it," Nikolai replied.

Juliet took another sandwich and held it in her hands for a while.

"Is everything ok?" Nikolai asked.

"I'm sorry if I appear rude or nosy, but I'm curious about your curse. Do you know who cursed you?" Juliet asked.

"No need to apologize. My parents told me it was a rouge

Gem user known as Mildred who did the deed. But the Prince of Darkness made the actual spell," he explained.

"I've never heard of her before," Juliet said, thinking. "I'm sorry. I can try looking in the library at home to help you."

"Don't be sorry. You have healed me twice and saved my life. I'm grateful," he smiled at her.

Juliet smiled and blushed at the compliment that Nikolai had given her. She loved helping people with her gift, that was given to her kingdom. She had been thanked by many people in the past, but something about Nikolai's praise made it extra special.

"How are you enjoying your time here?" Nikolai asked as he continued to eat.

"Your kingdom is beautiful, your staff are very lovely, and my maids are quite friendly and nice," Juliet explained as she sipped her water.

"Who are your maids?" Nikolai asked.

"Grace and Ruth," Juliet replied.

"I shall assign them to you when you move here," Nikolai said. "If that makes you happy."

Juliet smiled. "I would love that, thank you."

Nikolai and Juliet were suddenly interrupted by a knock at the door.

"Come in," Nikolai called out.

Grace and Theo came in and bowed.

"The funeral will be held in an hour," Theo advised.

"Thanks, Theo," Nikolai said.

"I better go get changed into something more appropriate for the funeral," Juliet said, standing up. "I'll see you soon."

She smiled at Nikolai before following Grace out the door.

CHAPTER NINE

*"A friend loves at all times,
and a brother is born for a time of adversity."*

Proverbs 17:17

Mildred kept to the back of the cave, while the other followers were eager to hear from the Prince of Darkness. After her previous encounter with the Master and his displeasure with her incompetence, she feared making a mistake again. But things were progressing. The Master was getting more robust, and the other followers were getting impatient. Mildred crept closer, trying to get a look at what the Master was doing.

A black book sat at his feet, opened. The Master, still bound, read a passage from the book. He whispered the book's contents to himself while the others stared in wonder and listened quietly, waiting for their instructions. Mildred sighed quietly. After the displeasing occurrence with the Master, she was second-guessing her allegiance to him, and she felt guilty and scared because of it. If anyone knew the doubts in her heart, she would be killed by the followers, or worse, have her soul eaten by the Master as an act of betrayal. Mildred shivered. It had gotten colder in the caves the deeper they went in, and she was getting restless. She needed rest. She looked at the others, who were waiting for the Master to speak. They looked like lost puppies, willing to do anything for him, even if it meant giving up their souls. One of the others looked over to Mildred and snarled at her. She was a shapeshifter, and could transform into a giant wolf. Her long black hair was tied up into a ponytail, and she had tribal markings all over her body. She was close to the Master, bringing him victims that stumbled across their cave by accident. The one thing that scared Mildred, was her red eyes glaring straight at her.

The Master opened his eyes and snarled. He looked around the room before setting his sights on one of his followers. He was a middle-aged man gifted with the strength of a hundred. The Master gestured for the man to come forward. The man smirked at the others as he confidently walked over to the Master, kneeling in front of him in a bowing stance. The Master lifted his hand to the man as far as the chains would allow, and snarled. Suddenly, the man started screaming as his bones began to break. His agonizing screams echoed throughout the cave, as his body began to wither away, as the Master ate his soul. Mildred looked away at the sight, and struggled to keep her last meal down. This part always scared her and made her feel faint. It's the reason why she didn't want to be a part of this anymore. What's to say the Master won't do the same thing to them once he is freed? The thought terrified Mildred. A few other followers backed away, scared at the sudden turn of events. The shapeshifter laughed, as the man's wrinkled and decayed body fell to the floor. The Master looked back down at the book and spoke.

"Arise from the gates of hell.
A beast of darkness is here to dwell.

Three heads are better than one.
One nasty bite, and it is done.
The eyes of that which is red.
A heart of stone which is now dead."

Black clouds came out of the book and made a circular portal in the air. Mildred backed away further as she heard several low growls, afraid of what would come through. A cerberus slowly walked through the portal and stood by the Master's side. Its fur was as dark as onyx, and its razor-sharp teeth became exposed as it growled at the others. Its three heads barked as a warning, and its venomous snake tail hissed from behind. The Master smiled as he patted the creature.

✦ ✦ ✦ ✦ ✦

Nikolai stood in front of the mirror dressed in black clothes, with a letter in his hand. The one his father wrote. His hatred for his father disappeared once he knew his father was being controlled. His father's letter was from the heart and showed much regret on his part. Nikolai felt guilty for not knowing. His father must have suffered a lot, but could not end it. He took one last look in the mirror, then headed to the church outside the palace. Once there, he was shocked to see how many people had shown up. He was quickly reminded by many people giving their condolences, that his father was once a very friendly and great King, and that everyone changes after losing someone they love.

Nikolai looked over and saw Juliet in a simple but elegant black dress. His feelings for her had increased over the past few days, and with the letter indicating a coming war, he feared losing her.

Priest Phil interrupted his thoughts as he announced that the service was about to start, so he walked over to Juliet and held out his arm. She smiled and took it. He led her to the front of the congregation, where they sat side by side in the front row.

Priest Phil spoke to the congregation about the late King, and all the good deeds he had done throughout his reign. He then talked about him in his last years. About his grief in losing the love of his life, and what that can do to a person. Nikolai was thankful to Priest Phil for portraying his father as a good person, just lost after his love passed. Juliet took Nikolai's hand in hers to comfort him. He smiled and squeezed her hand back in response, while they continued to listen to his father's eulogy.

Once Priest Phil had finished speaking, the late King who was laid to rest in a magnificent coffin, was placed into the ground. Nikolai stood up with Juliet by his side, and walked over to his father's grave. After saying a small prayer for his father, Nikolai placed a flower onto his coffin and stood beside Priest Phil. Others came up to say their prayers. After putting their flowers onto the late King's coffin, and sending Nikolai their condolences, they left the church. Once everyone had left, Nikolai stayed and watched as Priest Phil covered his father's coffin with dirt. He was thankful that Juliet was still by his side, giving him much needed support just by her presence. After his father's coffin was laid into the ground, Juliet and Nikolai walked back hand in hand to the castle.

"How are you feeling?" Juliet's quiet voice broke into Nikolai's thoughts.

"I wouldn't have made it through this afternoon without you by my side," Nikolai replied, kissing her hand. "So, thank you."

She smiled at him. "I'm glad I could help."

Once they entered the palace doors, Queen Julia and Captain Issac met them hand in hand.

"It was a lovely funeral, Prince Nikolai, but I'm afraid we

must leave for home," Queen Julia said.

"Of course," Nikolai said, turning to a passing servant. "Please prepare a carriage for the Queen, Princess and the Captain."

The steward bowed and went to organize Nikolai's request, as Queen Julia and Captain Issac went to gather their things.

"Be careful, please," Nikolai whispered. "There are people who are against the marriage alliance, and I fear for your safety."

"I promise I'll be careful," she whispered back. "You needn't worry. I have Issac and his men accompanying Mother and me home."

"I know," Nikolai sighed.

"Shall I write to you once I'm home?" Juliet asked.

"I would love nothing more," Nikolai replied, relaxing.

CHAPTER TEN

"Greater love has no one than this:
to lay down one's life for one's friends."

John 15:13

Nikolai paced in his father's office, waiting for news that Juliet and her mother had returned to their Kingdom safely. He had no doubts about Captain Issac and his capabilities, but his father's letter worried him about their safety.

To pass time, Nikolai went to see Priest Phil to make a date for the wedding. He then wrote a letter to Juliet explaining the details. After, he sent letters to the other kingdoms, inviting them to meet and discuss an alliance, and to inform them in person about the coming threat. After that, Theo arranged a public announcement for the people of the kingdom. There Nikolai informed them about the end of the war, and the marriage alliance. The people were overjoyed with the news of peace.

A knock at the door interrupted his thoughts, as he rested from his morning errands.

"Come in," Nikolai called out.

"Prince Nikolai, a letter has come for you," a servant said, as he came in with a note and handed it to Nikolai.

"Thank God," he said, quickly opening the letter and reading the contents inside.

He was relieved that Juliet and her mother had gotten home safely. He then handed the servant his letter to Juliet, explaining the wedding date.

"Please send this to Juliet," he informed the servant.

"Of course, Prince Nikolai," the servant replied bowing, before exiting the room.

As the servant was leaving, Theo came in and sat down exhausted.

"They make it back safely?" Theo asked.

"Yes, just got word," Nikolai said relieved.

"That's good," he said. "I spoke to my brother. I told him the bare minimum and asked him to make some more weapons for a possible war. I also asked him to keep an eye out for any odd or suspicious information."

"Thanks, Theo," Nikolai sighed.

"Wait, there's more. He wants to meet with you. He said your father came to him with a pretty weird request," Theo explained.

"What!" Nikolai exclaimed looking up from his work. "My father?"

Theo nodded.

"Where is he?" Nikolai asked.

Theo nodded towards the door.

"Come in Fitzwilliam," Nikolai called out.

Fitzwilliam walked into the room looking nervous and out of place. He bowed before Prince Nikolai and sat next to his brother.

"Relax, brother," Theo laughed.

"Easier said than done," he grumbled. "Forgive me, Your Highness, it's not you. I feel more comfortable in my workshop than in other places.”

“It’s all right, Fitzwilliam,” Nikolai said smiling, looking over at Theo, who was trying to hold in his laughter.

“Theo mentioned my father coming to visit you just before he passed?” Nikolai asked.

“Yes, Your Highness,” Fitzwilliam began. “It was quite odd, and he didn’t look very well. He asked me if I had a steel hammer in my workshop, so I got him one. He then asked me to smash a Gem. He looked relieved once it was shattered. Then he gave me an envelope saying it was for you.”

Nikolai stared at Fitzwilliam in shock.

“What color was this Gem?” Nikolai asked curiously.

“A light grey, and about the size and length of a dessert spoon,” Fitzwilliam explained, measuring an approximate with his fingers.

Nikolai turned to look at Theo, who was just as shocked as he was, about what they were hearing.

“No?” Theo questioned.

“It would explain the letter my father had left me just before he passed,” Nikolai stated.

Fitzwilliam looked from his brother to the prince with confusion and curiosity.

“My father left me a letter after his murder. He was being controlled by a rouge Gem user named Mildred, who gave him the moonstone Gem. The one you destroyed. My father used the Gem to control my curse and start this war. Mildred is also working to help release the Prince of Darkness, so he can start a war with all the kingdoms,” Nikolai explained.

“Why? What do they gain by controlling you to start the war, when they could have waited for the Prince of Darkness to rise?” Fitzwilliam asked.

“We don’t know,” Nikolai replied shrugging.

"We don't know much, brother. We are still looking into it. Nikolai has just sent a letter to all the other kingdoms asking for a meeting," Theo explained.

Fitzwilliam thought for a moment.

"I shall keep an eye and ear out for anything suspicious, or any rumors I hear of, and report back to you or Theo," Fitzwilliam said. "And it makes a lot more sense as to why you asked me to prepare some more weapons."

"Thank you, Fitzwilliam," Nikolai said.

"I'm assuming you're keeping this under wraps, until the other kingdom royalties arrive?" Fitzwilliam asked.

"I think it would be best," Nikolai replied.

"I think that is wise," Fitzwilliam said, picking up the envelope. "This envelope that your father gave me, holds instructions on how to earn the Sword of the Kings."

"The what?" Theo asked.

"The Sword of the Kings is supposedly a myth, but I believe it's real," Fitzwilliam said proudly. "I think that's why your father gave me the letter to give to you."

"I heard stories about it from my mother," Nikolai said nodding, as he took the envelope from Fitzwilliam. "I thought it was just that, a story."

"The Sword of the Kings is powerful. A topaz Gem is embedded in the sword hilt. It allows the blade to be covered in flames, giving one the upper hand in combat," Fitzwilliam explained. "It was known to be used by your grandfather. When one comes of age, they venture to where the sword is kept. They then have to pass a test, to see if they are worthy of holding the sword."

"That sounds like an awesome weapon," Theo exclaimed.

Nikolai opened the envelope and read it.

"It's in riddles," Nikolai said.

"It's not easy," Fitzwilliam explained. "It's in riddles because it's supposed to keep the sword hidden in the family, and not be found by an outsider."

"I can understand that," Nikolai said, reading the riddle. "The Sword of the Kings sounds powerful. At least I now know that my kingdom does have its own Gem."

"It would be beneficial in this upcoming war," Fitzwilliam said, standing up to leave. "I'll be praying for you, Your Highness. I best be off now, things to do."

"Thank you again, Fitzwilliam, for all your help," Nikolai said, feeling confident.

Chapter Eleven

*"Be kind and compassionate to one another, forgiving each other,
just as in Christ God forgave you."*

Ephesians 4:32

Early the following day, Nikolai sat on his bed re-reading the riddle his father had left him. He read it repeatedly, trying to figure out where the Sword of the Kings was hidden. He couldn't sleep properly as his mind was stuck on the letter, but he also couldn't think straight as a headache was beginning to form again. Nikolai sighed and got up to get a glass of water, hoping it would ease his pain. He walked over to the balcony from his room, with the glass in hand and breathed in the fresh air. It was a quiet and peaceful morning. He smiled as he thought of Juliet, excited that he would see her again in a couple of days. It made his heart race.

He was interrupted by a knock at his door.

"Come in," Nikolai called out.

Theo came in and joined his friend on the balcony.

"Couldn't sleep?" Nikolai asked him.

"Not a dam wink," Theo yawned. "I've been trying to figure

out that riddle your father left you, but my brain is all fried up."

"Yeah, mine too," Nikolai replied groggily.

"When is Princess Juliet arriving?" Theo asked.

"She should have left her kingdom yesterday; so, we should see her in a couple of days," Nikolai calculated.

"For the wedding," Theo grinned at him.

"For the wedding," Nikolai laughed.

"Maybe Princess Juliet would understand riddles better than us," Theo wondered.

"What makes you say that?" Nikolai asked.

"Well, she reads, doesn't she," Theo stated. "You know how women know things; maybe she'll know what the riddle means."

"I shall ask her," Nikolai laughed. "But not a word until after the wedding. I want that day to be special for her."

Theo grinned.

"What?" Nikolai asked.

"You've gotten soft," Theo laughed.

Nikolai laughed with him.

"Hey, Theo," Nikolai said. "Would you be my best man at my wedding?"

"I'm always your best man," Theo said, trying to crack a joke.

Nikolai laughed along with his friend.

"I'd be honored," Theo grinned.

✦ ✦ ✦ ✦ ✦

The Prince of Darkness was hungry for power and freedom. Chained up by the God of Light had been unfortunate, and a huge setback for his ultimate plan. He planned to rule in a world full of fear, darkness, and hatred because that was where he drew his power from. He loved spreading chaos and fear everywhere, and torturing people with their fears. But he had been trapped in this prison for over a thousand years now, and he was getting restless.

At one time, he thought someone would release him sooner, but that person had turned out to be weak. This time, he had found multiple people who he had manipulated into thinking the God of Light did not care about them, when he did. He laughed at how gullible they were. The only person he cared about was himself. He had promised them with riches and power, but it was a lie. They didn't need to know that, as he still needed them to set him free. Afterwards, he would not need them, and his creatures of darkness could feed on them.

"Selena, my precious," he called.

Selena was a shapeshifter who could transform into a massive wolf. She was brought up in the wild after her family had been murdered. Selina wasn't sure why she was the only one who lived. Nobody liked her, even her own family. Everyone around her thought she was odd, as she was seen always speaking to herself or an object.

Ever since she was little, she could hear voices whispering to her, guiding her, teaching her things, and telling her what to do. After the Prince of Darkness took her in the voices stopped, and she believed it was him who was the tiny voice whispering to her all along. When she asked him about it, he did not reply, only smiled. She still believed it was him.

Selina had long black hair braided into a ponytail. Her body was covered in tribal markings signifying different meanings, and her red eyes were sharp and always on the lookout.

"Yes, Master," Selina said bowing in front of him.

"I need you to retrieve a Gem. This specific Gem has the power to heal, and would be most beneficial to our cause. You can find it in the Kingdom of Elaxon. The Princess or the Queen will have one in their possession. Retrieve it, and bring one back to me," he said.

"Yes, of course, Master," Selina said bowing.

Selina got up and made her way to the entrance of the cave. Before she left, the Prince of Darkness called to her again. She turned to face him.

"Use whatever means necessary to get that Gem," he snarled.

Selina nodded and left the cave, transforming into her wolf form and running into the forest. She made it her mission to succeed, as she did not want to disappoint the Master like Mildred had.

CHAPTER TWELVE

*"And now these three remain: faith, hope and love.
But the greatest of these is love."*

1 Corinthians 13:13

Juliet could see the Kingdom of Zolatta through the carriage doors, and she was relieved that they were almost there. The carriage ride was uncomfortable and long, and she was eager to stretch her legs. The day was nearing the end, and she needed to rest before tomorrow, her wedding day.

"Don't worry, Juliet, just a few more minutes," her mother said, seeing how uncomfortable she was.

Juliet smiled at her mother. She wasn't just uncomfortable about the long journey. She was nervous about seeing Nikolai again and the wedding tomorrow. But she was also excited about the new chapter in her life. She was blessed that Nikolai was such a nice person, and that she had grown extremely attached to him.

"It's the Princess," she heard the townspeople say as they rode past.

"The Queen is also here," others gossiped.

"She's beautiful," others exclaimed.

Princess Juliet and Queen Julia waved to the townspeople as they rode past. Kids ran alongside the carriage, to give them some flowers they had just picked. Juliet thanked them and waved back.

"Everyone is so welcoming here," Queen Julia said, waving to the people as their carriage passed by.

"I guess they're excited about the wedding," Juliet said smiling.

The carriage stopped at the front of the palace, and Juliet saw Nikolai run to open the door, before the stewards could.

"Juliet, Queen Julia, welcome," Nikolai greeted, bowing, then looked around.

"Where is Captain Issac?" he asked.

"Here," Captain Issac said, dismounting his horse.

Captain Issac, Theo, and Nikolai quickly exchanged handshakes and greetings. Then Nikolai took Juliet's hand and helped her out of the carriage, and Captain Issac did the same for Queen Julia.

"I'm so glad you're here," Nikolai said.

"Me too," Juliet said smiling.

Nikolai led them up the stairs and into the palace. Juliet was amazed at how beautiful the decorations were for the wedding. Flowers and banners hung from the walls and ceilings. Servants, maids, and stewards were busy preparing extra bedding, cooking, and decorating the rest of the palace before the big day tomorrow. Juliet spotted Grace and Ruth, her two personal maids, running up to her and bowed.

"I'm sorry, Your Highness," both maids said bowing to Nikolai, "but we need to make sure Princess Juliet has everything ready for tomorrow."

"Of course," Nikolai said. "I'll see you at dinner."

Queen Julia and Juliet followed Grace and Ruth as they led

them to Juliet's bed chambers. Juliet and her mother sat on the bed, waiting to see what the maids wanted to show them.

"Ok," Ruth said, holding up the wedding dress. "I made this dress according to you and your mother's input; I hope you like it."

The gown was an elegant white, with a fitted bodice. It had an A-line shape, which started to flare out at the waistline, and into a triangular shape that was floor length. It had a scoop neckline, and long sleeves made with lace. There were embroidered sequins and beads throughout the dress.

"This is beautiful," Queen Julia gasped.

Juliet covered her mouth, gasping at how beautiful the dress was. It was fit for a Queen.

"This is stunning," Juliet told Ruth, almost in tears.

Grace came out and stood beside Ruth with the jewels.

"You will also be wearing these pearl earrings, with a matching necklace and bracelet," Grace said showing them the jewels.

"You girls are amazing," Queen Julia praised, admiring the gown and jewels.

"Ruth made the dress," Grace said smiling at Ruth. "I just have a talent for matching clothing with jewelry."

"Thank you, Your Highness," Ruth whispered, bowing shyly.

"Now we need to dress you for dinner," Grace said looking at Ruth.

"You are thinking of that dress?" Ruth asked.

"Defiantly that dress," Grace replied.

They both giggled and went to put the wedding dress and jewels back in the wardrobe ready for tomorrow. They came back holding a beautiful light pink knee-length dress with sleeves. Flowers were embroidered at the bottom of the dress in different shades of blue.

"I don't think Prince Nikolai will be able to look away from you," Queen Julia giggled. "That dress is stunning. Is this another one of your creations Ruth?"

"Yes, Your Highness," Ruth replied shyly.

"Would you be willing to make my wedding dress?" Queen Julia asked.

"Of course," Ruth beamed. "I'd be honored."

"Then it's settled." Queen Julia stood up happily. "I will see you at dinner Juliet."

She kissed her daughter on the cheek, and left the room to prepare for dinner.

"Here, Princess," Ruth said handing her the dress.

"Thank you," Juliet said, taking the dress.

Juliet stood up and headed to her room divider to change. Once the dress was on, she came out and sat at her vanity, where Ruth and Grace were waiting to do her hair and make-up.

"Simple?" Grace asked.

"Yes, please," Juliet nodded.

While Grace applied her make-up and Ruth did her hair, Juliet struggled to get her nerves under control.

Was this how my mother felt just before marrying my father? Is this normal? Juliet thought.

"Nervous, Princess?" Ruth asked.

"Is it obvious?" she whispered.

"It's normal to have pre-wedding nerves," Grace explained.

"Really?" Juliet asked.

"My sister and all my brothers had them," Grace explained. "And let me tell you a secret. My brothers were worse than my sister."

Juliet let out a breath of relief. "Thank goodness."

"You look stunning," Grace said, as both she and Ruth stood back to admire their work.

Juliet looked at herself in the vanity mirror and smiled. She looked and felt pretty, and she was grateful for Grace and Ruth's help. She then stood up and headed to the door. Turning around one last time, she looked at both Ruth and Grace.

"Thank you," she said smiling.

"You are very welcome, Princess," they both replied bowing together.

Juliet left the room feeling a little better than before. She headed down the corridor to the dining room but stopped just outside the door, as she saw Nikolai coming from the opposite direction in a nice suit. The moment their eyes met, they both smiled.

"You look stunning," Nikolai complimented.

Juliet blushed. "Thank you, Nikolai, you look very handsome this evening."

"Thank you," he laughed.

Nikolai held out his arm for Juliet, and she took it. Then he led her into the dining area. The others had not arrived yet, and Juliet felt that her mother had something to do with that. Nikolai led her to her chair.

"Allow me," Nikolai said, pulling the chair out for her.

"Thank you," she said, sitting down as he pushed the chair in slightly.

Nikolai then sat next to her at the head of the table.

"How did your journey go?" Nikolai asked.

"It was long, but we had no troubles," she replied.

"I'm glad. I must admit I was worried for your safety," he said, his eyes never leaving hers.

Juliet smiled and blushed again.

"How have you been?" she asked.

"Good, I've been working at getting the kingdom back up and running," he told Juliet.

"No troubles?" she asked.

"No troubles," he replied.

A servant came in and bowed.

"The Queen and Captain Issac send their apologies. The Queen is exhausted from the journey, and has requested dinner in her room tonight."

"Thank you," Nikolai said nodding.

The servant bowed and left.

After a few minutes, a servant filled the table with roast beef, vegetables, potatoes, and wine. Nikolai reached for Juliet's hand, and she gave it to him. Then they both gave thanks.

"Lord, thank you for this food before us. Thank you for Juliet and the Queen's safe arrival. I ask that you bless our day tomorrow. Amen."

"Amen," Juliet said, smiling.

The food looked amazing, so Juliet helped herself to a little bit of each dish.

"Your chief is amazing," Juliet exclaimed after taking a bite.

"He certainly is. I remember sneaking in there as a kid to get more dessert," Nikolai said, pouring her a drink.

"Thank you," she said taking the cup. "Did the chief ever catch you?"

He laughed. "Never, but I had Theo with me."

Juliet chuckled.

Nikolai held up his wine glass.

"To our future," he said.

'To our future," she replied, with her drink raised.

"So, Juliet, did you ever sneak into your kitchen when you were little?" Nikolai asked.

"A few times," she explained. "But I didn't go alone as well. I had someone on the lookout while I got enough snacks for the both of us."

"And who was this partner in crime?" he asked.

"Her name was Lacy and her mother worked at the palace," she replied.

"And what does she do now?" Nikolai asked.

"She owns her own bakery back home," she said.

"I guess all those kitchen heists were worth it," he laughed.

"I guess they were," she chuckled.

Juliet was surprised at how easy it was to talk to Nikolai. She felt safe with him and very happy.

As the servants took away the food, Nikolai looked over at her.

"Can I walk you back to your room?" he asked.

"It was such a long journey here, and I would like to stretch my legs," Juliet began.

"Then how about a walk around the garden?" Nikolai asked.

"I would like that," Juliet said, taking his offered arm.

The sun had set, and it was getting dark outside. Juliet was afraid she would not be able to see where she was going. As they arrived at the palace gardens, it was lit up with tiny fairy lights. There were also lights along a path that guided the way to a chair, that sat in the middle of the garden. It took Juliet's breath away.

"Who did this?" Juliet asked, taking in the beauty.

"I did, a few years back. I like to sit out here at night when I can't sleep. But it was too dark. So, I asked Theo if he would help me setup some lights," he explained, smiling at her reaction.

"It's beautiful," she commented. "The flowers."

"We're my mother's; she planted them," Nikolai said.

"They're beautiful," Juliet said, walking over to take a closer look.

"They helped calm me down, whenever I felt angry enough to change," Nikolai said picking one up.

"Can you still change into the fox spirit by yourself?" Juliet asked.

"Yes," Nikolai replied, moving closer to Juliet; he was inches away from her face. "Does that scare you?"

"No," she said, meeting his eyes.

He smiled.

"You're one brave woman," he said, placing the flower in her hair. "How did you know it was me, back when I almost-."

"Startled me," Juliet stated cutting him off.

He laughed and nodded in defeat.

"Your eyes were filled with fear when I saw you on the battlefield. When you startled me in the garden, they looked the same," she explained.

"I was afraid I was going to hurt you," he whispered.

Juliet caressed his cheek with her fingers. "But you didn't."

He held her hand and smiled at her.

"I thank the God of Light that he brought you to me," Nikolai said leaning in close to steal a kiss.

"Me too," Juliet replied returning the kiss.

CHAPTER THIRTEEN

"Never will I leave you; never will I forsake you."

Hebrews 13:5

"Princess," Juliet heard Grace's voice.

Juliet woke up to find Grace, Ruth and her mother standing over her bed. She sat up and yawned. She had gone to bed quite late last night, but did not regret it as she had been talking with Nikolai.

Juliet had learned a lot by talking with him last night. His favorite color was blue, he liked to read when he had the time, he loves horse riding, and he enjoys spending the evening in the training grounds, training in archery or sword fighting.

"What time is it?" she asked them groggily.

"Almost midday," Grace said.

"Midday!" she exclaimed, rushing to get out of bed. "I overslept."

"Juliet, my dear, we have plenty of time to get you ready," her mother reassured.

Juliet sat back down on her bed and sighed in relief.

"What time did you go to bed?" her mother asked.

Juliet looked up at her mother and smiled.

"Midnight," she said guiltily. "I'm sorry I didn't realize the time after dinner. Nikolai and I walked around the gardens talking. When it got too cold, we came back inside and went to the kitchen for some dessert. We talked until the midnight clock chimed throughout the palace."

"How romantic," Ruth exclaimed, clasping her hands together in excitement.

Grace giggled alongside her.

"Here, we saved you something to eat. There will be a banquet for Nikolai and you after the wedding," her mother said, giving her daughter a bowl of fruit.

"Thanks," Juliet said smiling.

"While you eat, I'll do your hair," Grace said, grabbing the brush.

Juliet walked over to her vanity, sat, and ate while waiting for Grace.

Grace walked over to Juliet thoughtfully.

"I'm thinking of putting your hair up into a loose bun, with braids entwined, leaving a few pieces dangling at the front, then adding some white roses to finish it. What do you think?"

"I think that sounds wonderful," Juliet replied.

"I agree," her mother said.

"So, when are you and Issac getting married, Mother?" Juliet asked, trying to distract herself from how nervous she was.

"We are planning it at the moment," Queen Julia explained.

"I'm so happy for you, Mother," Juliet said excitedly, "and for Isaac."

"How did you two meet?" Grace asked.

"Oh, it's a long story. I don't want to bore you," Queen Julia replied.

"I want to hear it again. Besides it will distract me from my pre-wedding nerves," Juliet pleaded.

Queen Julia smiled. "Ok. After Juliet was born, I lost my husband in a hunting accident. During that tough year, Issac came into our kingdom looking for work. He eventually found a job as a royal guard. During my time of mourning there were threats made to me, so the Captain of the Royal Guard assigned Issac to look after us. Issac never complained, slacked off, or took time off, and never let his feelings show until I almost got hurt. Juliet and I were horse riding one day and stopped to have lunch. Issac had been assigned to us for almost a year by then, and was teaching Juliet how to make rocks skip in the water. I was watching them both on the picnic rug behind them. He was such a good role model for Juliet. Suddenly, someone came up from behind me and threatened me with a knife to the throat. While playing with Juliet, Issac turned to see the horrible scene before him. Juliet was in tears when she saw me in that horrific situation. It turns out my attacker wanted our kingdom's Gem. Issac, who was always one step ahead of anyone, managed to trick the man into lowering his knife to my throat. Then Issac threw the rock that was still in his hand, and hit the man in the forehead. The man staggered back, and Issac lunged towards him, while I ran to Juliet to comfort her. After a few minutes quarrelling, Issac ended up having the man tied up. We ended the day quickly and headed back to the palace. Later that evening, I went to sit in the palace garden. Issac came up to me and asked if I was all right after what had happened earlier that day. I told him I was a little shaken up and worried for Juliet's safety, and he promised me then that he would always be there to protect me and Juliet. At that moment we shared our first kiss."

"How romantic," Grace exclaimed.

"I know, the story never gets old," Juliet said smiling. "I'm glad you and Isaac are getting married. I've always thought of him as a father."

"Issac will be pleased to hear that," her mother said, moved.

"Why did it take you both so long to think about getting married?" Juliet asked.

"After a while of stealing kisses in the hallway and meeting up to spend time together, Issac thought he wasn't the right person for me. I told him we were perfect, but I think someone may have said something because after that, he was different. He always addressed me as Your Majesty or My Queen," Queen Julia replied.

"What changed his mind?" Juliet asked, intrigued.

"The war. The thought of me in a marriage alliance with someone else," Queen Julia said simply.

"How romantic," Grace and Juliet said.

"He knew how precious time was, and didn't want to watch me marry someone else. He feared losing me," Queen Julia said blushing. "He also told me that the Captain of the Royal Guard before him, was considering Issac for the position when he retired. But thought Isacc wouldn't be right for the position, as he was so close to me."

"What," Juliet exclaimed, almost dropping her now empty bowl.

"After the war started and the previous Captain of the Guard was killed in battle, none of the other soldiers wanted to believe that Issac was their new Captain. They thought he got the position because of how close he was to me, not his skills. It took him a while to gain the trust of his men. But war changes everyone, and Issac and I aren't getting any younger. So, we decide to get married despite what people think. I love him, and he loves me," Queen Julia explained.

"Awe, that's sweet," Juliet, Grace and Ruth said.

"It's not fair that both of you had to suffer all these years,"

Grace said. "When you're in love, you want to be with that person, no questions asked."

"Thank you, Grace. Unfortunately, it is difficult for royals," Queen Julia said.

"Ok, hair is done," Grace said, stepping back to admire her work.

"Oh wow," Juliet said, staring at herself in the mirror. "Grace, this is amazing, thank you."

"I'm glad you like it," Grace said smiling.

"My turn," Ruth said with her make-up ready.

"I shall go and fetch the dress," Grace said excitedly.

"You both have such talents in make-up and hair. Who taught you?" Queen Julia asked.

"We taught each other," Ruth explained. "It's better to have multiple talents in this line of work. Grace and I like to switch roles now and then to keep our talents up to date."

"You girls sure are talented," Juliet complimented.

"Thank you, Princess," Ruth replied cheerily.

Juliet sat as still as she could while Ruth did her make-up, being careful not to move too much. Grace came back with the wedding dress in hand with a big grin on her face. Queen Julia got up and started admiring the dress again. The wedding dress Ruth had made Juliet was stunning. She was lucky to have her as one of her maids. She was incredibly talented, hardworking and a good friend. Ruth tilted Juliet's head as she applied the lipstick and stood back to admire her.

"You look magnificent," Ruth said, packing up.

Grace and Queen Julia stopped what they were doing and looked over to Juliet. Their stunned faces told Juliet that Ruth had done a fantastic job. Juliet stood up, and Grace handed her the wedding dress. She walked behind her room divider and got changed. Juliet had to get Grace to help her, as she didn't want all her hard work on her hair to come undone.

Once Juliet had the dress on, she stared at herself in the mirror, feeling beautiful and full of nerves. Grace and Ruth had outdone themselves to make this a special day for her. Juliet walked out of her room divider and showed everyone the finished results. She was met with gasps, awes, and eventually tears.

"My baby girl has grown up," Queen Julia cried, bursting into tears.

Grace and Ruth handed Queen Julia a box of tissues, but not before they took one for themselves. Juliet went over to her mother and hugged her.

"I love you, mother," Juliet whispered.

"I love you too," Queen Julia whispered back. "I'm so proud of you."

CHAPTER FOURTEEN

*"So, they are no longer two, but one flesh.
Therefore, what God has joined together, let no one separate."*

Matthew 19:6

Nikolai woke up suddenly when his bedchamber door slammed shut, and found Theo poking at him to get up. He sat on the side of the bed, yawning.

"Someone had a late-night last night," Theo grinned.

"I'm a gentleman, Theo," Nikolai said tiredly. "I would never do that to Juliet."

"I know," Theo said. "So, what did you guys get up to last night?"

Nikolai yawned.

"Juliet was restless after the long journey, so we walked around the gardens. Then, it got too cold to stay out there, so we returned inside and headed to the kitchen for dessert. We stayed up till midnight talking with each other. We had no idea it was midnight until the clock chimed throughout the palace. We then went to our separate bed chambers."

"I bet you're excited about your wedding day," Theo said. "How's Princess Juliet feeling? Did you get to know her a bit more. Considering you've only met her a few times when you were young."

Nikolai laughed.

"Yes, I am excited, and she's doing fine. I learnt a lot about Juliet. She loves to read, go horse riding, is an amazing healer, loves the colors green and blue, and loves to help people. But before heading to bed, I may have stolen a kiss or two from her," Nikolai laughed.

"I'm glad you're happy. Even though you may think you don't deserve it, you do deserve happiness," Theo said happily.

"Thanks, I just hope you find love soon," Nikolai said.

"When I do, you'll be the first to know," Theo replied.

Nikolai's manservant, Levi, walked into the room.

"Ready to dress, Your Highness?" Levi asked with the clothes in his hand.

Nikolai got up and took the clothes from Levi, thanking him, then went behind his room divider to change.

Nikolai had chosen black dress pants, black leather shoes, a long white cotton shirt, a black vest, and a black coat to finish the look. He hoped he looked okay. He remembered seeing a picture of his parents on their wedding day, and based his outfit on what his father had worn. Although with a few changes, as his father's outfit was a bit out of fashion.

Nikolai came out dressed and sat in the chair provided by Levi, so he could get a clean shave. Theo took the time to tell him about the morning he'd missed. Juliet wasn't at breakfast, so he assumed she had slept in like him. Queen Julia and Captain Issac were at breakfast. They had told him they were getting married, and that he and Nikolai were invited to celebrate their special day. And the preparations for the wedding were being finalized.

Once Levi had finished, Nikolai got up and looked in the mirror.

"How do I look?" Nikolai asked Theo and Levi. "Honest opinions."

"You look good, Your Highness," Levi replied bowing.

"You look nervous," Theo said.

"I am. I don't know why, but I am," Nikolai said, feeling the pre-wedding nerves.

"Relax, Nikolai," Theo said, putting his hand on his friend's shoulder as comfort. "I can see the way Juliet looks and acts around you, and the way you look and act around her."

He laughed.

"Thanks, Theo," Nikolai said, feeling a lot better. "Okay, I'm ready."

"Okay, I'm ready," Juliet said, looking at herself for the last time in the mirror.

"Wait, Princess," Grace said, running towards her with a veil.

"Oh, we can't forget that," Queen Julia said, helping Grace fix the veil into Juliet's hair.

"There, perfect," Queen Julia said, and Ruth and Grace nodded with approval.

"Where's Issac?" Juliet asked.

"He's waiting at the front," Queen Julia replied.

"Okay," Juliet breathed. "Let's go."

Juliet walked out of her bedchambers with her mother, Ruth, and Grace behind her. As they walked down the corridors, Juliet was congratulated by many staff. She bowed and thanked them as she walked past them, and was relieved to find Captain Issac waiting at the palace's front steps. He and his men were waiting outside to escort them to the church, where Nikolai awaited her arrival.

"You look magnificent, Princess," Captain Issac complimented as he bowed.

"Thank you," Juliet replied.

"And you, my dear Queen, look breathtaking," Captain Issac said, walking over to Queen Julia and kissing her cheek.

Juliet smiled at them. She was happy that they were finally together after all these years. Juliet exited the front doors and walked down the palace stairs, to where Captain Issac's soldiers waited. She stopped and looked around at all the townspeople who gathered to greet her. She waved at them and smiled as a group of children approached her and gave her flowers.

"Thank you, they are beautiful," Princess Juliet said smiling.

The children bowed and ran back to their parents happily. The party continued to walk down the street towards the church, while the townspeople cheered and gave their blessings.

After a short walk, they arrived at the front entrance to the church, where Juliet stood speechless. The church was covered in different types and colors of roses. The staff had hung banners beautifully along the entrance, and an arch was filled and entwined with white and pink roses that led to the door. Grace and Ruth took one more look at Juliet, to ensure everything was perfect before heading inside to sit. Her mother and Captain Issac came up, taking turns to hug her.

"I'm so proud of you," Queen Julia whispered, before letting her daughter go.

"Thanks, mother," Juliet whispered back to her.

"You've done great, Princess," Captain Issac said.

Queen Julia and Captain Issac started to head into the church, but stopped when Juliet called out to them.

"Issac," Juliet called, feeling nervous. "Will you walk me

down the aisle as my father?"

Captain Issac was speechless, and her mother was moved. Both looked like they were about to cry.

"I'd be honored," Captain Issac replied smiling, wiping away a tear.

"Thank you," Juliet said.

Queen Julia went into the church with such joy. Once she had taken her seat, the music began. Captain Issac offered his arm to Juliet, and she took it.

Prince Nikolai was standing at the front of the church, looking very handsome. His face lit up when he saw Juliet coming down the aisle, and they exchanged smiles with one another. There were so many people in the congregation. Pastor John from her home country was there with his wife. They smiled and waved, and Juliet waved back at them. She also saw Lacy with her family and smiled. She was happy to see them all here. Once they were at the front of the church, Captain Issac took Juliet's hand and gave it to Nikolai.

"Treasure her," Captain Issac said to Nikolai.

To which Nikolai replied. "Always."

"I'm so proud of you, and I'm so glad I can call you my daughter," Captain Issac said to Juliet.

"Thank you," she replied.

Captain Issac went to sit with Queen Julia, as Nikolai and Juliet walked up to Priest Phil hand in hand.

"Welcome everyone to this very special day, as we celebrate the wedding of Prince Nikolai and Princess Juliet," Priest Phil spoke to the congregation.

"Let me start by reading from the Tanakh. So, they are no longer two, but one flesh. Therefore, what God has joined together, let no one separate. The book of Matthew, chapter 19, verse 6," Priest Phil declared. "Be completely humble and gentle.

Be patient, bearing with one another in love. Make every effort to keep the unity of the spirit, through the bond of peace. Ephesians chapter 4, verses 2-3. You have declared your commitment to one another. May God, in his goodness, strengthen your commitment and fill you both with his blessings. May God bless your lives together and bring about many good things. Amen."

"Amen," both Nikolai and Juliet replied.

As Nikolai and Juliet turned to one other, Theo and Grace came up and handed them both their rings. Nikolai took Juliet's hand and placed the wedding ring on her finger. Juliet then took Nikolai's hand and did the same. Then Nikolai took Juliet's hand and drew her in closer, as they both shared a kiss as husband and wife.

The whole congregation applauded, cheered, and shouted their blessings.

Nikolai and Juliet turned to face the congregation, as Priest Phil spoke to them again.

"Now to bestow the Crown Jewels onto the Prince and Princess of Zolatta. And to announce their new titles," Priest Phil declared. One of the church helpers came forward, carrying the Crown Jewels in an ancient beautifully decorated chest. He stopped beside the priest and waited for further instructions.

"Do the people here today accept and recognize Prince Nikolai and Princess Juliet as their King and Queen?" Priest Phil asked the congregation.

"Yes, we do," the congregation replied. Priest Phil then turned to Nikolai and Juliet.

"With this crown, do you promise to rule peacefully, and uphold mercy and justice in all the laws?" Priest Phil asked Nikolai and Juliet.

"I do," they both replied with confidence. Priest Phil then turned to his helper, and took the crown out for Nikolai. He held it up in front of him as he spoke.

"I now pronounce you King Nikolai of Zolatta," Priest Phil declared, placing the crown on his head.

The people applauded.

Priest Phil took the other crown from the helper, and turned towards Princess Juliet.

"I now pronounce you Queen Juliet of Zolatta," Priest Phil declared, as he placed the crown onto her head.

King Nikolai and Queen Juliet stood hand in hand, while the people of Zolatta applauded their new King and Queen. Nikolai then led his new bride down the aisle and out of the church, to where an open carriage waited, to take them back to the palace. Juliet's smile never left her face as she and Nikolai walked up to the carriage. Once Nikolai helped her into the carriage, he sat beside her, sharing another kiss as the townspeople cheered. The carriage started to move as it took them both through the town and back to the palace. The townspeople were cheering, singing, and dancing in the streets with joy. Nikolai and Juliet waved at the people as they passed by. This was a happy day for the King and Queen, and the people of the Zolatta and Elaxon kingdoms.

Once they returned to the palace, Nikolai helped Juliet down from the carriage, and they both went inside. After the doors closed behind them, Nikolai took Juliet by the hand and swung her around to face him. She smiled as he touched her waist and leaned in to kiss her. She put her hands around his neck and kissed him back.

"You look stunning," Nikolai whispered while brushing his fingers across her cheek.

"Thank you, you're looking very handsome yourself," she replied smiling at him.

He smiled back at her. "Thank you."

"Shall we grace everyone with our presence in the dining

hall?" Nikolai asked, offering his arm to her.

"Yes, I am quite hungry. I missed breakfast this morning," she replied, taking his offered arm.

"So did I," he laughed, leading her down the hallway and into the dining area.

As they both entered the dining area, the minstrels were already singing and dancing. The room was filled with all the Lords and Ladies, along with others that Juliet and Nikolai knew personally. Among the crowd was Queen Julia and Captain Issac, Lacy and her husband, Priest John and his wife, Priest Phil and his wife, and Theo and his brother Fitzwilliam.

Once the bride and groom sat down at their seats, the rest of the guests sat down with them at their allocated seats. As the servants brought out the food, they talked amongst one other. The table was filled with roast pork and chicken, with a side of vegetables, potatoes, and multiple imported wines from across the country.

Queen Julia and Captain Issac were seated next to Juliet on her right. To Juliet's left was Nikolai, Theo, then Fitzwilliam. The rest of the guests sat at multiple tables in front of the newlyweds, as they feasted and celebrated this special day. While they ate, they enjoyed the performances from various singers and dancers. Juliet was so happy to see some familiar faces, especially her childhood friend Lacy, who approached them both and bowed.

"Congratulations, Queen Juliet, Your Highness," Lacy said.

"I'm so happy to see you here, Lacy. How are you and the family? Is business good?" Juliet asked.

"The family and I are doing well. The bakery is doing good, too," Lacy replied.

"Nikolai, this is my friend Lacy, the one I was telling you about," Juliet explained.

"It's a pleasure to meet Juliet's partner in crime," Nikolai greeted, shaking her hand.

"I told him about our kitchen heists when we were kids," Juliet told Lacy.

"We were pretty sneaky. We never got caught, although I think the kitchen staff knew already, but didn't want to spoil our fun," Lacy chuckled.

"I thought that too," Juliet laughed.

Over the next few hours, Juliet had spoken to Priest John and his wife. They had opened and now ran an orphanage right next to the church back home. As so many children had lost one or both parents during the war. Nikolai then introduced Juliet to Priest Phil and his wife. She thanked them for the lovely wedding ceremony. Then Juliet had the privilege of meeting all the Lords and Ladies, who helped oversee all the lands King Nikolai owed. After eating and drinking all evening, people started to leave around eleven as it was getting late.

"You look exhausted, my dear," Nikolai said kissing Juliet's cheek. "Let's retire for the night."

Nikolai helped Juliet to her feet, holding her hand as they walked to their bed chambers.

"Did you enjoy tonight?" Nikolai asked.

"I did, thank you. Did you?" she asked, yawning.

"I did," he replied, kissing her hand.

When they entered their bed chambers, Juliet was amazed at how big the room was. To the left was a balcony looking toward the beautiful mountains. The view was amazing, and there were curtains along the side for when summer came. They could leave the balcony doors open but close their blinds, making it cooler inside. To the right was their bathroom, wardrobes, a vanity set for herself, and a mirror for Nikolai. Right in the middle of the room stood their bed. It was a huge bed; one fit for a King and his Queen. Juliet smiled to herself as she walked over towards the balcony. The view was beautiful. The balcony backed onto the beautiful garden that Nikolai and his mother had decorated. Behind the garden was a huge forest that went on for miles, which gave them some privacy. Nikolai came up behind Juliet, wrapped his hands around her waist, and rested his head on her shoulder. She held his hands as they admired the view.

"It's beautiful, isn't it," Nikolai whispered into her neck.

"It is," she agreed, leaning into his touch.

They stood there for a moment, before Nikolai took his hand and gently moved Juliet's hair away from her neck. She felt his lips touch her neck a second later, as he slowly planted multiple kisses. He turned her around and pressed his lips onto hers. Juliet kissed him back as she wrapped her hands around his neck. Nikolai then lifted his bride into his arms and carried her to their bed. Gently laying her down, they continued to kiss and embrace each other passionately.

CHAPTER FIFTEEN

"In addition to all this, take up the shield of faith, with which you can extinguish all the flaming arrows of the evil one."

Ephesians 6:16

Selina, in her wolf form, ran for miles and miles until she reached the border to the Kingdom of Zolatta. She was angry when she found out that the Princess and Queen, who held the Gems of healing, were not in their own kingdom but in the Kingdom of Zolatta for a wedding. She was tempted to wreak havoc in the Kingdom of Elaxon, because of the time she had wasted. However, she decided against it as she didn't want to be on the wrong side of the Prince of Darkness, like Mildred had. She didn't have any patience with Mildred, and felt happy when the Prince of Darkness showed Mildred how displeased he was with her. She thought he would feast on her soul. She was counting on it. But when he only threatened her, Selina wasn't satisfied. She loved being the person that the Prince of Darkness trusted and relied on the most. She felt good, valued, and wanted. And she wanted it to stay that way. That is why she must complete this mission no matter what. Or die trying.

She continued running past the border and into town, arriving after midnight. There was no one about, which was a relief to Selina, as she didn't want to give up her element of surprise. When she got to the palace, she stopped and counted how many guards there were. There were quite a few patrolling the grounds, and they were armed. She only needed to remove a few guards patrolling where the Princess or Queen slept. She sniffed the air and was delighted when she caught the scent of the one Mildred had cursed as a baby. The prince who was cursed to transform into a fox spirit. Selina wanted to fight him but restrained herself, knowing she must complete her mission first. Who knows, maybe if she was lucky, she could challenge him.

Her nose caught the scent of the Princess first. She cautiously followed the scent that trailed to the Princess's bed chambers, keeping an eye on the guards patrolling the palace. She suddenly stopped. An armed guard patrolled the lower grounds near where the Princess's balcony overlooked. She lowered herself to the ground, ready to attack and waited. The guard stopped and surveyed the scene around him, then turned around and headed toward Selina. When the guard was close enough, Selina pounced on him, sinking her teeth into his neck, killing him instantly. She looked up towards the balcony smirking to herself.

She had found her next victim.

Nikolai startled awake; sensing danger was near. He quickly sat up and looked around the room, but nothing was there. He looked down to find Juliet still fast asleep. She looked beautiful and at peace. But he still couldn't shake the feeling of danger. He kissed Juliet on the forehead, before climbing out of bed. He picked up his clothes from where he had thrown them on the floor only hours before, and put them on quickly. He scanned the room again, looking behind everything, but still couldn't find the source of the danger. He sniffed the air and froze. Fear coursed through his body, mainly for Juliet's safety. He recognized that smell; it was the smell of a giant wolf. Nikolai rushed to the balcony and looked outside, sniffing the air to find the source. His fox spirit instincts and sense of smell, told him the threat was outside, watching him from the bushes. He heard a low growl coming from the bushes to his right, and knew he was right about the danger.

Nikolai rushed out of his bed chambers and ran down the steps to the garden outside, where he had heard the sound. Once outside he slowly moved forward, while trying to listen for movement within the area. In times like this, he was glad for his fox spirit curse, which allowed him to hear and smell things for miles. He heard a rustle in the bushes to his left, and quickly turned to scan that area. Deep red eyes stared back at him as the growl continued. If there were ever a time to willingly change into the fox spirit, it would be now. Juliet was asleep in the palace and out of harm's way, and he had to protect her.

Nikolai felt himself slowly and painfully transform into the fox spirit. His bones began to break and expand as his body became a fox. Once his transformation was complete, he concentrated on finding the wolf's location again. His hearing told him it was still to his left, but closer to the palace, right under the balcony. Nikolai panicked as it was getting closer to Juliet. He turned and ran towards the wolf with his teeth bared. The wolf moved away just in time to miss the swipe of his long, sharp claws. Nikolai turned around to find the wolf out of hiding, and ready to pounce. He stood his ground analyzing, until he knew what his best move would be. The wolf's weakness was its neck, according to the Mythical Creatures book he read after discovering his curse. He would try to injure it in that spot, to have the upper hand in this fight.

Nikolai already had two advantages against the wolf. One, this was his ground. He knew it better than the wolf did. Two, he had six tails to help him fight. Nikolai had good odds of winning this fight, or at least injuring it enough for it to flee.

The wolf did a half circle around him before pouncing on him at the last minute. With its teeth bared and claws ready, the wolf collided with Nikolai, causing him to fall onto his back. Before the wolf could bite him, he used his back hind legs to push it off. He then made himself upright and faced the wolf again. This time, Nikolai charged at the wolf with his claws and teeth bared, ready to attack. Nikolai's claws sunk into the wolf's side, causing it to howl in pain. The wolf's teeth then found Nikolai's shoulder and bit down hard.

Nikolai also let out a howl.

Pain throbbed through his shoulder, and he could feel the blood running down his fur. He used his other claw to dig into the wolf's other side. It howled in pain and fought to free itself from Nikolai's hold. Scratching at Nikolai's chest with its claw, the wolf finally broke free and bolted away from him, stopping at a safe distance. It stood at the edge of the bushes, panting from exhaustion. It turned back to face Nikolai and growled before running off into the night. Nikolai sat on his hind legs panting with exhaustion and pain, due to his wounded shoulder. He winced as the pain began to throb even more. Digging his claws into the dirt, he tried to relieve the pain, but with little effect. His long ears twitched at a sound to his right. He turned his head weakly, whimpering in pain, to see the source of the sound. He found Juliet standing there in her nightgown, hands clasped to her mouth with tears in her eyes. She started walking towards Nikolai with a blanket, but he moved back, afraid he would hurt her.

"Please," Juliet begged through tears. "Let me help you."

Nikolai howled.

The pain was intense, and he knew Juliet could help him. Feeling defeated and weak, Nikolai slowly lay down on the grass, signaling to Juliet that he was okay with her approach. Juliet wasted no time as she ran up to Nikolai and started healing his wounded shoulder and chest. Nikolai watched her as she used her healing powers on him. Juliet didn't look afraid, which made him relax and feel much better. Nikolai then nuzzled his furry face against her face, making her laugh. She took his face and stroked the fur on his nose and ears. He licked her cheek, making her laugh again. Relief flooded through Nikolai; he was in control, and she wasn't afraid of him.

The wound on his shoulder had fully healed, and he noticed that Juliet was shivering. Nikolai started returning to his human self. Once completed, Juliet placed the blanket she had brought, over his shoulders to hide the chill. Nikolai stood up, covered the blanket over him, and embraced Juliet.

"Thank you," Nikolai whispered.

"You're welcome," Juliet whispered back.

Nikolai took her hand, and they both walked back into the palace.

When they entered their bed chambers, Juliet quickly tended to the fire to warm the room, while Nikolai closed the doors and the curtains to the balcony. He then sat on the chair in front of the fire, shivering as Juliet came and sat beside him.

"Shall I call for some tea?" Juliet asked.

"No, thank you. I'll be fine," Nikolai said, caressing her cheek. "Unless you want some."

"I'm ok. I was just worried about you," Juliet replied.

"I'm good, thanks to you," Nikolai assured.

"Then let us head back to bed where it's warmer," Juliet

suggested, taking Nikolai's hand. Nikolai followed her as she guided him back to bed. Once they were back, Nikolai wrapped his arms around Juliet and pulled her into a hug, their faces only inches apart. He started to feel warmer and noticed Juliet wasn't shivering anymore. As Nikolai stroked Juliet's hair, she drifted off to sleep in his arms. He stayed up for a while thinking of what just happened in the last half hour, fearing for Juliet's safety. He had hoped to hear from the other kingdom's about a meeting, but had yet to receive a letter. He needed to talk to Theo, Queen Julia, Captain Issac, and Juliet tomorrow. He would also need to speak with Captain Oberon and his men, so they can be ready and prepared.

But all that must wait until morning. Nikolai then closed his eyes and drifted off to sleep not long after that.

CHAPTER SIXTEEN

"Is anyone among you in trouble? Let them pray.
Is anyone happy? Let them sing songs of praise."

James 5:13

Juliet woke up to Nikolai's arms around her. She lay her head on his chest and snuggled in closer, while he caressed her back. He brushed her hair out of her face and smiled at her. She smiled back. Last night, before the attack, had been fantastic. Nikolai and Juliet spent the night in each other's arms, as husband and wife.

"Morning," he said, smiling down at Juliet.

"Morning," Juliet replied. "How's your shoulder?"

"It's good, thank you," Nikolai replied.

"What happened last night? Why were we attacked?" Juliet asked.

She felt Nikolai sigh, as he hesitated for a moment.

"I am going to call a meeting today to inform everyone, including you," Nikolai explained. "But this attack, I believe, was not a coincidence."

"Oh," Juliet said worriedly. "Do you suspect that the wolf will come back."

"Yes, but don't worry, I won't let anything bad happen to you," Nikolai reassured her.

"Thank you," Juliet said, as Nikolai leaned closer to steal a kiss. Juliet wrapped her arms around his neck and pulled him closer. When their lips parted Nikolai stared at Juliet with admiration.

"Is everything okay?" Juliet asked.

"I am surprised you feel so at ease around me, especially with my curse," he replied, surprised.

"I trust you," Juliet told him.

"That means a lot, thank you," Nikolai said. Juliet pulled apart and held her hand up to Nikolai for him to listen, as she heard something going on outside.

"You hear that?" Juliet asked him.

Outside, they could hear people shouting and panicking. Nikolai and Juliet got up and quickly dressed into something simple, then headed out to where the noise was. Theo met them in the hallway, looking pale.

"What is it?" Nikolai asked, holding Juliet close.

"There's been an attack," Theo replied. "A guard has been killed." Nikolai let out a long sigh and rubbed his eyes.

"I need you to gather Queen Julia, Captain Issac, Fitzwilliam, Captain Oberon, Finnick, Jarreth and yourself, and meet me in the conference room," Nikolai commanded.

Theo nodded and quickly ran off.

"I want you close to me, Juliet," Nikolai said worriedly.

Juliet nodded and took his hand as he led her down the corridor. Something was wrong, if it caused Nikolai to be this protective of her, but she didn't ask. She would wait until he explained it to everyone else as a group. They stopped by his office and went inside. Juliet stood at the door waiting for Nikolai, while he picked up a few things he might need during the meeting. Afterwards, they headed to the conference room.

On the way, Nikolai stopped a servant, and asked him if he could organize breakfast to be brought in for everyone in the conference room. He had also asked the young man if any letters had arrived. To Nikolai's disappointment, no letters had come. He told the servant to find him immediately if any letters do arrive. He also organized another servant to find Priest Phil, and ensure that the body of the fallen soldier was moved to the mortuary.

Once they entered the conference room, Nikolai prepared his notes as Juliet sat beside him waiting patiently. After several minutes, everyone Theo had gone to find, made their way in and sat around the table.

"Juliet, Queen Julia, Captain Issac, this is Captain Oberon. He is Captain of the Royal Guard in Zolatta. Next to him is First Lieutenant Finnick and Second Lieutenant Jarreth, and Fitzwilliam," Nikolai introduced.

"It's nice to meet you," Juliet acknowledged.

"You too, Your Highness," Fitzwilliam replied.

Captain Oberon just grunted his reply with his arms folded over is chest. He looked like a serious man.

"Don't mind him, he's grumpy around everyone," Finnick laughed.

Finnick was very carefree and friendly, while Jarreth nodded politely.

"Jarreth's mute; he doesn't say anything," Finnick said. "But he's a dam good fighter."

"It's nice to meet you all," Juliet replied.

Nikolai sat at the head of the table with his hands clasped, leaning on the table, and sighed.

"Last night, I woke up to find a wolf just outside mine and Juliet's balcony. It had tried to get to Juliet, but I injured it enough to make it flee. This morning, Theo told me that one of our soldiers had lost his life last night on duty," Nikolai explained.

"Oh my," Queen Julia said worriedly.

"After my father passed, I found a letter in his room that was very concerning to me, a possible threat," Nikolai went on.

"Excuse me, Your Highness, but if this possible threat was so concerning, why are we just hearing about it now?" Captain Issac questioned.

"I wanted to see if I could organize a meeting with the other kingdoms, because it doesn't just affect us. It affects all four kingdoms. I sent a letter two weeks ago and still haven't received a reply. I wanted to tell everyone simultaneously. I thought it was the best course of action," Nikolai explained.

Captain Issac nodded. "I understand, I'm sorry for questioning you."

"It's okay. I can understand your concern," Nikolai assured.

"This letter you found, how much did your father explain about the possible threat?" Queen Julia asked.

"He spoke of the Prince of Darkness and his army of dark creatures. He said that people were working on releasing him. He explains that the only way to defeat him and his army, is to unite the four kingdoms and use the power of our Gem's," Nikolai explained.

"Wow," Finnick said, "I thought the Prince of Darkness was just a story, you know, to scare the kids."

"The Prince of Darkness is very true. Have you not read the Tanakh?" Fitzwilliam asked Finnick.

"No, I haven't," Finnick said guiltily. "I'm not much of a reader."

"Well, lad, maybe it's time you started reading it. Just so you know who we're going up against, and how powerful he is," Fitzwilliam suggested.

"What do you want us to do, Your Highness?" Captain Oberon asked.

Nikolai thought for a moment.

"Fitzwilliam, I need you to go to Ashmore and speak to Lord Blackstone, and give him a letter I have prepared," Nikolai told him.

"Will do," Fitzwilliam replied.

"Oberon, I would like you to travel to the Kingdom of Neylon, as an ambassador, and deliver a letter," Nikolai told him.

Oberon nodded.

"Finnick, Jarreth, I need you to go and deliver a letter to Lord Hain, then deliver one to the Kingdom of Kudzu."

"Of course, Your Highness," Finnick replied.

Jarreth nodded his understanding.

"Queen Julia and Captain Issac, I suggest you return to your kingdom and prepare for the coming threat. We can correspond our plans and updates through letters," Nikolai suggested.

"I agree," Queen Julia said. "We'll let you know of any updates and news from our end."

"Thank you," Nikolai said. "Theo and Juliet, I will need your help here."

"Of course," Theo said.

"I'm here for you, always," Juliet replied.

"Okay, let's disperse. If anyone has any concerns, report to me. And thank you for your time and support," Nikolai finished, standing up.

Before the others left the room, Nikolai gave them each the letters they were to deliver. They each then left the room to prepare for their mission. Juliet followed Nikolai out of the conference room, and into his office. She organized for a servant to bring tea, hoping this little gesture would help Nikolai even a little bit.

Nikolai then hugged her. She wrapped her arms around him,

and they stood momentarily embracing each other. She could feel his heartbeat returning to normal, and knew that last night's attack, the dead guard, and the threat were wearing him out. He broke the embrace, looked at her and smiled.

"Thank you," he whispered.

"I haven't done anything," Juliet said, confused.

Nikolai raised an eyebrow at her.

"You've healed me multiple times, you've been looking out for me since we met, you're not afraid of my curse, and you're an amazing and supportive wife. I love you, Juliet," Nikolai said with affection.

Juliet blushed. "I love you too."

A smile lit up on his face, and Juliet blushed in embarrassment. He hugged her again, chuckling at her embarrassment.

"How's your headache? Would you like me to heal it?" Juliet asked him.

"Thank you, but I feel a lot better at the moment. Being around you makes me relaxed and calm. I will let you know if I am in need," he said, stroking her hair.

Juliet smiled and hugged him tighter.

"During the meeting, you said that you needed my help with something. What is it?" Juliet asked him.

"Something my father wrote to me. It doesn't make sense," Nikolai said, reaching for the letter on his desk. He turned back to Juliet and handed it to her.

"Theo and I can't make any sense of it, but maybe you can," Nikolai told her.

A knock sounded at the door, and a maid came in and curtsied with the tea tray.

"Thank you," Juliet said, gesturing for her to put it on the desk. She quickly placed it on the desk and curtsied before leaving the room. As Nikolai made tea, Juliet read his father's letter.

"My Son, I'm sorry. I hope this letter will make up for all my past mistakes. Be careful about who you show this letter to. The Sword of the Kings is not just a story. It's a real sword, only for our ancestors and future generations to wield. I wielded the sword at one point. Unfortunately, I had to hide it again shortly after I met Mildred, and had enough strength to break free from her control for a few hours. I was lucky she hadn't known about the sword's existence. If this sword ended up with the Prince of Darkness, I'm afraid there would be no hope for the future. I've given this letter to Fitzwilliam to give to you because I trust him. I hope you find this sword to protect the people you love.

I love you, son,
Your loving father."

Juliet turned the letter over and found a paragraph written by the late king.

It's dusty and dirty with insects and darkness.
With stones and chains, it's only for the heartless.
One may dwell in this place for long.
The only people who leave, are the ones who are strong.
It's guarded by one but seen by many.
One can leave its place, by spending a pretty penny.
Three meals a day with nothing to do. I hope this letter serves as a clue.

Juliet reread the letter multiple times, thinking about the answer to the riddle. Nikolai came up to her and handed her a cup of tea.

"Thank you," Juliet said, taking a sip.

She looked down at the riddle and thought to herself. Three

things stood out to her; it is somewhere dark, holds chains and is guarded by one.

"The dungeons," Juliet said, looking up at Nikolai.

He thought for a moment, then laughed. "Of course. Thank you. I can't believe Theo or I didn't get it."

"Well, to be fair, you and Theo have had much on your minds lately," Juliet said smiling. "What is the Sword of the Kings?"

"Long ago, the God of Light gave this kingdoms' ruler a topaz Gem. The Gem gave us the means to control fire. The first king gave it to the blacksmith, and asked him to insert the topaz Gem into his swords hilt. In doing so, it enabled the sword's blade to engulf in flames when in battle. But only the true heir to the kingdom can wield its power. That is why it vanishes when the king dies, or if the king has no need of it, he goes and returns it himself. That way the next generation must pass a test, to see if they are worthy to wield it," Nikolai explained.

"Luckily, your father hid it before the Prince of Darkness got his hands on it," Juliet said, drinking her tea.

"Yes, I'm glad he did, too," he replied.

"At least we have two Gems so far that can help defeat the Prince of Darkness and his army," Juliet said, feeling confident.

"Yes, but the question is, am I worthy to hold such a sword?" Nikolai questioned nervously. Juliet put her tea down on the desk and took Nikolai's hands.

"You'll be fine. I have faith in you, and so did your father, considering he left you the instructions to find it," Juliet comforted.

"Thank you for your support," Nikolai said.

A sudden knock sounded at the door.

"Come in," Nikolai called.

Theo and Captain Oberon came in.

"Is everything alright?" Nikolai asked.

"Yes, my men are ready for their mission. We will leave at

dawn tomorrow," the Captain explained.

"Perfect," Nikolai said relieved.

Captain Oberon then bowed and left.

"Queen Julia and Captain Issac will be leaving tomorrow morning, too," Theo said.

"Thanks, Theo. We will have one more dinner with them before they depart," Nikolai said. "I also have great news, Juliet figured out the riddle."

"That's great," Theo said excitedly. "What was the answer?"

"The dungeons," Nikolai replied.

"What! I feel kind of embarrassed we didn't get that," Theo said sheepishly.

Juliet smiled at Nikolai.

"Have you been down to check it out?" Theo asked.

"Not yet," Nikolai replied.

"Well, we do have time before dinner. And there is nothing else to be done," Juliet hinted.

"You want to check it out?" Nikolai asked, surprisingly.

"Yes, I think it's exciting," Juliet replied. Nikolai looked at Theo who shrugged.

"Your call. I'm just as surprised that her Highness is not afraid to get her hands dirty," Theo said.

Nikolai laughed. "Okay."

They all left the office and made their way down to the dungeons. The closer they got to their destination, the fewer people they encountered. Nikolai took the lamp at the entrance and opened the door. Theo and Juliet went in first while Nikolai held the door open, then followed them inside. They took the steps down carefully as mice and insects scurried about. The further they went down, the colder it got. Nikolai gave Juliet his jumper after he noticed she was shivering. They reached the bottom of the dungeons and looked around. There were no prisoners, which was good, but the place felt eerie.

"Did the note say anything else?" Theo questioned.

"No, it didn't," Nikolai said, looking around.

Juliet walked around the place, looking for anything out of place or unusual. Most of the cells showed a small bed, table, and toilet. Chains were fixed to the walls in multiple cells, and insects were crawling around in the dark shadows. She walked up to the stone wall and ran her hand across it, hoping there was a secret door. The wall was cold and rough, as she walked along the wall inspecting it. She stopped as her hand came across a dent. She looked at the wall and found a small opening. It was small enough to hide if you weren't looking for it. And it was small enough for a key.

"Nikolai," Juliet called out. He and Theo walked towards her.

"Did your father give you a key?" Juliet asked, showing him what she had found.

"No, he didn't," he said, inspecting the small opening.

"Maybe something of value," Theo suggested. "Maybe a key was too obvious."

"Maybe something he gave you?" Juliet asked.

"No, nothing," Nikolai said looking upset.

"Back to square one," Theo said unamused.

"Maybe I got the riddle wrong," Juliet said, feeling foolish. "I'm sorry."

"Don't be. Theo and I never came up with locations. We were stumped the minute we read it," Nikolai reassured her.

"Thank you, but I would like to have another look at the letter," Juliet said with determination.

"Well, let's head back up for now. It's almost time for dinner. Then we will think things through, and talk about them later," Nikolai advised.

"Sounds good. I'm starving," Theo said, walking out of the

room. Juliet took Nikolai's offered arm as they walked out of the dungeons.

✦ ✦ ✦ ✦ ✦

Selina was angry that she couldn't get her hands on the healing Gem. If the Prince of Darkness found out, he would have been very displeased. That is why she couldn't go home, not without the Gem. She would find some other way to get her hands on it and, in the process, get revenge on the Fox spirit who had injured her into fleeing. Selina had found a small cave outside the kingdom to hide in, and gather her strength. On the way there, she found aloe vera plants for her injuries, and tea tree plants for inflammation. She ground them up and added water to make a paste, before applying them to her wounds. She had lain down to rest, plotting her next move, when she heard something outside the cave. Her instincts told her it was just a small animal, so she didn't bother getting up.

Selina slept all night and didn't get up until just after dawn the next day. She felt well-rested, and her wounds had gotten better. She had decided last night that she would try and get the healing Gem from the Queen of Elaxon this time. Selina felt she was an easier target than the Princess, and knew she would be victorious with the Queen. She rose and left the cave, drinking from her water flask. A big grin formed when she imagined what it would be like, handing over the healing Gem to the Prince of Darkness. How pleased he would be with her, unlike Mildred. She was ready, and this time failure wasn't an option.

CHAPTER SEVENTEEN

"Do not be anxious about anything, but in every situation,
by prayer and petition, with thanksgiving,
present your requests to God."

Philippians 4:6

Nikolai felt at peace as Juliet's head lay against his chest. He stroked her hair, knowing that the gesture relaxed her. The night was getting chilly, so Nikolai covered Juliet and himself with a blanket and snuggled her closer to him. It had been a long and busy day, and Nikolai and Juliet didn't get much chance to be alone until now.

After dinner with Queen Julia and Captain Issac, Juliet and Nikolai decided to have an early night as they were exhausted. When alone, they finally made up for the lost kisses throughout the day by embracing each other, and spending a blissful evening together. While Nikolai lay there with Juliet in his arms, he thought about the riddle, and the small indent they had found in the dungeons that afternoon. Nikolai tried to figure out the key, but got nowhere. Indeed, his father would have given him another clue if there was one. But what if there wasn't another clue? The palace was huge, and it would take him months to find the sword. He needed to stop stressing and overthinking things, and trust in the God of Light.

At dinner, Nikolai and Juliet had filled in Queen Julia and Captain Issac, on the discovery of the Sword of the Kings. They were just as keen to find it as Juliet, Theo, and Nikolai were. They had all agreed that it would be a massive advantage for the coming war, and would help wherever needed.

The following day, Nikolai woke up with Juliet still in his arms. He smiled down at her and kissed her forehead. She lifted her head to see Nikolai and smiled groggily. Today, Queen Julia and Captain Issac would be leaving to head back to their kingdom. As for Captain Oberon and his lieutenants, they would have already left for their missions hours ago.

"Are you ok?" Juliet asked.

"Yes, just thinking about the riddle," Nikolai said. He brushed some loose strands of Juliet's hair behind her ears and smiled. At that moment, Juliet noticed a different ring on one of Nikolai's fingers. Curiously, she took his hand and inspected it.

"What's this ring?" she asked. Nikolai looked down and saw which one she had pointed to.

"It's a signet ring that belonged to my father. It's custom for a father to give one to his son, but my father never did. Once he passed, Priest Phil gave me my father's one, just something for me to remember him by," he explained. Juliet was quiet for a moment, studying the ring.

"Is everything alright?" he asked.

"This ring looks like it could fit in that small opening we found in the dungeons," Juliet stated.

Nikolai lifted his hand to have a closer look. Juliet was right; it could fit.

"Your right. It only makes sense," he said. "Let's give it a go. It's the only lead we've got."

"Right," Juliet said, wriggling out of Nikolai's embrace. "We'll go and see after we see my mother and Issac off," Juliet said getting up and heading to the bathroom.

Nikolai watched her go, praying a silent prayer of thanks to the God of Light, for bringing this wonderful woman into his life. He smiled and went to get dressed for the day.

After breakfast, they all made their way to the front of the palace, where a carriage stood ready to take Queen Julia and Captain Issac home. Captain Issac and Juliet hugged for a moment and exchanged a few words. Juliet then hugged her mother, as she spoke words of comfort to her. Captain Issac walked over to Nikolai and exchanged handshakes, wishing him the best in this challenging situation.

"Have a safe journey," Nikolai said, waving to Captain Issac as he mounted his horse. Nikolai heard Theo yawning from behind him and laughed. Theo stood beside Nikolai and waved to Queen Julia and Captain Issac, as they departed. Juliet came and stood by Nikolai. He held out his hand for comfort, and she took it smiling. But Nikolai could still see the tears in her eyes.

"Are you alright?" Nikolai whispered to her.

"Yes. I did not realize it would be so difficult to say goodbye to my mother," Juliet said, wiping her eyes.

"Not goodbye, but until next time," Nikolai said smiling. She smiled back.

"Any time you miss her, she is always welcome here. And if you wish to visit your home country, I would love for you to show me around," Nikolai explained.

"Thank you," she beamed.

"I'm still here," Theo said with a yawn. Juliet and Nikolai laughed.

They stood hand in hand, as they watched the carriage move further and further away from the palace.

"There better be a good reason as to why Levi came pounding on my door so early," Theo said, half asleep.

"Looks like you had a late-night last night," Nikolai stated.

"Fitzwilliam had some news to share about our current situation, so we went to the tavern for a drink, and stayed out a little too late," Theo said, rubbing his hands over his face.

"Well, Juliet and I have some news, too," Nikolai said, patting Theo on the shoulder. "But first coffee for you."

"Oh yes please. It's like heaven in a cup," Theo said, almost running back into the palace. "Thank you, God, for coffee."

Juliet and Nikolai followed Theo back into the palace. They headed into one of the sitting rooms, while the servants brought them something to eat and drink. Theo collapsed on the chair and accepted the coffee the servant had made for him.

"What's your news?" Theo asked, consuming the coffee he had just been given.

Nikolai looked at Juliet and nodded, wanting her to speak since it was her theory.

"I thought Nikolai's signet ring might be the key, to opening the small passageway in the dungeons," Juliet said hopefully.

Theo thought for a moment before replying.

"That would make sense. It's usually passed down from generation to generation," Theo said.

"I thought we'd try it today," Nikolai said energized, looking at Juliet and Theo.

"I'm keen," Theo said, grabbing another drink.

"Me too," Juliet replied.

"Great, we'll head down there after we've had something to eat," Nikolai said, handing Juliet a plate.

"So how is Fitzwilliam?" Nikolai asked.

"He's good, but he heard some bad news," Theo said, putting food onto his plate.

"What could be worse than letting the Prince of Darkness free?" Juliet asked.

"Creatures of darkness," Theo said. "There have been some sightings and people are afraid."

"Do we know who they are targeting?" Nikolai asked.

"No, it's all just random at the moment," Theo replied, concerned.

"What are the creatures of darkness?" Juliet asked.

"Wolves, cyclops, basilisks, minotaur's," Theo listed them off. "Just to name a few."

"The Prince of Darkness must be summoning them somehow, because these creatures were killed off thousands of years ago," Nikolai said, thinking.

"It would make sense," Juliet said. "Bringing back what people feared the most."

"Tell Fitzwilliam to be careful," Nikolai said, concerned.

Theo nodded. "Will do."

"And since we are now aware of these creatures of darkness, we should research them to be prepared. We may have to encounter them in the coming war," Nikolai explained.

"I agree. I'm happy to do that and pass on the information I find," Juliet offered.

Nikolai nodded a thanks.

"Ok, before we meet in the dungeons, Theo, I want you to prepare some eagles to send to Oberon, Finnick, and Queen Julia. Juliet and I will write the letters explaining the news of the creatures."

"On it," Theo said, getting up.

"We'll meet at the entrance to the dungeons in an hour," Nikolai said to Theo.

They all walked out of the room with purpose and determination. Finally, things were looking up on their side. Nikolai hoped the messages would get to the others quickly, before they got into any kind of trouble.

✦ ✦ ✦ ✦ ✦

In the cave of Akuma, Harkin sat against the wall with his arms crossed, watching, and waiting for his orders. His hair was light brown, and he had striking blue eyes. Harkin was bullied as a child and preferred to go at things alone. One evening, when he was young, he had run into the forest to escape his drunken father, and got lost. He cried out to whoever would listen, and asked them to make him strong so he wouldn't be bullied by anyone again. Minutes after he had cried out, he was bitten by a bat. At first, he thought the incident was unfair, but he was proven wrong.

After the bat incident, he had finally found his way home. He washed his wound the best he could and stumbled into bed. In the middle of the night, he was awakened by a sharp pain coursing through his body. He stumbled onto the floor in pain and cried out. Enormous black bat wings broke out from the skin on his back. Once the pain was through, he realized that the bat biting him in the woods was a gift. He wasn't sure who gave him this gift, but he was finally strong enough to stand against his bullies.

Over the next couple of days after the incident, he realized it wasn't just the bat wings he had gotten, but incredible speed, strength and far sight. While testing his new gifts, a red-haired woman approached him. She told him she knew who had given him the gift, and asked him if he wanted to meet that person and get stronger. Harkin agreed and followed the red-haired woman. The Prince of Darkness had greeted Harkin like a long-lost son. He promised him revenge on all the people who had wronged him in the past, but needed his help with something first. Harkin agreed without question.

Harkin watched the Prince of Darkness from the back of the caves, while he summoned his beasts of darkness.

"An eye of one, but teeth of many
This massive giant is anything but friendly.
It preys on the weak and anything in its path.
When one encounters the beast, it will see their wrath."

A black portal appeared inside the cave, and another cyclops came forward holding a mallet. It let out a furious roar.

"Go to your brothers who are in the Kingdom of Neylon, and make sure there are no survivors," the Prince of Darkness ordered.

The cyclops grunted its reply, then left the cave, heading to the Kingdom of Neylon. Harkin watched it go and thought to himself how dumb cyclops were. They looked furious and scary on the outside, but they were terribly slow, and simple-minded creatures who were easy to control.

"Harkin, my son," the Prince of Darkness called. Harkin got up, walked over to the Prince of Darkness, and bowed before him.

"Yes, Master," he replied.

"I have heard that there are people in this world who are against me and my plans," he growled.

"What would you like me to do?" Harkin asked without hesitation.

"Kill them," the Prince of Darkness rasped. "One is already near the cyclops. Leave him. There are others who are getting close to what is left of the Kingdom of Kudzu. I'll leave them to you."

"As you wish," Harkin said, bowing again before leaving the cave. As soon as Harkin left the cave, he spread out his bat-like wings, and flew toward the Kingdom of Kudzu. Using his far sight, he saw the two soldiers riding towards Kudzu, and knew that these were his next victims. They had only a few more days of riding before they saw what was left of the Kingdom of Kudzu. So, Harkin increased his speed to catch up to them, and started planning.

CHAPTER EIGHTEEN

"For those who are led by the Spirit of God
are the children of God."

Romans 8:14

Selina quickly picked up the Queen's scent after leaving the cave. She was thrilled when she learned that the Queen was about to journey home. She would have her chance to steal the Gem for her Master. She watched from afar at the interaction between the Queen and her daughter. Her anger flared at the sight of Nikolai, the Fox spirit, standing near the Queen's daughter protectively. She wished she could fight him again after their last battle. But the mission had to come first. He would suffer later; she would make sure of it.

Selina watched as the carriage drove away from the palace, and she silently followed on foot. She counted the guards accompanying the Queen, to determine what strategy to take. She only saw eight guards. Four on horseback and four walking beside the carriage. This was too easy. She smiled to herself. She would wait until they stopped for the night to attack. She would transform into her wolf form, and finally take the Queen's Gem.

Later that night, when the Queen and her guards had stopped at an inn for the night, Selina transformed. She let out a howl once her transformation was complete. The change was painful every time. That is why she preferred to stay in her wolf form most of the time. It was more accessible and convenient, and she liked it that way. She sniffed the air to catch the Queen's scent, following as soon as she found it. Being careful not to alert any of the guards, she quietly made her way towards the Queen's room. She stopped outside her bedroom window, and listened to see if the Queen was asleep.

She heard rustling behind her and turned to see Issac poised with a sword, ready to fight. Selina let out a low growl and turned her attention fully to Issac. She lunged at him with her teeth bared, but Issac moved quickly and brought his sword down onto her side, slicing through her thigh. Selina yelped and turned towards Issac with hatred in her eyes. She ran towards him again, jumping on him, and knocking him to the ground, trying to bite into his neck. Issac winced in pain as Selina cut through his chest with her claws. Using every bit of his strength, Issac pushed Selina off him and quickly stood up. With his sword ready, he ran up to Selina and stabbed her in the leg. Selina howled in pain as she tried to stand up, but Issac quickly attacked again, causing her to fall. She whined and struggled but managed to stand up again, ready to defend herself. Issac ran up to the wolf and wounded it in the stomach, causing Selina to collapse.

"Are you ok, Captain Issac?" asked a guard running to assist.

"Yes. Thank you, Lieutenant," Captain Issac replied.

Captain Issac and the Lieutenant stared down at the wolf. Selina looked up at her would-be killers and winced in pain. She knew she was going to die. She had failed her Master. The only person who ever cared for her. Or so she thought.

"What do you want to do, Captain Issac?" the Lieutenant asked.

"Even though I punctured a vital organ, it'll be a long and painful death," the Captain said. "I'm not a fan of animal cruelty, so let's put it out of its misery."

As the Lieutenant lifted his sword, he stopped and looked at the wolf. Then bringing his sword down, Selina breathed her last breath, as the life faded from her eyes forever.

"Maybe you should get Her Majesty to heal that wound of yours," the first Lieutenant suggested, looking at his Captain's wounded chest.

"First things first, tell the men to be extra observant tonight. Get everyone to pair up. We don't know if there are others around," Captain Issac ordered.

"How did you know it was following us?" the first Lieutenant asked.

"Very observant Lieutenant. I'm a skilled tracker," Captain Issac said, sheathing his sword. "I'll check on the Queen. Be careful."

Captain Issac walked to the front of the Inn, and opened the door to find Queen Julia, the Inn's owners, and staff huddled together looking frightened.

"It's dead," Captain Issac reassured them all. They all sighed with relief, then resumed their duties while Queen Julia approached the Captain, looking worried.

"Can you please get some water and bring it here?" Queen Julia asked one of the staff.

"Of course," one replied, bowing before going to fetch it.

"Let me heal that for you," Queen Julia said, leading Captain Issac towards the dining room table.

Captain Issac sat down, took his shirt off, and smiled when he saw Queen Julia blush. Queen Julia turned towards the staff that came with the water and thanked them, while placing the water on the table. She grabbed a cloth and started to clean Captain Issac's wound. Once cleaned, she used her Gem's power to heal the rest. While she concentrated on the injury, Captain Issac stared at her with admiration and love, and smiled to himself.

"What are you smiling about?" Queen Julia asked curiously.

"You," Captain Issac said.

"Me?" Queen Julia questioned.

"How amazing you are," Captain Issac said, caressing her face. She smiled and blushed. Once she had finished healing the wound, Captain Issac took Queen Julia's hand, kissing it gently.

"Thank you," Captain Issac said, leaning in to steal another kiss. Queen Julia kissed him back.

✦ ✦ ✦ ✦ ✦

Oberon stopped to rest just after midday, after travelling for hours. He had left at dawn like the others and had decided to go alone, because having a second person would only slow him down. He was fit and healthy for his age, and could travel further than the others without resting. The only other person who could match him was Finnick, and that took him years to accomplish. He knelt beside the stream to fill his flask. Once done, he resumed his mission to the Kingdom of Neylon. It would be a long journey, but he was always up for a good challenge. It had turned out to be a nice clear day, but rain was coming soon. He could smell it, and the clouds were getting greyer as he walked on.

Oberon suddenly stopped. He looked down at the ground and saw a colossal footprint outlined in the dirt. He knelt for a closer look.

Impossible, he thought to himself. He looked ahead and found another footprint, and another one in front of it. They were heading in the same direction he was.

"This is not good," he said to himself. "Not good at all."

He looked up and stared into the distance, calculating how long it would take to reach his destination. He could make it in half the time if he ran, and didn't stop for the night. He thought about it and decided that would be best. He could manage it. That's why he preferred to travel alone. If the King and Queen of Neylon were in trouble, helping them might benefit his kingdom in the coming war. And Oberon always did what he thought was right. That was what his father had taught him. He stood up, stretched his muscles, and took a long drink out of his flask before filling it up again and putting it away. Then he started running towards Neylon, hoping he wasn't too late.

Oberon ran for half the day before stopping to fill his flask in a nearby stream. While filling up his flask, he noticed some berries growing nearby. He stood up and inspected them to see if they were edible. The berries were mulberries and were just ripe for the picking. He unfolded the cloth he had, for his already eaten food, and began picking the berries. Once he had enough, he secured them safely in his bag and resumed his mission.

Before he had even started to run, he felt the ground shake with a slow thump. He stopped and listened to see which direction the sound was coming from. He looked behind him but saw nothing, as there were many tall trees about. He stood for a moment listening carefully, then what he feared the most came out from behind the trees. A cyclops. The fearsome beast stared back at Oberon with its one big eye. Its massive hand tightened around its mallet, as it let out a furious roar. Oberon stood ready with his broadsword out, and ready to attack.

The cyclops ran towards him, baring its teeth and raising its mallet. Oberon dodged the cyclops's mallet at the last minute, letting the mallet hit the tree he had left behind. Oberon quickly tried to think of its weak spots, and how to effectively attack and defend himself from this creature. He looked around at his surroundings, while the cyclops tried to hit him, missing every time. Sheathing his sword, Oberon started running in the direction he was heading to. The cyclops ran after him with its mallet raised and gave a loud and ferocious roar. It was angry. Oberon kept running until he found a massive tree. He turned around and stood in front of the tree, ready to move out of the way. Once the cyclops was close enough, Oberon jumped out of the way. The ground shook from the impact, as he heard a loud thump. The cyclops collided head-first into the massive tree. Oberon quickly unsheathed his sword, ran up onto the creature's back, and brought his sword down onto the cyclops neck, before the beast knew what had happened. The cyclops fell to the ground with a loud thud. Oberon stood there panting, wondering how many he would find when he got to the Kingdom of Neylon. Fearing the worst, he took a quick drink, then ran towards the kingdom again, praying he wasn't too late.

CHAPTER NINETEEN

"So do not fear, for I am with you; do not be dismayed,
for I am your God. I will strengthen you and help you;
I will uphold you with my righteous right hand."

Isaiah 41:10

Finnick and Jarreth were getting their horses ready to leave Lord Hain's estate. They had arrived the night before and were greeted by Finnick's father, Lord Hain, who held a feast late into the night. Finnick's father told him that he would help the King, and contact him the following day, which relieved Finnick. His father could sometimes abuse the power the late King had given him. Finnick would worry about his servants and the household, having grown up there with them. Now, his father was getting older and grumpier in his old age.

After serving as his Captain, the late King made Finnick's father a Lord, to honor him. He gave him an estate which was a two-day ride on horseback from Zolatta. Finnick hated it when others would address him as Lord Hain, because of how his father can get at times. When his father passed, that would be when he would take on that title, the estate, and the responsibilities that came with it.

After saying his goodbyes to his father, Finnick and Jarreth set off to the Kingdom of Kudzu. They left at dawn, hoping to get a good start on the day. With their horses saddled up and ready, they walked out of his father's estate. Finnick waved to all his friends, and the servants he had grown up with. Then the two lieutenants mounted their horses and began to head out. As the horses started trotting, the kids ran after them at a safe distance, waving and laughing, as they tried to keep up with them, making Finnick smile. He waved to them one last time before getting his horse to go into a full gallop.

At midday, they stopped to let their horses drink and rest, while they had a quick lunch break and rest, before heading out again. Jarreth noticed the dark clouds and pointed upwards to Finnick.

"It looks like a storm is heading our way," Finnick agreed.

Even though Jarreth said nothing, Finnick and Captain Oberon would always know what he meant. When they first met Jarreth, he was an orphan, and they decided to take him under their wing, and train him to become a Royal Guard. After that, they trained together almost daily. After a few months, Captain Oberon and Finnick began to learn how to use sign language, to understand and communicate with Jarreth, which made Jarreth come out of his shell around them even more so. Jarreth's strengths were archery and stealth, and he was the best in his field. Even though he was mute, he was one of Captain Oberon's most trusted lieutenants, alongside Finnick.

Jarreth looked to the sky and sniffed. He frowned.

"What is it?" Finnick asked.

"Birds are fleeing from our direction, and I can smell smoke," Jarreth signed to Finnick. Finnick looked up and saw Jarreth's concern.

"We should probably head out now," Finnick said, packing

his lunch. Jarreth did the same. Once the horses were ready, they resumed their journey at full gallop.

Finnick trusted Jarreth, that is why he pushed for Captain Oberon to give the second lieutenant position to Jarreth, even though he could not communicate well.

But Jarreth performed his duties as second lieutenant so well, that even Caption Oberon, who always had a poker face, was impressed and proud of how far Jarreth had come since meeting him.

After riding from midday to dusk, both lieutenants decided to stop and rest. While Finnick tied the horses up, Jarreth began to scout the surrounding area. With his dagger in his hand, Jarreth slowly and carefully looked for anything out of ordinary. He looked for any signs that would hint at them being followed, and looked for any dangers that might be present. The fleeing birds and the smell of smoke still worried him. Jarreth pulled his black scarf up around his neck and mouth, to block out the smoke smell, but it did not work. The closer they got to their destination, the stronger the smell got. And Jarreth had a gut feeling that their destination would be a sad one. Once he felt that the surrounding area was safe, he returned and sat down with Finnick, who gave him something to eat.

"First watch or second?" Finnick asked. Jarreth held up one finger.

"Ok, wake me up at midnight," Finnick said, rolling over to sleep. Jarreth watched the surrounding area like a hawk with his dagger ready. He had a feeling that something was out there watching him and Finnick. A rustle of leaves to the left caught his attention, and he jumped up to scan that area.

Just a tiny animal, Jarreth thought, sitting back down.

But the sensation of being watched never left him. So, he prepared his weapons just in case.

CHAPTER TWENTY

"The Lord is my strength and my shield, my heart trusts in him."

Psalms 28:7

Nikolai stood outside the dungeons with Juliet and Theo.

"Ready?" Nikolai asked them both.

"Yes," they both replied, looking nervous. They took the steps down to the dungeons one by one, and came and stood before the small hole in the wall. Nikolai took off his signet ring, studying his family's crest that was embedded on it. Turning to the stone wall he put the ring into the small opening, and turned it clockwise, but nothing happened. He then turned it anticlockwise and heard a click. They all looked around the dungeons excited.

"Look," Theo called, pointing to the second cell. The second cell's stone wall opened like a door. Through the door was a long corridor, with lamps on each side to light the way. At the end of the corridor was another door.

"So, what's the plan?" Theo asked, inspecting the open door.

"I'm afraid it's going to have to be me moving forward from now on," Nikolai said. Nikolai saw Juliet's worried look.

"I'll be ok," Nikolai reassured her.

"I'll be praying for you," Theo said.

"Thanks, Theo," Nikolai said, walking towards the newly opened door.

Once Nikolai was inside, the door closed behind him, preventing anyone else from coming in. The light from the lamps hanging on the wall, were brighter now that there was no open door. Nikolai walked cautiously down the corridor, keeping an eye and ear out for any traps. Insects crawled across the floor in a hurry as Nikolai walked past. Spiderwebs hung in the corner of the walls and around the lamps, showing that this place had been cut off from the world for a while. The closer Nikolai got to the door, the chillier it felt. He wondered if he was heading lower into the kingdom's catacombs. Once he reached the door, he opened it and was greeted by cold air.

"Dam," Nikolai said, wishing he had brought a jumper. He walked through the door, and found a stone table in the middle of the room. The room also had three doors, each leading to somewhere unknown. Nikolai walked up to the stone table and read the inscription that was carved into the table.

"Three doors lay before you.
Choose only one and disregard the others.
One holds riches for the taking.
One holds the deceased King and Queen.
One holds the gift of wisdom."

Nikolai re-read the inscription, making sure what he was reading was true. His thoughts instantly turned to his mother. The idea of bringing her back overwhelmed him with grief and happiness. Nikolai braced himself on the stone table and wept. He wished he could choose his mother or father to come back, and help him with this new threat, because he was struggling. He needed his father to show him how to run a kingdom, and be a proper and good king. He also had so many things that he wanted to tell them both. But deep down, he knew it was the wrong choice. After wiping the tears away, he stood up and re-read what each door held.

"Deceased, wisdom or riches," he said to himself. "I don't want riches. I've heard what that can do to a person, especially after the stories Finnick told me about his father. I can't bring back my parents, even though it pains me to say it. Then there is wisdom," Nikolai said.

He thought to himself for a moment.

"If any of you lacks wisdom, you should ask God, who gives generously to all without finding fault, and it will be given to you. James chapter 1 verse 5," Nikolai quoted out loud.

Nikolai remembered his father reading that from the Tanakh for him as a kid. He smiled, knowing which door he would be taking. Nikolai walked over to the entrance of wisdom and walked through it, making his way down the long corridor. After a while he came to an opening, and inside he saw the Sword of the Kings. It was floating just above the ground, and shone with a warm golden color. He could see the topaz Gem sparkling on the sword's hilt. He looked around the room and saw other weapons on the wall.

That's weird, Nikolai thought, *why would there be other weapons in here.*

Nikolai started to walk towards the sword, but stopped after hearing a low growl from behind the floating sword. He cautiously took a step back, trying to get a look at what was growling at him. Its blue eyes shone in the darkness, and it growled at him again, showing its teeth as it moved forward into the light. A white wolf stood in front of the Sword of the Kings, guarding it.

"Ok, that explains the multitude of weapons here," Nikolai said, taking a quick look at the wall.

Nikolai had to think of a strategy quickly. He looked towards the wall of weapons again, then back at the wolf. Nickolai didn't want to hurt the wolf, but didn't want to get killed by one either. He sighed to himself. He didn't want to hurt the animal. He had always loved them, and really wanted a dog as a pet when he was younger. The wolf began to slowly walk towards him while still growling. It lunged towards Nikolai, but he quickly got out of the way in time. While the wolf righted itself, Nikolai quickly looked to the wall of weapons again and found a shield.

Perfect, he thought to himself.

He ran over to the wall to grab it, but was tackled to the ground by the wolf. As he lay on his stomach, the wolf bit down on his foot causing Nikolai to scream. He turned over onto his back and kicked the wolf with his other foot. The wolf let go, and Nikolai, unable to stand, crawled towards the shield on the wall.

"God of Light, help me, please," Nikolai prayed, catching his breath.

Nikolai noticed the wolf limping as it made its way over to him. It lunged at him again, but this time, Nikolai was prepared. He protected himself with his hands, moving the wolf's teeth away from his face. Nikolai then saw an arrowhead stuck in the wolf's right paw. While Nikolai held off the wolf with one hand, his other hand tried to remove the arrowhead.

"I'm sorry, but this is going to hurt," Nikolai told the wolf.

Nikolai ripped the arrowhead out and pushed the wolf away. It fell towards the ground and whimpered, licking its paw. Nikolai sat up, gasping for breath. He looked at the wolf, then at the arrowhead in his hand, then at his bleeding foot.

He sighed.

The wolf then got up and started to walk towards Nikolai. Out of fear, Nikolai moved back using his arms, trying for the shield again. But instead of attacking Nikolai, the wolf whimpered as it approached him. When it reached him, it licked his face.

"You were just in pain," Nikolai said, stroking its white fur. The wolf stood near Nikolai as he attempted to get up. Once up, he made his way over to the Sword of the Kings. When Nikolai was in reaching distance, he looked down at the wolf who came and stood by his side panting. Nikolai smiled and patted its head. He then turned his attention back to the sword, reaching for it. Nikolai held the sword in his hands, weighing it and admiring the details of the blade. It was lighter than he thought it would be. The wolf suddenly started whining and moved closer to him, sensing something. Nikolai turned around to see what was bothering the wolf and gasped, almost dropping the sword. His mother and father stood there in white, smiling back at him.

"Hello, son," Nikolai's father greeted smiling.

Chapter Twenty-One

"For the Lord is the great God, the great King above all gods."

Psalms 95:3

Jarreth poked at Finnick until he woke up groggily.

"My turn for guard duty?" Finnick asked, yawning.

Jarreth nodded.

"Ok," Finnick said, standing up to stretch. "Anything happen while I was out."

"Nope, but this place doesn't feel right," Jarreth signed.

"Ok," Finnick nodded. "Get some sleep and we'll leave early in the morning."

Jarreth laid to rest as Finnick did some stretches to wake up properly. While Finnick stretched, he scanned the area around him. He trusted Jarreth, and when Jarreth thought something wasn't right, it usually wasn't.

After stretching, he grabbed his weapon just in case and sat down near the fire, waiting, and watching. Hours went by without anything happening, and soon the sun began to rise. Finnick stood up and went for a walk, making sure to stay close to their camp just in case. Suddenly, something hit him from behind, causing him to lose his balance and fall. He quickly stood up with his axe and looked around, poised, ready to strike. No one was there, and Jarreth was still sleeping at their camp. He then lowered his axe and started walking back to camp, hoping Jarreth wouldn't mind being woken up earlier. He wanted to leave earlier, as this place didn't feel right.

Whoosh.

Finnick looked up towards the strange sound above him, but saw nothing. He looked around alarmed, but nothing was out of the ordinary.

Something strange is happening, he thought.

He quickened his pace to their camp, but was suddenly snatched from the ground. Whatever had him, threw him to the ground forcefully. He rolled over and looked to the sky; nothing was there. He tried to stand but fell to the ground, wincing in pain. He looked at his now broken leg, and thought what kind of animal would have the strength to lift him from the ground. He scanned the sky again but couldn't see anything. He looked over to where Jarreth lay.

"Jarreth," Finnick called.

Jarreth woke up alarmed by Finnick's cry, and jumped up, ready with his weapon as he scanned the area. When he saw Finnick on the ground clutching his leg, he raced over to him, kneeling beside him.

"Something attacked me," Finnick whispered looking around.

Jarreth looked around and saw nothing.

"It snatched me from the ground, so keep your eyes on the sky as well," Finnick said, grimacing from the pain.

"Keep a look out while I set your leg," Jarreth signed.

Finnick nodded and took his axe in his hand, ready. Seeing that Finnick was distracted, Jarreth pushed the bone back into place, causing Finnick to scream in pain. Jarreth quickly took the first aid kit from his belt, and looked around for a stick strong enough to function as a splint.

Whoosh.

"Look out," Finnick said, pointing at the sky.

Jarreth saw a man with enormous black bat wings flying straight towards them. Jarreth took out his bow and arrow and held it steady, eyeing his target. The man with bat wings flew closer and closer towards Jarreth and Finnick. Jarreth continued to hold his position with his bow and arrow aimed, ready to strike. He had to wait for the right time. Otherwise, the man could easily avoid it.

"Jarreth," Finnick yelled.

Jarreth didn't move from his position. He held his bow and waited for the right time to shoot.

"Anytime now," Finnick yelled, looking worried.

Jarreth closed one eye and made the shot.

"*Dam*," he thought, taking another arrow out.

The enemy dodged at the last minute, causing the arrow to pierce his shoulder blade instead of his wing. Jarreth looked around to see where he went, while trying to find a good shooting spot. He needed to shoot from another angle to get a good shot, preferably with his back to the sun.

"*The trees*," Jarreth thought.

Jarreth ran for the nearest tall tree, keeping his eyes on the sky for the enemy. He circled once, looking around, but couldn't find the enemy. Then, with sudden dread, he looked directly up from where he stood.

Whoosh.

The enemy came down and attacked Jarreth, forcing him to the ground. Jarreth rolled onto his back and removed a knife from his boot, after misplacing his bow and arrow. The enemy got a hold of Jarreth's dagger, coming down again with force, hoping to plunge the dagger he now held into Jarreth's heart. As Jarreth held the enemy's blade away from himself, the enemy tried to use more force to impale him. Jarreth needed to think of a new plan and fast. He looked around, saw that his bow and arrow were only a few meters away, and got an idea. He used as much force as he had left and punched his attacker, causing him to stumble back, giving Jarreth the advantage to reach for his bow and arrow.

Jarreth quickly put an arrow into his bow and stood poised, ready to attack. The enemy slowly stood up, wincing, and wiping blood from his mouth.

"You got me there," the enemy said, surprised.

"What do you want?" Finnick asked.

"Name's Harkin, and I serve the Dark Master," he said, smirking.

"The Dark Master?" Finnick questioned, looking at Jarreth.

Jarreth just shrugged, lowering his bow.

"The one you lowly humans call the Prince of Darkness or the Dark One. The one the God of Light banished, to rot in a cave chained to a wall for eternity," Harkin spat.

"Ooooooooh", Finnick said, stretching the word out, and nodding sarcastically to Jarreth. "That guy. The depressing fellow who likes to manipulate and torture people, and make a pain of things."

Jarreth smiled at Finnick's humor.

"How dare you make fun of the Dark Master," Harkin yelled. "I will kill you both, so that there are less filthy humans like you in our new world."

Finnick put his hand on his heart, looking hurt.

"Oh no, we're not invited anymore," he said sarcastically.

Harkin looked at both lieutenants with pure hatred.

"I think you mean His new world, not Ours. Because of his

manipulative nature I doubt he's going to share it, even if he promised. Cause that is who he is," Finnick explained.

Harkin's rage increased, as he clenched his fists so tightly, they turned red.

"Ready, Jarreth," Finnick whispered.

Jarreth signed yes with one hand, as he slung his bow over his shoulder and held his hands in fists, standing in a fighting stance.

Harkin came at full speed to attack Finnick, but Jarreth jumped in front of him and held Harkin's hands at bay, preventing him from attacking. Harkin tried to pull his hands away, but Jarreth had a good grip on him and was not letting go. Jarreth smiled at Harkin before kicking him in the stomach and punching him in the jaw. Harkin fell to the ground, wiping the blood from his mouth, and stood up to face Jarreth. He was angry.

"You both are going to regret this," Harkin said, flying to the sky.

Jarreth watched as Harkin flew to the sky and out of reach, laughing like he had won.

But Jarreth had other plans.

He took out his bow, placed the arrow in the bowstring, and pulled the arrow back as far as he could, ready to attack. He watched the sky, searching for Harkin with his bow and arrow ready. The sun shone as the day began anew. Jarreth knew he had to finish this battle soon otherwise, the sun would work as a disadvantage for him, and an advantage for Harkin. He saw Harkin, a couple of meters away, flying in his direction with his dagger ready to attack. Jarreth closed one eye and focused on his target.

Harkin came closer and closer. But Jarreth held his bow and arrow steady, prepared for the right time. When Harkin had gotten close enough, Jarreth let the arrow fly towards his target, hitting him where he intended.

Harkin fell to the ground, clutching his chest. Blood covered his hands as he tried to stand up, but he collapsed to the ground again. Coughing up blood onto the ground, Harkin's anger turned into fear. The Prince of Darkness had promised him eternal life and riches, but that wasn't going to happen. Harkin fell to the ground, clutching his bloody chest, then breathed his last breath.

Jarreth stood up and walked over to Finnick. He didn't look so good. Finnick had ripped a piece of his jacket sleeve off, and wrapped it around his wounded leg to stop the bleeding. But he was still getting paler and weaker from the blood loss. Heading towards Finnick, Jarreth picked up a strong-looking stick, hoping to bandage and splint Finnick's leg back into place, before any damage was permanently done.

As Jarreth got closer to Finnick, he noticed he was now lying unconscious from the loss of blood. Jarreth quickly began to set Finnick's broken leg, bandaging it up, and creating a splint with the stick he had found. Once Finnick had been taken care of, Jarreth began to pack up their camp. He tied their bags and belongings to their saddles quickly, knowing they couldn't stay here. Finnick needed help, and the closest place that could assist him was the Kingdom of Kudzu.

Even then he wasn't even sure they could help.

CHAPTER TWENTY-TWO

"In him we have redemption through his blood, the forgiveness of sins, in accordance with the riches of God's grace."

Ephesians 1:7

The Prince of Darkness yelled with anger and frustration. His spies had returned with news of Selina and Harkin's death, to only mere human beings. He would have to find more people to manipulate, if he wanted his plans to go well. He opened the book of darkness in front of him, extending his hands upwards, and started chanting words from the book.

"A face like a bull and a body of a man
One cannot defeat it without a grand plan.
With an axe in hand and the strength of a hundred
It will devour anyone when it is hungered."

The Prince of Darkness laughed as a minotaur stepped through the dark portal, with a spiked axe. Mildred kept in the shadows to the back of the caves, watching the Dark Master with the minotaur.

The creature looked frightening and hungry, and she shuddered in fear. She didn't want to be part of the Master's plan anymore, and she hated herself for falling for his promises. Or better yet, his fake promises. The promise of power and eternal life. But who would want to live in a world full of loneliness, death, pain, and destruction ruled by the Dark Master and his creatures of darkness? She was too gullible, and she fell for the bait. And it was too late now.

Still, she would try and get the word out to someone to warn them. To give them a fighting chance, and an advantage in this coming war. But first, she waited for the right moment to flee.

"Mildred," the Master bellowed.

Mildred walked over to the Master and bowed before him, trying with all her might not to show her fear.

"I've sent Jorogumo ahead to the Kingdom of Kudzu. She will have prisoners captured there. Bring them back to me so I can consume their souls, and finally break free from this prison," he said hungrily.

"Of course," Mildred replied.

Yes, my second chance, she thought.

Mildred stood up and walked out of the cave, but stopped just before exiting, as the Master called after her.

"Do not disappoint me, or there will be consequences," he growled.

Mildred swallowed the lump in her throat and nodded. "Yes, Master."

As soon as Mildred left the cave and was a reasonable distance away, she sighed with relief. She wouldn't bring anyone else to the Master. She would try and make things right, but she didn't know where to begin.

"Maybe it's a hopeless case after all," Mildred sighed, feeling her hopes shattered.

Her head shot up at a horse neighing, and hooves trotting in the distance. She looked for a hiding place, not knowing whether the rider was a friend or foe. She dived behind a bush as the horse entered the clearing, and peeked through the bushes to see who it was.

"My dear child, you don't need to hide from me," said a soft voice.

Mildred saw a beautiful white unicorn and looked up to see the rider. The rider was dressed in white and had a kind smile. Immediately, Mildred felt at peace. She stood up and walked over to the unicorn and its rider.

"It's beautiful, isn't it Mildred," said the rider, smiling.

Mildred looked up at the man who called her by her name.

"How do you know my name?" Mildred asked curiously.

"I know everything about you, Mildred," the man replied.

Mildred looked horrified.

"I know that you were bullied as a child by your parents and peers. I know you felt unworthy of love after your first husband was cruel to you. I know that you deeply regret the life choices you've made, by following the Dark One. And I know that you want to prove yourself, by helping spread the word of what the Dark One is doing," the man replied.

Mildred gasped in shock and started to move away slowly, thinking it was a trick sent by the Master, as he was known to do.

"Relax, child. My name is Malachi. I am a messenger of the God of Light, and I've come to help you."

CHAPTER TWENTY-THREE

*"Until now you have not asked for anything in my name.
Ask and you will receive, and your joy will be complete."*

John 16:24

"Mom, Dad," Nikolai said, running up to hug them both.

"Nikolai, I'm sorry for all the hurt I caused you," his father said.

"I know, I found your letter, and I forgive you," Nikolai told him.

"I'm so proud of you," his mother said kissing his forehead.

"Thank you, mum," Nikolai replied.

"Congratulations on completing the test," his father said quite proudly.

"Test?" Nikolai questioned.

"You didn't think we purposely trapped a wolf in here, did you?" his father laughed. "No, it was a test to see if you are worthy of the Sword of the Kings. Being a King is difficult, but extremely rewarding. You must be open to new ideas, learn to give people a second chance at redemption, and not judge someone by their appearance."

The wolf came up and stood beside Nikolai, and he patted its head.

"He really likes you," his father said smiling.

"It seems so," Nikolai laughed.

"You know this wolf is special. The proper given name for this wolf is the Arctic wolf. You know, because it has white fur and all," his father explained.

"It's also very loyal to one person its entire life, and it seems to have chosen you," his mother said happily. "It will protect you no matter what."

Nikolai looked down at the wolf and smiled, as it started to lick his hand. Nikolai laughed and patted its head again.

"I think I'll call you Nix," Nikolai said.

"Nix is a perfect name. It means snow in Latin," his mother explained.

Nikolai stared at both his parents sadly.

"What's wrong, son?" his father asked.

"I just wish you were here with me," Nikolai said.

"But we are," his mother said smiling.

Nikolai laughed. "Not like this, but-"

"I know," his mother said sadly.

"I wish you could meet Juliet, my wife," Nikolai said. "You would have loved her."

His father sighed with relief. "I'm glad I made it in time."

"Fitzwilliam told me about you breaking the moonstone Gem. Thank you, father," Nikolai said earnestly.

"Yes, well," his father laughed, trying to hide his shame.

"Dad, I don't blame you for anything. I know now that you were being controlled," Nikolai said.

"Thanks, son," he replied.

"I need some advice with this threat you were talking about in your letter. Is there anything you can tell me about it?" Nikolai asked both parents.

His father let out a long sigh.

"The Prince of Darkness is starting an army. He has followers to whom he has given supernatural powers, which gives them special abilities. I met one who had bat wings, and another who could transform into a basilisk. These people will give up anything for power, but the Prince of Darkness has manipulated them. He's also summoning the creatures of darkness to help him win this war. My advice for you would be to unite all the kingdoms together for this war. Find as many Gems as you can, and train in that Gem's power. Then use it against the Prince of Darkness."

"I thought the only people who held the Gems were royals. Also, didn't the God of Light trap the Prince of Darkness? He can't do much being trapped," Nikolai questioned.

"Last time I was there, he was feeding off people's souls. If he has enough, he has the strength to break free from his trap," his father replied.

Nikolai sighed and thought for a moment before speaking again.

"I have sent letters to each kingdom asking for an alliance, but none have replied," Nikolai explained. "But I have sent people to act as ambassadors to those kingdoms."

"Smart move, son, I'm proud of you," his father said.

"Thanks, Dad," Nikolai replied.

"Just remember you have the God of Light to help you. Trust in his strength, and in your friends. Don't judge someone without hearing both sides of the story. Give people second chances, and always ask for advice if you are unsure," his mother told him. "It's what makes a good King."

"Thanks, Mum," Nikolai said.

"About the use of Gems, only the mighty ones are given to the royalties, by the God of Light. The other Gems must be found, and only if you complete the test can you take the Gem," his father explained.

At that moment, Nikolai looked at his parents in shock as they started to fade away.

"What's happening to you?" Nikolai asked, reaching out to them.

"We can't stay any longer, my son. We must move on. The God of Light is waiting for us. I love you, son," his father said, disappearing.

"I'm so proud of you. I love you, Nikolai," his mother said, as she kissed his forehead, just before disappearing.

Nikolai stood looking at the now empty space, where his parents had just been standing. He knew they were in a better place, and he felt peace at the thought of that. He looked down at the sword in his hand.

"I'm glad we now have the upper hand in this coming threat," Nikolai said aloud, patting the wolf's head. "Let's go home, Nix."

CHAPTER TWENTY-FOUR

"Have I not commanded you? Be strong and courageous.
Do not be afraid; do not be discouraged,
for the Lord your God will be with you wherever you go."

Joshua 1:9

Jarreth let Finnick sleep most of the day, while he packed up the rest of their camp. He would eventually have to wake Finnick up, if they wanted to reach the Kingdom of Kudzu before the end of the day. They were close but still far from the kingdom, and Jarreth knew it would take a little longer to get there because of Finnick's condition. Jarreth calculated they would probably reach the kingdom by nightfall.

He looked to the sky hearing a screech, only to see a falcon. He shielded his eyes from the sun while looking out for the bird. After realizing the falcon was from the Kingdom of Zolatta, he extended his arm for it to come down. Once the bird landed on his outstretched arm, Jarreth removed the letter attached to the falcon's leg then released it. Jarreth looked down and read the letter that the King had written.

The Prince of Darkness is summoning the creatures of darkness, Jarreth read. *That makes things difficult, and it also explains why the man with the bat wings attacked us.*

Jarreth sighed silently.

He looked over to see Finnick still asleep but also grimacing in pain. They needed to get to the Kingdom of Kudzu, and fast. They would have herbs there to help with Finnick's condition. Jarreth folded the letter, tucked it in his pocket, and went to Finnick. Kneeling, he shook Finnick's shoulder.

"What," Finnick said yawing.

Jarreth, using sign language, explained what had happened to Finnick and where they needed to go.

"I hope they have some alcohol there," Finnick said, grimacing as he sat up.

Jarreth smiled. His friend was going to be okay.

Jarreth helped Finnick to his feet as best he could without causing him too much pain, but Finnick's leg was broken, so the pain was intense. They both slowly walked over to the horses, that were ready and waiting. When Jarreth finished helping Finnick onto his horse, he then mounted his. After tying Finnick's reins to his saddle, he nudged his horse into a walk to see how Finnick would handle it with his pain. He was doing okay, thank God. Jarreth was also relieved they could finally move away from this part of the forest.

After riding the horses for hours throughout the evening at a walking pace, Jarreth was relieved to see the Kingdom of Kudzu. The kingdom was rumored to be beautiful, surrounded by forests and rivers to attract wildlife. The kingdom's amethyst Gem, was rumored to have the power to take on any animal's abilities, and communicate with them. According to King Nikolai's intel, the King and Queen who ruled the Kingdom of Kudzu, were King Eros and Queen Athena, with their daughter Princess Iris.

As Jarreth got closer to the village surrounding the kingdom, he felt something wasn't right. There was no one around, not even the animals. When he and Finnick reached the entrance to the village, they both stared at the scene before them in horror.

"What the hell happened here?" Finnick exclaimed.

The village surrounding the kingdom was deserted. Buildings were burnt down from a fire that had been and gone. Soot covered the buildings and grounds, and the half-eaten bodies of animals, were left to rot in the middle of the road. The once beautiful Kingdom of Kudzu, that was surrounded by beautiful and exotic animals, flora, and fauna, was now destroyed and in ruins. The wildlife that had once been living here in the village, had fled, or been killed and left to die on the streets.

Jarreth turned to Finnick with a worried look.

"Where are the bodies?" Jarreth signed.

"That's a good question," Finnick said, looking around. "I don't like this."

"Something doesn't feel right here," Jarreth signed.

"I agree," Finnick said.

"Let's find somewhere safe to camp, and I'll scout for survivors" Jarreth suggested, signing.

"I don't think it's safe to go alone," Finnick said hesitantly.

"I have to. I need to find some herbs for you and any survivors. There must be someone who knows what happened here," Jarreth signed.

"I don't know what happened here, but I doubt there will be any survivors," Finnick said. "But I understand where you are coming from. I could use some pain relief or, better yet, some alcohol."

The two lieutenants rode through the deserted village trying to find a safe place to set up their camp. Sadly, most of the houses were burnt to the ground, and the smell of smoke and blood was overwhelming. They eventually chose a little cottage outside the village that was only partly damaged.

Jarreth dismounted his horse, tied it up to the fence, and went to help Finnick down from his horse. After getting Finnick down, Jarreth helped him enter the cottage and onto the couch. Jarreth then brought their belongings in and placed them near Finnick. He began looking around the house to find some herbs and water. He opened every cupboard in the kitchen, before finding some turmeric and water. He went back to Finnick with both in hand.

"Thanks, man," Finnick said, gulping down the water and turmeric Jarreth gave him.

"I'm going to scout the area," Jarreth signed.

"Be careful," Finnick cautioned.

Jarreth nodded, then took his leave, shutting the door behind him.

Only two hours of sunlight left, Jarreth thought, looking at the sky. *Better check the village now and leave the palace until tomorrow.*

Jarreth started running from house to house, checking everywhere for any survivors. He noticed that most homes still had cutlery and food on their tables, as if they'd be back for dinner. There were no signs of forced entry or any evidence of where the bodies were. Jarreth stopped at one of the houses, as he caught sight of something dark moving from the corner of his eye. He ran to the side of the house where he had seen the figure, but nothing was there. The sound of bins being knocked over startled him, and he turned around hoping to catch the culprit, but nothing was there. He moved closer to inspect, taking out his dagger just in case. He checked the bins, then looked around the area and still couldn't find anything.

This is weird, Jarreth thought. *I better finish my scouting, then head back to the cottage.*

He went to the last couple of houses and did a quick check for survivors and medicine, but to his dismay, there were no survivors or herbs he needed inside. Jarreth circled back to the cottage. He would check the palace tomorrow, hoping for better results. But if Jarreth had only turned around then, he would have seen the creature that had been stalking him in the shadows for hours.

Its eyes followed Jarreth, as he ran back through the village and to the cottage. After it saw Jarreth heading into the house for the night, its long legs clattered along the dirt path and back to its master, who resided in the palace.

CHAPTER TWENTY-FIVE

"I can do all things through him who gives me strength."

Philippians 4:13

Oberon stopped at another stream to refill his water flask, and to have another drink. Running nonstop for days with four hours of sleep each night, had made him hopeful that he would reach his destination that afternoon.

The Kingdom of Neylon.

The closer he got to the Kingdom, the more signs of destruction he saw. Trees that once stood high, were snapped and broken, big footprints were embedded in the ground, and wildlife carcasses rotted on the road leading into Neylon.

Oberon splashed water onto his face to relieve the heat. He then stood up and went over to the cliff's edge. Looking down, he saw a sharp drop with rocks and trees.

He sighed.

He would have to find a safe path down, or find another place to descend. Walking a bit further he saw a man-made path, which still looked dangerous due to the surrounding destruction. In the distance he heard an explosion, and saw black smoke rising from Neylon. He looked back at the man-made path, and began to descend quickly but carefully. He hoped Finnick and Jarreth were having an easier time reaching their destination than he was.

A falcon screeched; notifying Oberon of its presence. Oberon looked up and whistled to the bird. It flew down gracefully and landed on his outstretched arm. Oberon took out the note that was attached, and read the contents within.

Oberon sighed. It's what he feared the most.

The Prince of Darkness was bringing back the creatures of darkness, which explains why a cyclops attacked him. He folded the letter and placed it in his pocket. He then took out a clean sheet of paper and pen, and began writing back to the King about his findings. Once done, he folded the letter, tied it around the falcon's leg, and released the bird.

Once he was safely at the bottom of the cliff, Oberon saw farms outside the main village, that were still unaffected. He began running to one of the farmhouses, hoping to get a horse and some answers. Coming up to one of the houses, Oberon pounded on the door. The door opened a crack, showing just the eyes of a man.

"I don't want any trouble. I just need information and a horse," Oberon told him.

The villager looked him up and down and thought for a minute, before opening his home to Oberon. Once Oberon stepped through, he found at least fifty other villagers huddled in the house, afraid.

"Oberon, Captain of the Royal Guard from the Kingdom of Zolatta," he greeted, extending his hand to the homeowner.

"James," was all the civilian said.

"James, how long has your kingdom been under attack?" Oberon asked.

"Um, a couple of weeks now, I think," James replied.

"Why haven't you asked for aid from the Kingdom of Zolatta? My King sent a letter to your King but heard no reply," Oberon explained.

"Every time we tried to send someone with a letter, they never come back. We hear their screams coming from the forest, and a roar from some creature guarding it," James replied, terrified.

Oberon nodded. "Lucky for you I have come across this creature, and can tell you with confidence that it is now dead."

The villagers murmured happily.

"Thank you," James said.

"Where is your King?" Oberon asked.

"At the palace fighting with others who can fight. The ones who cannot are hiding out here in different farmhouses," James replied.

"Do you have a horse you can spare?" Oberon asked.

James nodded and led the way to the stables, with Oberon following behind. James went ahead and saddled his horse for Oberon, then gave him the reins.

"Thank you," James said.

"Don't thank me yet, we don't know how the people are doing at the palace," Oberon said, mounting the horse. "Thank you for your kindness."

He ushered the horse into a full gallop and headed to the palace. The closer he got, the more destruction and chaos he saw throughout the village, and surrounding the castle. People's homes and buildings were smashed into rubble. Blood soaked the grounds from the dead who fought for their kingdom, and big footprints marked the land.

The cyclops were here.

Oberon dismounted, then carefully made his way up to the castle's front doors, hoping not to alert any cyclops who may still be alive and hiding.

Thump, thump, thump.

Oberon turned, looking for the source of the sound.

Thump, thump, thump.

Oberon suddenly saw two knights running from one of the houses, along with the survivors. Right behind them was a cyclops, axe in hand, chasing after them. Oberon ran to help the survivors and soldiers, as the cyclops gained on them fast. He unsheathed his sword, running past the survivors and up towards the giant beast. Oberon skidded down to his knees and sliced the beast's ankles, causing it to stumble in pain. To give the survivors more of a head start, Oberon quickly got up and stabbed the creature's hand, which held the gigantic axe.

Thump! The weapon dropped from the creature's hand.

The creature roared in pain while looking around for its attacker. But Oberon remained out of the creature's line of sight, causing it to get even angrier. Oberon then came behind the creature, and used his sword to slash the creature's back legs. The cyclops roared furiously, turning towards Oberon, only to see him running away. The cyclops ran after its new victim with rage, forgetting its weapon.

While Oberon ran, he saw some rope hanging off a broken wagon, and instantly a plan formed. He grabbed the rope and ran with it, trying to find somewhere to lay his trap. He ran past multiple houses and buildings, but none fit his plan, so he circled back towards the kingdom. On his way back, he found the perfect spot to set his trap. He quickly tied one end of the rope to a pole, then tied the other end to another pole across the street. He then turned around to face the creature coming for him. The cyclops reached out to try and grab Oberon, but instead it tripped over the rope. The cyclops fell to the ground with a loud thud, that echoed throughout the village. Before it could get back up, Oberon brought down his sword, slicing into the creature's neck. The body went limp. He took out his sword and walked away from the dead cyclops, taking a moment to catch his breath.

"Wow, that was some move," said a voice behind him.

Oberon turned to see the two knights, who had rescued the survivors.

"It's not my first, and it won't be my last," Oberon stated, sheathing his sword. "Oberon, Captain of the Royal Guard from the Kingdom of Zolatta."

"Nice to meet you. My name is Kirsten, Captain of the Royal Guard for Neylon," she introduced, shaking hands with Oberon. "This is my 1st Lieutenant, Ethan."

Oberon nodded. "Nice to meet you."

"Likewise. Nice move with the cyclops. I haven't seen anyone who can finish one off by themselves," Ethan said with awe.

"So, what brings you here?" Kirsten asked.

"I need to speak with your King," Oberon said.

The two knights waited to see if Oberon would elaborate.

"It's urgent," Oberon said.

"Right, I shall introduce you to our King," Kirsten said, walking towards the palace.

Oberon followed along with Ethan, as Kirsten led them into the palace. Once inside, Oberon saw at least a hundred people, who had sought shelter from the attack. Women, children, and the elderly huddled in fear, while the men sharpened their weapons, and some women looked after the wounded. Kirsten led Oberon to a separate room where the King sat, trying to figure out the next battle plan.

"Your Highness," Kirsten greeted, bowing.

The King looked up and nodded for Kirsten to continue.

"This is Oberon. The Captain of the Royal Guard from the Kingdom of Zolatta. He wishes to speak with you," Kirsten explained.

"Very well," the King said, looking up.

Oberon bowed before the King.

"You may rise, Oberon of Zolatta. Your bravery has spread across the palace, and I thank you for your help. I am King Jabari."

"Thank you for your kind words, Your Highness," Oberon said. "I have come with a letter from the King of Zolatta."

He took out the letter and handed it to the King. There was silence in the room as the King read the letter.

"I see," King Jabari said. "Your messengers were probably killed by the cyclops guarding the forest to our Kingdom. I am sorry for your loss. We have lost a few trying to get word out to our allies."

"The cyclops patrolling your forest is now dead," Oberon stated.

King Jabari raised an eyebrow, clearly impressed.

"If there are any more threats, I'm happy to assist before my departure home," Oberon offered.

"Thank you for your bravery, but you have already defeated our two most problematic creatures," King Jabari explained. "The creature guarding the forest, and your latest victory within the village, were a bit smarter than the rest. Hence why it was difficult for us to defeat them. They were getting smarter with each kill, and knew how we fought just by watching us."

Oberon nodded.

"You can tell your King that he has me as an ally," King Jabari said.

"Thank you," Oberon said bowing. "If you no longer require my services, I shall take my leave. I do not like to be away from home too long, with this threat looming."

"Of course," King Jabari said. "Kirsten, Ethan, prepare a horse for Oberon, and some food for his departure."

"Of course, Your Highness," Kirsten said bowing. "Follow

me, Oberon."

Oberon bowed to the King then followed Kirsten, who led him to the stables while Ethan went to gather the food.

"Are the rumors true?" Kirsten asked. "That the Prince of Darkness has come back and declared war."

"Yes," Oberon replied without explanation.

"It's scary to think the creatures of darkness are coming back, after being destroyed almost a hundred years ago," Kirsten said while saddling a horse.

"Keep up your training and don't play the hero, and you'll be fine," Oberon said, taking the reins from her.

Kirsten laughed. "Will do."

Just then Ethan came out with a cloth full of food, as Oberon mounted his horse.

"Fruits, nuts and two flasks of water," Ethan said, handing the wrapped cloth to Oberon.

"Thanks," Oberon said as he urged his horse to a trot.

Leaving behind the Kingdom of Neylon, Oberon was relieved that King Nikolai had King Jabari as an ally. But deep in the forest a giant wolf had emerged, and saw everything that had happened. Growling with hatred, the wolf turned and ran to tell the Master everything he had seen and heard, knowing he would not be pleased.

Claud entered the cave of Akuma, and raced to inform the Master about what had happened in Neylon. He transformed from wolf to human, before bowing before the Master.

"What news do you have for me, my spy?" the Master smirked.

"The cyclops have all been killed, and the King of Neylon has agreed to ally with the King of Zolatta," Claud explained.

The Prince of Darkness was filled with fury.

"Those lowly humans have proven themselves yet again, by defeating my creatures of darkness," the Prince of Darkness replied, strangely calm.

Claud stepped back, careful not to get involved in the Master's fury.

"Where is Mildred?" the Prince of Darkness commanded. "I need more souls so I can be strong enough to break free."

There was silence among the Master's followers.

"Where is she?" he demanded.

"She has chosen a different path," Claud replied. "I saw her speaking to Malachi, the Angel."

"She will regret that decision," the Prince of Darkness said, reaching for his book. "She will indeed."

Laughter filled the cave, as the Prince of Darkness began reading from his book of darkness.

CHAPTER TWENTY-SIX

"Trust in the Lord with all your heart
and lean not on your own understanding."

Proverbs 3:5

Mildred quietly sat around Malachi's campfire, watching him unpack the food he had brought. He handed her some bread and cheese, then poured some wine.

"You said you could help me reach people, to tell them about the Dark One's plans," Mildred said.

"Yes, I did," replied Malachi.

"How are we going to do that?" Mildred asked.

"We are going to request an audience with the King and Queen of Zolatta," Malachi explained.

"Oh," was all Mildred could say.

Malachi looked at her questionably.

"Last time I was there, I did something terrible," Mildred said regretfully.

Malachi stopped what he was doing and looked at her.

"I-," Mildred stammered.

"Everybody makes mistakes; you are only human. The God of Light did not make anyone perfect besides his Son, who came down to die, to save everyone from their mistakes, including you Mildred," Malachi explained.

"But what if I hurt someone quite badly?" Mildred asked.

"Like murder?" Malachi asked.

Mildred looked down in shame. "I-."

"There is no mistake too big, that the God of Light won't forgive. If you repent, and not make that mistake again, and ask the God of Light to forgive you, then you will be forgiven. The God of Light will then put it in the past and forget it," Malachi explained.

"How do I tell him I'm sorry?" Mildred asked, eager to put her past behind her.

"Pray," Malachi said.

"Pray?" Mildred questioned.

"That is how people talk to the God of Light; they pray," Malachi said simply.

Mildred looked at him thinking. She hasn't prayed in such a long time.

"If you are worried about praying, the God of Light knows you and your heart," Malachi began. "It doesn't matter if you have been praying for years, or if it's your first time. He knows you."

"Ok," Mildred replied with a little more confidence.

"I will leave you for a bit so you can talk to him. I will go and fetch more firewood. It's going to be a chilly night," Malachi said, standing up.

Once Mildred saw Malachi disappear through the trees, she sighed.

I can do this, she thought.

"God of Light, please hear my prayer," Mildred said aloud. "I messed up big time, and I realize I am a sinner, who has made lots of mistakes. I know I could never reach heaven alone. I place my faith in you. Please forgive my mistakes and help me to live for you. I give my heart to you and trust in you. Amen."

Immediately, Mildred felt like a weight was lifted from her shoulders. She felt lighter and more at peace and began to cry.

"It's ok, child," Malachi said, placing his hand on her head for comfort. " It's ok."

✦ ✦ ✦ ✦ ✦

Sitting in his office, Nikolai thought about everything that had happened in the dungeons. He was happy to have had the chance to speak to his parents, and was relieved that he retrieved the Sword of the Kings.

When he returned from his test, Juliet awaited him and immediately healed his injuries and Nix's. Nix had returned with him and usually stayed by Nikolai's side or Juliet's, growling at anyone who got too close. Things were coming together slowly, but the people sent to the Kingdoms of Kudzu and Neylon, still hadn't replied, and Nikolai was getting worried.

A knock at the door interrupted his thoughts as Juliet entered his office. She went straight to Nix, giving him a good pat which he loved, then kissed Nikolai.

"Afternoon," Nikolai said smiling.

"Hi, how are you feeling?" Juliet asked.

"Better," Nikolai said. "And you?"

"Good, I just got these letters from Theo. They're from my Mother, Captain Oberon, and Lieutenant Jarreth," Juliet explained.

She handed him the letters, and Nikolai opened the one from Oberon first, reading the letter's contents.

"Captain Oberon has fought with a cyclops. He thinks they

have attacked the Kingdom of Neylon, and is almost at his destination. He will inform us soon once more information has been collected," Nikolai said, reading aloud.

"I hope the Kingdom of Neylon is ok," Juliet said worriedly. "That's probably why we didn't hear back from them."

"That would make sense," Nikolai replied. "What news from your mother?"

"Mother was being stalked by a shapeshifter who could turn into a wolf, but Issac killed it. They are also safe back at home," Juliet read.

"That's good to hear," Nikolai said.

"What does Jarreth's letter say?" Juliet asked.

"Jarreth said Finnick has been injured, but is doing fine. They were attacked by a man with bat wings, who was sent by the Prince of Darkness to kill them. The enemy has been eliminated, and they are almost to the Kingdom of Kudzu. They will check in once they have arrived," Nikolai began. "My father warned me about some of the followers of the Prince of Darkness. He told me they were rewarded with supernatural abilities for serving him. My father remembered a man with bat-like wings amongst others."

"How horrible, who would do that to themselves?" Juliet asked horrified.

"People who want power, to hurt others, to rule," Nikolai replied, naming a few. "But I reckon the Prince of Darkness is manipulating these people."

"It's sad to think so, but I agree," Juliet said sadly.

Nikolai put his arm around her waist and hugged her.

"I wish we knew more about the Prince of Darkness's plan," Juliet sighed.

"Me too," Nikolai said, kissing her forehead. "Me too."

"Have you tried using the sword yet?" Juliet asked.

Nikolai sighed and looked over at the sword leaning against the wall of his office.

"Not yet. I was hoping to wait till Oberon came back. He's a skilled swordsman, whereas I'm more of a skilled archer," Nikolai explained.

"Fair enough," Juliet said. "Also, I did some research on the different creatures of darkness."

"What did you find?" Nikolai asked with curiosity.

"Well, nothing good for starters," Juliet said, getting a book out. "The wolf that attacked Mother, had the same description you told me about the wolf that you fought. But it's no ordinary wolf. They're known as shapeshifters. They can transform from human to wolf, and have the same kind of abilities as a wolf."

"What makes shapeshifters different from werewolves?" Nikolai asked.

"Werewolves change at every full moon. Also, when a werewolf bites you, you become one," Juliet read from the book.

"Well, I'm glad I fought a shapeshifter instead of a werewolf," Nikolai said relieved. "What else have you found?"

Juliet flipped the pages until she found what she was looking for, then began to read.

"Cyclops, meaning circled-eyed giant. They are known to be cannibals. They are a wild race of lawless creatures, with neither social manners, nor fear of God. These creatures are quite dumb but are vicious in a fight, and there are no known weaknesses."

"That's ok because Oberon managed to defeat one. We'll ask him how when he gets back," Nikolai said, writing down some notes.

"Next one is a minotaur. It's the body of a man, and the head and tail of a bull. It's a vicious beast and a cannibal. It also fights with a gigantic axe. A minotaur can be killed with its own horn, when stabbed in the chest or neck area," Juliet read.

"That is going to be a difficult one to beat. I hope we never have to deal with one," Nikolai said, writing down some more notes.

"I agree, we may need more than one person to defeat a minotaur," Juliet suggested.

"I agree. The more people we have, the better chance we have of defeating it," Nikolai agreed. "What did you find next?"

"We have the basilisk, known as the King of Serpents. A basilisk is said to have the power to cause death with a single glance. It can also spit deadly venom. To kill a basilisk, one must reverse the direction of its glare back to the basilisk itself," Juliet said, closing the book.

"Reverse its glare back onto itself. Is that it?" Nikolai asked, astonished at how something so simple can be a basilisk's weakness.

"That's what the book says," Juliet said, putting the book away.

"I just thought it'd be more difficult. Thank you for doing all this research," Nikolai said, putting his notes away.

"There's still so many different creatures of darkness out there. We won't know which of these creatures has been summoned, until the war begins. And then it may be too late," Juliet said, rubbing her eyes.

Nikolai took Juliet's hands, kissed them gently, and hugged her.

"We've got a start. That's better than nothing at all," Nikolai encouraged.

Juliet started to relax in his embrace. Everyone felt the pressure of this coming threat, and Nikolai needed to think of some strategy to prevent burnout or a breakdown. He needed everyone's help to achieve his goal of defeating the Prince of Darkness. But not if they are overworked and stressed.

"Juliet," Nikolai said putting her hair behind her ears. "Let's do something together, anything you want."

Juliet smiled at him. "How about a picnic by the lake?"

"That's sound very relaxing and inviting," Nikolai said, kissing her forehead. "Let's do it."

"Really," Juliet said excitedly. "Now."

"I've got nothing planned. Besides it will be nice just to sit back and relax," Nikolai said smiling at her enthusiasm.

She smiled back and kissed him. "I'd love to."

CHAPTER TWENTY-SEVEN

"May the God of hope fill you with all joy and peace
as you trust in him, so that you may overflow with hope
by the power of the Holy Spirit."

Romans 15:13

The next day Jarreth was up at dawn. He was eager to put this village behind him, after he searched the palace to be sure they didn't miss any survivors. Finnick stirred from across the room, in the only decent bed in the house.

"Morning," Finnick said, sitting up in bed. "How'd you sleep?"

Jarreth nodded, then pointed to Finnick.

"I'm okay. Still in quite a bit of pain, but I'll live," Finnick said, looking down at his leg.

Jarreth walked over and inspected Finnick's wound himself.

"It looks to be healing well," Finnick said, looking at Jarreth. "Do we have any more turmeric?"

Jarreth nodded, went to the cupboard where he initially found it, and got more for Finnick.

"Thanks, man," Finnick said, taking the herb.

"I'm going to scout the palace. If there are no survivors, then we leave this place and report back to the King," signed Jarreth.

"Be careful," Finnick replied, nodding.

"Always am," Jarreth signed.

Jarreth packed up a supply bag just in case, then left the cottage. He closed the door behind him, hoping Finnick would be safe enough while he was gone. Jarreth then looked up at the sky. The sun was out but you could barely see it, as there was still a lot of smoke in the air, making the sky darken with a smoky haze. He covered his mouth with the scarf he always carried, trying to block out the smell of smoke. He shouldered his backpack and saddled his horse, then cantered off to the palace. While riding, he noticed the amount of debris on the road and wondered what creature caused this. Still unsure of what he was dealing with, he cautioned his every move just to be safe. The closer he got to the palace, the more signs of destruction he saw. He stopped his horse when he noticed an animal carcass lying on the ground, covered in something white. He dismounted and knelt to check the animal.

Cobwebs, Jarreth thought confused. *Surely a spider couldn't do this much damage; unless the Prince of Darkness tampered with it.*

He looked up and checked his surroundings, noticing more cobwebs covering the palace and surrounding area. Jarreth unsheathed his knife from his pocket and looked around cautiously.

No movement. No animals. No insects. And no humans. Strange.

He mounted his horse again and continued to the palace. Once at the gate, he tied his horse up and continued on foot. He walked up the front steps, and slowly opened the front doors.

The palace inside was dark and filled with dust, as if no one had occupied it for a long time. He scouted the palace's ground floor first, before circling back to the front door. Not a single person was found. He then went up to the second floor and scouted the area. He couldn't find anyone or anything, to inform him about what happened to this once-thriving kingdom. He then heard something fall from behind him. He spun around quickly, knife in hand, ready to attack.

No one was there.

Curious, he walked over to the area and inspected it. He picked up the candlestick that had dropped, and placed it back on the bench. He turned around to continue his mission, but stopped short. Standing before him was a massive spider, roughly forty centimeters in length. It was black, red, and poised, ready to attack him. It came at Jarreth with supernatural speed, shooting out its web, to try and capture its prey. Jarreth kept moving, trying to avoid being hit by its web, while finding an opening to attack. While running, he took out his bow and arrow then spun around to face the oncoming spider. Drawing his bow, he aimed it at the spider's body, letting the arrow fly straight into its flesh. Its legs slowly curled over its body as it died. Jarreth shook off the uneasiness. He could deal with the tiny everyday house spiders, but this was too big. It wasn't your average size spider. The Prince of Darkness definitely tampered with it.

He continued to scout the second floor, finding nothing in the process. Upon opening one of the bedroom doors, Jarreth stopped and stared wide-eyed. At least five spiders clung to the wall, while three were on the ground, working hard to ensure their new prey wouldn't break free of their cobwebs. The prey caught in the spider web was a tiger, struggling to free itself from the web. But against eight spiders, it was proving difficult, so it gave up and went limp as it accepted its fate. Jarreth held up his bow and arrow and began shooting the spiders individually, until they were all dead on the floor. He cautiously approached the tiger, and began to rip the cobwebs off its body until it was free. The tiger rubbed its head against Jarreth's leg, showing gratitude. Jarreth smiled and patted its head, before turning towards the door.

He left to continue his mission. After finding nothing in the main area of the palace, he decided to go down and check the dungeons. He noticed the tiger following him, and was glad he didn't have to face whatever the dungeons held alone. He slowly descended the dungeon's stairs, watching for any movement. The further he went down, the more he was consumed with darkness and dust. Opening the door to the prison cells, he stopped midway to avoid detection. Peeking through the door, Jarreth saw over a hundred bodies cocooned inside cobwebs, unable to move, hanging by a web from the ceiling. Jarreth's heart pounded as he scanned the area, trying desperately to find someone alive. He crept slowly to the nearest body and began cutting through the web with his knife. He pulled at the web covering the victim's face and checked for a pulse, nothing. He scanned the area again, trying to find the culprit.

He thought his eyes were playing tricks on him, as he began to see multiple dark shapes moving towards him. Or maybe his eyes weren't tricking him, and something was really coming after him. After a moment of hesitation, Jarreth turned around and ran back through the door, with the tiger close behind him. The sounds behind him grew louder and louder, as he ran back up the stairs to the palace. The tiger followed closely behind him, eager to get out.

Once Jarreth reached the front doors, he opened them and ran outside with the tiger. Now that he was in daylight, he turned around with his bow and arrow, and found himself face-to-face with a giant spider. This spider was bigger than the ones he had previously faced. Moving further and further away, Jarreth let his arrow fly straight into the spider's body, causing it to stumble a little before continuing to chase its prey. Jarreth dodged the spider's web attacks by moving around constantly. He used the buildings and debris to avoid being hit, all the while shooting his arrows at the spider. After a bit of cat and mouse shooting and dodging, Jarreth began to slow down as the spider got weaker and slower, before dropping to the ground dead. Jarreth stood there panting with exhaustion and fear, at how giant and fast the spider was. His knees gave way, and he collapsed onto the ground. The tiger approached him and licked his face. Jarreth patted the tiger while catching his breath.

That answers the question of where the bodies are, Jarreth thought. *But surely there must be survivors.*

From the corner of his eyes, Jarreth saw movement and readied his bow and arrow at the target, but lowered it after seeing it was just a boy. The boy was in his teens, with blonde hair and blue eyes. He held his bow and catch of the day in one hand. Witnessing Jarreth's encounter with the giant spider, the boy, wide-eyed, raced over to see Jarreth. Jarreth stood up as the boy got closer, and put his weapons away.

"That was amazing," the young boy exclaimed.

Jarreth smiled and nodded.

"I'm Lucas," the boy said, dropping his catch to shake hands.

Jarreth nodded and shook his hand.

"What's your name?" Lucas asked.

Jarreth hesitated, then bent down to the ground, and wrote his name in the dirt. He then pointed to the scars on his neck. The boy read the name, then looked at the wounds Jarreth was pointing to.

"It's nice to meet you, Jarreth," Lucas beamed.

Jarreth gestured to the kingdom around him.

"You're asking what happened here?" asked Lucas.

Jarreth nodded.

"I can't answer that, but I can take you to someone who can," Lucas said, picking up his catch.

Lucas turned around and headed deeper into the forest, as Jarreth followed behind him with the tiger. The deeper they walked into the woods, the more signs of life he saw. People gathered around in makeshift tents, along with several types of animals. Fires had been set up as people cooked and talked around them. Jarreth felt relief seeing how many people survived. Lucas stopped before one of the makeshift tents.

"Princess Iris," he called out.

Jarreth stared at the woman who emerged from the tent. The young woman looked to be in her late twenties. She had light brown skin and short purple hair, with beautiful brown eyes. She walked up to Jarreth with a beautiful smile, and that was when Jarreth noticed two striking things about her. One, she had orange and black tiger-like ears, her nails were long and sharp, and she also had a tail that was moving as she walked. Two, she was wearing a beaded crown with an amethyst Gem, that dangled from a bead in the center of her forehead.

"Lucas, what have I told you about bringing strangers into our camp," Iris scolded.

"I-," Lucas began. "I saw him defeat one of Jorogumo's minions. A massive one, all by himself."

"Really?" Iris asked, turning to stare at Jarreth, amazed.

Jarreth blushed and smiled at the Princess.

"And what's your name, sir?" Iris asked.

"He's mute, but his name is Jarreth," Lucas said.

"Mute?" Iris asked.

Jarreth nodded, embarrassed, and tightened the scarf around his neck.

"Well, come inside, and we can talk," Iris said, gesturing into the tent.

Jarreth followed Iris inside the small tent, and sat at the table across from her. Her servants poured some tea and placed some biscuits on the table, before standing to the side.

"You can use sign language; I can understand," Iris reassured.

Jarreth nodded, then began using sign language to explain everything that had happened to him and Finnick, and why he was here.

"Is your friend still in the cottage?" she asked.

Jarreth nodded.

"Okay, I will organize one of my scouts to fetch him, and bring him here to be treated," Iris said, gesturing to one of her servants to complete the task.

"Princess, what can you tell me of the creature in your kingdom," Jarreth signed. *"Lucas mentioned Jorogumo. Who's that?"*

"Jorogumo is a spider demon who is working for the Prince of Darkness. She has three forms. The first is a human being, the second is half spider-half human, and the third form is fully spider, and a big one at that," Iris explained.

"You know about the Prince of Darkness?" Jarreth asked, signing.

"Yes. I believe our kingdom was attacked by him first," Iris said sadly. "We lost a lot of good people, because Jorogumo deceived us in her human form for a long time."

"Why did you not seek help from the other kingdoms?" Jarreth asked, signing.

"You don't think I've tried," Iris said offended.

"I'm sorry, I didn't mean to assume. It's just that my King has sent a letter and has been waiting for a reply," Jarreth signed, apologizing.

"I'm sorry, too. I didn't mean to get worked up. We have been trying to get word out. But when we tried sending people to get help, Jorogumo sends her minions after them," Iris said.

"*I'm sorry*," Jarreth signed.

"I'm curious," Iris said, staring at Jarreth intently. "How did you manage to get through unharmed?"

"*Unharmed! My friend is injured, and a follower of the Prince of Darkness attacked us*," Jarreth explained. "*I only just managed to kill our attacker before he killed us.*"

"Right, sorry. I'm finding it hard to trust people since Jorogumo deceived us," Iris apologized.

"*I understand*," Jarreth signed.

Princess Iris smiled and stared at Jarreth with wonder and excitement. These feelings she had once locked away long ago, have resurfaced with the young man before her. She began to feel her cheeks go hot. Jarreth smiled back at her.

"I've sent scouts to retrieve the young man's friend. They will return shortly. It's not that far, so they should be back in about twenty minutes," Iris's maid informed, bowing.

Jarreth nodded.

"Thank you, Edith," Iris said.

"What did your King's letter say?" Iris asked.

Jarreth took out the King's letter and handed it to the Princess.

"*Everything you need to know is in there*," Jarreth signed.

Princess Iris took the letter and began to read. Jarreth stared at her, thinking how beautiful she was. After a couple of minutes of reading, Iris looked up at Jarreth.

"Princess Iris," a soldier interrupted them.

"You may come in," Iris called out.

A soldier came in and bowed.

"We have brought the young man's friend. He is in the medical tent," the soldier informed.

"Thank you, you may go," Iris said.

But the soldier remained where he was.

"What is it, Erick?" Princess Iris asked annoyed.

"If I may speak freely, since this young man has survived the night in the kingdom, let me take a few men to go scouting for survivors. With your permission, of course," Erick suggested.

"*There are no survivors*," Jarreth signed and shook his head.

Erick looked at Jarreth with insignificance and raised his eyebrow.

"No offence, but let the soldiers deal with this matter. We have years of experience in fighting," Erick sneered, smiling a little too much.

"That is enough, Erick. Jarreth is the 2nd Lieutenant from the Kingdom of Zolatta, who has kindly shared what he knows about our kingdom's ruined state," Iris barked. "Jarreth has already told me there are no survivors, and I trust him."

Erick looked at Jarreth angrily, nodded to the Princess, and left.

"I'm sorry," Iris began.

Jarreth held up his hand to stop her, then signed, "*It's okay, I'm used to it.*"

"Just because you're used to it, doesn't make it right," Iris replied, smiling at him.

Jarreth smiled back.

"*May I see my friend?*" Jarreth signed.

"Of course, let me show you to the medical tent," Iris said, standing up.

They left the makeshift tent together, and Jarreth followed Iris to the medical tent. Jarreth saw kids playing without a care in the world, as people gathered around the fire to help prepare the next meal. He saw others helping older and younger people; a real community coming together to help each other out. Iris went into the medical tent and over to where Finnick lay.

"And where have you been?" Finnick asked, arms crossed.

"You had me worried."

"*Sorry*," Jarreth signed, smiling, then sighed. "*I didn't realize the time.*"

"I can see that," Finnick said, looking to Princess Iris, who was talking with the nurse.

Finnick turned back to Jarreth with his eyebrows raised, and a big goofy smile on his face. Jarreth ignored his friend's implications and began signing.

"*Princess Iris lost half her kingdom to a spider demon who is working for the Prince of Darkness.*"

"Uh huh," Finnick said, still eyeing Jarreth.

Jarreth continued to ignore his friend's implications.

"*How's your leg?*" Jarreth asked.

"A lot better. The nurse gave me a herb that's taken the pain away completely, and some other herb to help with healing. I will only need crutches for a month," Finnick said. "Have you told her of our mission?"

"*Yes, I just gave her the letter from the King, just as you arrived*," Jarreth signed, watching Princess Iris approach them.

"You're both welcome to stay here until Finnick's leg heals enough to ride. I've just spoken to Lucas, and he has a spare room for you, Jarreth. Finnick will stay here in the medical tent to recover," she offered.

"Thank you, Princess Iris," Finnick said.

"*Thanks*," Jarreth signed.

"You're welcome. I shall speak to you both tomorrow regarding the letter, once I've had a chance to read it," Iris said, before leaving the tent.

Jarreth watched Princess Iris as she left the medical tent. He was looking forward to seeing her again tomorrow, as something stirred inside him for the first time. He was never good with women. That was always Finnick's strength. Plus, all the women at home thought he was disabled because of his muteness. But there was something different about Iris, and Jarreth felt something more than friendship with her.

"Earth to Jarreth," Finnick whispered.

Jarreth looked over at his friend, who was grinning at him.

"Looks to me like someone has caught your eye," Finnick said grinning.

Jarreth smiled at his friend. Just then Lucas burst into the tent and ran up to Jarreth.

"Princess Iris said you are bunking with me. Let me show you where you'll be staying," Lucas said excitedly.

"Go on, I'll be fine. I need to rest," Finnick said smiling, as Lucas dragged Jarreth out of the tent.

Jarreth followed Lucas until they reached his tent. Once inside, Lucas showed Jarreth where he was sleeping and the toilets, which was quite a walk away. You needed a torch and a second person for safety.

"So, how long are you staying?" Lucas asked.

"*Until my friend is able to ride home*," Jarreth wrote on Lucas's paper.

"Awesome, we can hang out all day," Lucas said excitedly, then stopped. "Unless you don't want to hang out with a kid."

Jarreth smiled and wrote to Lucas. "*I don't mind. You are the second nicest person here.*"

"You've met Erick, I'm guessing," Lucas said with disgust.

Jarreth nodded.

"He bullies me," Lucas said sadly.

"*Why?*" Jarreth asked, tilting his head to one side.

"Because I'm still a kid. But I want to learn to fight. So I can defend myself and others. But he said I'm too young," Lucas moped.

"*I learnt to fight when I was fifteen*," Jarreth wrote. "*Better to start young, I reckon.*"

"So, you'll teach me?" Lucas asked excitedly.

"*If your parents say it's okay, then yes*," Jarreth wrote.

Lucas stopped short and looked towards the ground.

"My parents died during the Jorogumo attack," Lucas said. "It's why I want to learn to fight, so that I can help others."

Jarreth looked at Lucas with sympathy.

"*We start training tomorrow*," Jarreth wrote.

CHAPTER TWENTY-EIGHT

"Even though I walk through the darkest valley, I will fear no evil,
for you are with me; your rod and your staff, they comfort me."

Psalms 23:4

Mildred helped Malachi pack up their camp, so that they could have an early start to the day. Travelling to the Kingdom of Zolatta didn't seem like a burden anymore, since Mildred gave her heart to the God of Light, and trusted fully in him. She still couldn't see how it would work out, but she trusted in the God of Light that it would, somehow.

Mounting her horse, she followed behind as Malachi led the way. She watched closely for the Dark One's followers, as they rode throughout the day.

"What is wrong, child?" Malachi asked.

"Just worried about unwanted company," Mildred replied.

"You need not worry about the Dark One and his followers," Malachi reassured her.

"Can I ask you a question?" Mildred asked.

"Sure," Malachi replied.

"Can all angels read minds?" Mildred asked curiously.

"Child, I cannot read your mind; only the God of Light can," Malachi laughed. "But I can read your facial expressions."

Mildred chuckled. "That obvious?"

"In the Tanakh, it is written, 'Do not fear, for God is with you,'" Malachi explained.

"I have to remember that one," Mildred replied, making a mental note.

"You are safe with me," Malachi reassured.

"Thanks, and sorry for stressing," Mildred said.

Malachi smiled. "It's ok."

Malachi and Mildred stopped near a small lake for lunch. After dismounting their horses, Mildred led them to the lake to drink.

The lake was crystal clear, with beautiful flowers surrounding the edge, and a small waterfall in the middle. Mildred's horse moved away from her, and began to make its way deeper into the water. Her horse stopped once it was submerged entirely, except for its head.

The water then started to glow. The other horse trotted away, startled at the unexpected, but Mildred stood there in awe. The horse showed no fear, as the water around it began to glow.

"What's happening?" Mildred asked Malachi, who came and stood next to her.

"The God of Light's gift, to aid the Kingdom of Zolatta with this coming threat," Malachi explained.

"I don't get it," Mildred said, confused.

"Just watch and see," Malachi said, gesturing to the lake.

The horse suddenly grew beautiful, white wings, which blended in with its white body. A golden horn appeared on its head, and its mane and tail turned white like snow, with little bits of gold in them. Once the transformation was complete, the horse left the water and trotted up to Malachi and Mildred.

"It's beautiful," Mildred beamed. "But is it a pegasus or a unicorn?"

"When a horse has wings and a horn, it's called an alicorn," Malachi explained. "Your mission, given to you by the God of Light, is to bring this alicorn to the King and Queen of Zolatta."

"My mission?" Mildred asked, patting the alicorn's head.

"Yes," Malachi said. "Do you accept?"

"Yes," Mildred said, smiling.

"Before we continue with our journey, you must eat," Malachi said, handing her some fruit and nuts.

"Thank you," Mildred said.

Mildred took the offered food and sat on a rock on the edge of the lake. She watched the alicorn spread its wings to stretch, and was in awe at the majestic being before her. This was a truly magnificent creature. She thought back to her time serving the Dark One, remembering that his creatures were all terrifying and scary. Thinking about what she had just witnessed from the God of Light, his creatures were magnificent and unique.

The alicorn came up to her and sniffed her food. Mildred laughed and gave her an apple. Once the alicorn took and ate the apple, Mildred began patting its head. The golden streaks throughout its mane shone in the sunlight, creating a glitter effect.

"What's her name?" Mildred asked.

"She doesn't have one yet. Why don't you pick one for her," Malachi suggested.

Mildred thought momentarily. She wanted the name to fit perfectly.

"What about Amisha?" Mildred suggested. "It means pure, truthful, beautiful and a heart of gold."

"I think it's perfect," Malachi replied.

Mildred smiled as she continued to eat, feeling happy for the first time in a long time.

CHAPTER TWENTY-NINE

"And do not forget to do good and to share with others,
for with such sacrifices God is pleased".

Hebrews 13:16

Jarreth was woken up the next day by an extremely excited Lucas, who wanted to start his training as soon as possible. Jarreth held his hand up in defeat, to let Lucas know he was getting up. He tapped his wrist, showing Lucas what he wanted.

"It's eight o'clock," Lucas replied.

Jarreth nodded then got up. After a quick wash and shave, Jarreth met Lucas outside, who was trying to wait patiently. Jarreth smiled at Lucas's eagerness to train.

Lucas then dragged Jarreth to the tent where they were serving breakfast. The older adults of Kudzu were working together to ensure that everyone was well-fed, and that there was enough food to go around. Lucas led Jarreth to the end of the line, where they waited for their turn.

"What training are we going to do first?" Lucas asked.

Jarreth took out his small knife, showed Lucas, then put it

back in his pocket. He then used his hand to show him throwing something.

"Knife throwing, awesome," Lucas said excitedly.

Jarreth smiled.

"Training him is useless, you may as well give up now," Erick sneered, as he came and jumped in front of Lucas and Jarreth.

"Hey, no fair, we were here first," Lucas barked.

"What are you going to do? Fight me," Erick taunted.

Before Lucas could move, Jarreth stopped him and shook his head.

"Hmp, smart move," Erick said, facing Jarreth. "You know the Princess may trust you, but I don't. I'm surprised they let a mute like you become a soldier."

Jarreth held back Lucas for the second time, before Lucas could hit Erick.

"That's right, listen to your new friend. He may be mute, but he's smart," Erick laughed.

Erick turned back around to find Finnick leaning on his crutches, staring intently at him. Erick stood back, being suddenly caught off guard.

"Why are you glaring at me?" Erick asked, annoyed. "What's your problem?"

"I'm hoping you'll unexpectedly explode, if I think about it hard enough," Finnick said, glaring at Erick.

Lucas laughed, while Jarreth smiled.

"Freak," Erick spat, storming off to the back of the line.

"Serves him right for cutting in front, without an invitation," Finnick said.

Jarreth gestured for Finnick to hop in line in front of them.

"Why thank you, my good sirs," Finnick said, in a funny voice, tipping his imaginary hat.

Lucas laughed. "That was awesome."

"Nobody bullies my friends," Finnick said. "You okay, Jarreth?"

Jarreth nodded.

"Next," the elderly lady called to the line.

Finnick, Jarreth and Lucas picked up some plates from the table, and walked towards the older woman who called out.

"Morning Lucas, and who might your friends be?" the elderly woman asked, placing food on each of their plates.

"This is Jarreth," Lucas said, pointing towards him.

Jarreth nodded.

"Man of a few words, aren't you? Nice to meet you," she greeted. "I'm Dottie."

"I'm Finnick. Jarreth and I are from the Kingdom of Zolatta," Finnick introduced himself.

"You're the lads who defeated the bat boy, I heard," Dottie said.

"You heard correctly," Finnick laughed.

"I don't understand why someone would give themselves up for experiments, for the Dark One," Dottie said, shivering. "That's just nasty."

"I saw Jarreth kill one of Jorogumo's minions. It was gigantic and scary," Lucas exclaimed.

"Really now," Dottie said, impressed, looking at Jarreth.

Jarreth gave a sheepish smile.

"Well, extra servings for all three of you, for your bravery," Dottie said, filling up their plates even more.

"Awesome, thanks," Lucas and Finnick said excitedly.

After, Finnick and Lucas went to find a seat, while Jarreth waited for his plate to be filled.

"Don't take to heart what Erick said," Dottie whispered to Jarreth.

Jarreth smiled and nodded, then walked off to join his friends.

"*How's your leg?*" Jarreth signed.

"A lot better, but still hurts a bit. They gave me crutches to walk around in, so I don't lose my mind by being confined to bed," Finnick explained.

Jarreth laughed silently.

Once they had finished their breakfast, Lucas took Jarreth and Finnick to a clear spot behind his tent so they could train. There were a few trees around to use as targets for knife throwing. Jarreth chose one, marked it with his knife, then stood back with Lucas and Finnick. Jarreth held his knife up towards the side of his face, then let it fly towards the tree, hitting it dead on center.

"Wow," Lucas said in awe.

Jarreth collected his knife, then returned to where Lucas and Finnick were waiting.

"*Can you help me translate?*" Jarreth signed to Finnick.

"Sure. Lucas, I'm going to translate everything Jarreth says. It's easier that way, otherwise, we'll be here all day," Finnick explained.

"Okay," Lucas said, waiting patiently.

"When practicing knife throwing, ensure everyone stands behind you to prevent injuries. First, aim at your target. Second, just as you let go of the knife, use as much force as you can while throwing it, so it can pierce its intended target. In your case, it'll be the spider. You want to injure it, so using as much force as possible will ensure you hit it, and injure it simultaneously," Finnick interpreted for Jarreth.

"Okay," Lucas said, listening.

"Now give it a try," Finnick interpreted.

Jarreth gave Lucas one of his knives and stood back to watch. Lucas held the knife in his hand momentarily, then brought it up near his face. Concentrating, he flung the knife with as much force as he possibly could at the target. The knife hit the tree, stayed there for a couple of seconds, and then fell out.

Lucas let out a sad sigh.

"Hey, that was good for your first time. It stayed in the tree for a couple of seconds. Just keep practicing and you'll get better," Finnick translated. "Jarreth didn't get it his first time either, and he didn't get to where he is today without plenty of practice."

Lucas smiled, nodded, and ran to the tree to collect the knife.

"Princess Iris," Lucas exclaimed, running back to them as Iris came up towards them. "Jarreth and Finnick are teaching me to fight."

"I hope you don't mind, he insisted. He said he wants to defend himself and help others," Jarreth signed.

"Not at all," Iris said. "It's good to see that he wants to help."

"With the right training, he'll be a good soldier in the future," Jarreth signed.

"That's great to hear," Iris said. "Can we talk about the letter?"

Jarreth nodded, then looked at Finnick.

"Sure," Finnick said. "Sorry Lucas, break time."

"Awe, okay," Lucas replied in defeat.

Jarreth and Finnick followed Princess Iris as she led them back to her tent. Once inside they all gathered around the table.

"So, regarding your King's letter, I'm happy to ally with your kingdom," Iris said.

"That's great news," Finnick said. "Our King and Queen will be pleased to hear that."

"Thank you," Jarreth signed.

"I have written a letter to your King and Queen, so you can take it with you when you depart," Iris said, handing the letter to Jarreth.

"Will do, Princess," Finnick said.

"When do you think you will depart?" Iris asked.

"Nurse says I can ride tomorrow," Finnick said.

"Tomorrow," Iris said. "So soon."

"Yes, I'm afraid our King and Queen need us back once our mission is done," Finnick replied.

"I understand," Iris said sadly. "I'll let you get back to training with Lucas. I'm sure he'll want to get as much practice in before your departure."

"Thank you, Princess," Finnick said, rising.

"*Thank you*," Jarreth signed.

Jarreth, Finnick and Princess Iris left the tent. As they headed back to Lucas, Jarreth watched the Princess walk in the opposite direction to them.

Finnick put his hand on Jarreth's shoulder. "Go talk to her, I'll train with Lucas for a while."

"*Thanks*," Jarreth signed, smiling.

Jarreth ran up to Princess Iris and stopped beside her in a walk.

"What can I do for you, Jarreth?" she said smiling.

"*Just making sure you're okay*," Jarreth signed.

Princess Iris smiled at Jarreth.

"Mysterious and caring," Iris said, looking at Jarreth.

Jarreth smiled and blushed.

"I'm doing okay, considering what's been happening around here," Iris said. "Just glad we're allies now."

"*Can I ask you something?*" Jarreth signed.

"Sure, go ahead," Iris replied.

"*Your kingdom's Gem power can communicate with animals, right? Have you tried to communicate with the spiders that attacked your kingdom?*" Jarreth asked, signing.

"Tried and failed. They only follow Jorogumo's orders," Iris explained.

"*Right, I'm sorry*," Jarreth signed.

"It's okay," Iris said smiling at him. "Can I now ask you a question?"

Jarreth looked surprised, and nodded a yes in reply.

"Did you happen to find Jorogumo's nest?" Iris asked.

Jarreth hesitated for a second, before signing. *"Yes, I did."*

"What did you find there?" Iris asked.

Jarreth stopped and turned to face the Princess with sympathy. She stopped and stared at him, waiting for him to reply.

"Your people are cocooned in cobwebs," Jarreth signed, then stopped for a moment. *"I cut one open to check the victim's pulse, but there was none. Jorogumo has multiple gigantic spiders that reside down in the dungeons, who guard the cocooned people."*

Princess Iris let out a sigh, then nodded.

"I'm sorry," Jarreth signed.

"No, don't be. I wanted to know," Iris said, beginning to cry.

Jarreth wiped away the tear that ran down her face. He let his hand linger for a moment, before pushing a loose strand of hair behind her ear. Princess Iris leaned into his touch, as Jarreth embraced her.

From a distance away, Erick watched with fury at what he saw, storming away to meet his new friend. He thought to himself that he would make Jarreth regret he ever lived, by making a deal with Jorogumo. He smirked to himself before heading back to camp.

Jarreth smiled while walking back to where Finnick and Lucas were training. He had never felt this way about a woman before, and was a bit upset when Princess Iris was called away to meet with the elders.

When Jarreth got to the training spot, he saw Finnick and Lucas being bullied by Erick and a few others. One pushed Lucas around while the other stole Finnick's crutches, causing his friend to stumble. Jarreth ran over and stopped Erick just before he pushed Lucas again. Finnick came up behind Lucas slowly, favoring his good leg, and massaging a bruised jaw.

"The mute has arrived," Erick and his friends laughed.

"Stop it, he's twice the soldier you are," Lucas cried.

Erick was about to shove him again, but Jarreth stood before Lucas.

"I think you guys should leave," Finnick suggested.

"Are you telling us what to do?" Erick laughed.

"Just a suggestion," Finnick replied.

Jarreth and Erick stared at each other for a few minutes, before Erick finally spoke. "Fine, let's go," he grunted.

Jarreth turned towards Lucas and Finnick to see if they were okay. He saw that Lucas only had a few cuts and bruises, and Finnick was only sporting a bruised jaw. Nothing serious. Finnick came up slowly to Lucas and patted his head.

"You okay, buddy?" Finnick asked.

Lucas nodded, wiping his eyes.

"Why is Erick such a jerk?" Finnick asked.

"Behind you," Lucas cried, pointing behind Jarreth.

Jarreth turned quickly and stopped an incoming punch from Erick. Holding onto Erick's arm, Jarreth pulled him closer while twisting his arm down, then slamming Erick towards the ground. Erick's friends stared at Jarreth with shock and fear, before backing away slowly.

"Should we help?" Lucas asked Finnick, shocked.

"I don't think Jarreth is the one that needs the help," Finnick laughed.

Erick groaned in pain on the ground, as Jarreth turned back towards Finnick and Lucas. Erick's friends quickly came, picked him up, and took him away.

"That was awesome," Lucas exclaimed. "Can you teach me that?"

Jarreth smiled and nodded.

"That showed him," Finnick said. "Hopefully, he won't bother

Lucas when we leave."

"Leave," Lucas said sadly.

"Our mission here is over, and we must head back home. Our King and Queen need us," Finnick explained.

"Not to mention our Captain," Jarreth signed.

"Yes, and our Captain too. Sorry sport, but we must leave tomorrow," Finnick said. "But after lunch today, we can continue with your training. We will get as much done before we leave."

"Awesome," Lucas said. "Let's be the first in line for food, so we can eat quicker and train earlier."

Lucas ran off to the tent where they served food, while Jarreth and Finnick followed behind laughing at Lucas's enthusiasm.

After lunch, they returned to training for the rest of the evening. The more times Lucas threw the knife, the better he got. He continued practicing until he finally got the blade to stay in the tree. Jarreth walked up and inspected the knife; it was embedded deep into the tree trunk. He turned around and gave a thumbs up to Lucas, who then ran around excitedly, while Finnick stood laughing.

Later at dinner, Lucas told anyone who would listen, about his training exercises with the two lieutenants. Erick and his friends looked scared of Jarreth and, as soon as dinner was over, left the area. Others stayed and listened to the story of how Lucas and Jarreth first met. The event shocked many because Jarreth had killed one of the giant spiders guarding their home. People then asked questions about Jarreth and Finnick's rank, and their kingdom, leading them to talk late into the night. Once it got too late, everyone went to their tents and settled in for the night.

As Jarreth lay on his makeshift bed, he wondered if Lucas would be alright after they left, and if he would see Iris again. He had feelings for the Princess and wanted to pursue them. But two things stood in the way. One, he was just a soldier and not of royal birth. Two, he wasn't sure how it would work out, as they lived in different kingdoms.

Jarreth and Finnick had a quick breakfast with Lucas the following day, before saddling their horses for departure. Lucas hung out with them while they readied their supplies and horses.

"Will I see you guys again?" Lucas asked.

"I hope so," Finnick said.

Jarreth nodded.

"I'll make sure I practice every day," Lucas said, determined.

Jarreth gave him the thumbs up, then went to Finnick and helped him onto his horse.

"*You okay*," Jarreth signed.

"Yup, just a bit sore, nothing serious," Finnick reassured.

Once Finnick was safely on his horse, Jarreth approached Lucas and knelt at the boy's height level. He took out one of his throwing knives and handed it to Lucas.

"For me?" Lucas asked excitedly.

Jarreth nodded.

"Thank you," Lucas said, hugging him.

Behind Lucas, Jarreth saw Princess Iris walking towards them.

"Morning Princess," Finnick greeted.

"*Morning. Thank you for your hospitality and for healing my friend*," Jarreth signed.

"Thank you both for your kindness and bravery," Iris said.

She walked up to Jarreth, and out of earshot to the others.

"I hope to see you again soon," Iris whispered, reaching for his hand.

"*Me too*," Jarreth signed, smiling, taking her hand in his.

Iris and Jarreth smiled at one another for a moment, before Jarreth mounted his horse.

"*Until next time*," Jarreth signed.

Princess Iris nodded and smiled. "Until next time."

As Jarreth rode away with Finnick, he prayed to the God of Light that he would see Iris again soon.

217

CHAPTER THIRTY

*"And while they were eating, he said,
"Truly I tell you, one of you will betray me."*

Matthew 26:21

Erick left his tent in the middle of the night, and headed out to one of the guards on duty around their camp.

"Captain!" one of the guards said, surprised to see him about.

"Go get some sleep; I'll take your shift," Erick told the guard.

"Thanks, Captain," he replied heading off.

Erick smiled to himself while watching the guard return to his tent. Once the guard closed his tent door, Erick turned and started walking towards the Kingdom of Kudzu.

While walking back to his home kingdom, Erick kept an eye and ear out for any dangers from Jorogumo and her followers. To his luck, it was a quiet walk back.

Anger coursed through him, as he remembered seeing Jarreth and Iris together that evening. He hated Jarreth for that, and planned to take revenge soon.

Erick and Princess Iris were childhood friends. Growing up,

Erick's mother had abandoned him. Erick spent most of his time with the Princess, teaching her how to fight and defend herself. He often took her horse riding to get her away from her palace duties. But things changed when Princess Iris and Erick got older. Erick had joined the Royal Guard to escape his abusive father, and Princess Iris took on more royal duties as Princess of Kudzu.

After a few years, Princess Iris and Erick grew distant, mainly because Princess Iris saw how Erick treated the palace staff, and his men. Once when Princess Iris was kidnapped by a group of mercenaries, Erick got her back unharmed. In doing that, the King rewarded him with Princess Iris's hand in marriage. But Princess Iris had refused Erick.

When her kidnappers were holding her captive, she discovered that Erick had orchestrated the whole thing, because he wanted Princess Iris as his wife. After the incident, Princess Iris brought the matter about Erick's involvement in her kidnapping, to her father's attention. Her father was furious, that he went and investigated the matter personally, but couldn't find a reason to arrest him. Unknown to Princess Iris, all of Erick's men had vouched for him, out of fear or loyalty. Regardless, she knew never to trust Erick again, even after the previous Captain of the Royal Guard chose Erick as his successor. Princess Iris, knowing his true nature, had spies keeping an eye on him for her.

As Erick continued walking back to his home kingdom, he thought that if he couldn't have Princess Iris for himself, no one could. He would ensure that, even if it meant going through Jorogumo to achieve that goal.

Erick took out his water flask and drank all the alcohol inside, before chucking the flask to the ground behind him.

"Finally," Erick laughed as he saw the Kingdom of Kudzu within view.

Erick slowed his pace and drew his sword out for protection.

Being suspicious of everything that moved, he carefully walked closer to the kingdom. He knew Jorogumo's minions were about. And he didn't want to end up dead by one of them, before he spoke to Jorogumo himself, so he tried to be as quiet as possible. Erick gave away his position when he unintentionally stepped on a fallen twig.

"Damn!" he whispered standing still, while listening to the forest around him.

When satisfied that he hadn't woken up the whole forest, he continued to the Kingdom of Kudzu, but stopped short when he heard a noise behind him.

Erick jumped back startled, holding up his sword. A spider about the size of a standard wall clock, jumped out in front of him with its two fangs raised, ready to attack.

"Oh dam, you're a big one, aren't you?" Erick said, scared.

The spider stood there ready to attack, waiting to see what Erick would do.

Erick was filled with panic. He hated spiders. Always had. The one standing before him was a huge one, compared to the everyday ones you deal with. Even the ones that attacked his home kingdom a while back, weren't as big as this one. But he guessed they worked well in numbers and not size. Erick stood as still as he could while he thought of a plan. He didn't want to attack one of Jorogumo's minions and fail at getting her help. But he also didn't want to be attacked by one of her spiders.

There was a rustling in the bushes nearby, and another spider jumped out.

This one was a little bigger.

Erick panicked and started running in the direction of the Kingdom of Kudzu. He looked back and swore to himself, after seeing both spiders chasing after him. Erick felt something hit his shoulder, and turned to see cobwebs covering it. Peeling it off, he continued to run towards the kingdom.

Looking back, he saw the two spiders shooting cobwebs in his direction, one after another. Once Erick came out of the forest, he saw a cottage outside the village and headed in that direction. Just before he reached the cottage door, he fell to the ground. His legs were covered and bounded by cobwebs, from the incoming spiders. He used his sword to cut into the web, and was surprised at how strong and thick it was. Once the spiders got within reach, Erick had to kill them with his sword.

After, he removed the cobwebs around his legs, and stood up, shaking off the fear. He looked down at the two spiders that lay at his feet, now dead. He sighed with relief and dread. He just hoped Jorogumo wouldn't take offence to him killing her kind.

Once Erick entered the Kingdom of Kudzu, he raised his sword and walked around cautiously, trying to find Jorogumo's nest, and not more of her minions. Cobwebs covered houses, trees, and buildings, the closer he got to the palace. He knew he was getting close to her nest.

Opening the palace doors quietly, he snuck in and looked around. Dust and cobwebs covered the furniture and walls. The smell of mold made him gag, and Erick had to cover his nose with his hand to block out the smell. Looking around the room, Erick almost stumbled over from shock. He could see different sized spiders resting on the palace walls.

He started to panic at the different sizes.

"I hope they don't get any bigger than what's on the walls," Erick said, shaken.

He slowly walked down the steps that led to the dungeons. Once he reached the bottom, he stopped and stood there in shock. At least a hundred villagers were cocooned in cobwebs, while others were trapped and bound to the wall, witnessing what would soon happen to them.

"Ahhh, fresh meat," a soft, seductive voice whispered.

Erick felt a cold shiver and turned to find Jorogumo above him, looking down. She was half-human and half-spider, with red and black markings across her spider body, and her human figure. She had long black hair and red eyes. Her smile was contagious, and her beauty was like that of a goddess. It was difficult to look away, and Erick wasn't sure if he should run, or gaze upon her beauty and suffer the consequences.

"What brings you down here? Usually, we must hunt for our prey," Jorogumo asked, slowly eyeing her prey.

"Um, I-," Erick couldn't find his words.

"What a cute little thing you are, speechless for words," Jorogumo laughed.

Erik shook off the fear and walked towards Jorogumo unafraid.

"I need you to do something for me," Erick said boldly.

Jorogumo's laughter echoed throughout the dungeon.

"How bold of you," she said, walking around Erick.

Erick watched as Jorogumo circled him carefully, being mindful to move when her long black spider legs got too close. Erick noticed that Jorogumo's much larger spider minions came into view, to watch their master. Jorogumo, seeing the panic and fear in Erick's eyes, ordered her minions to keep their distance for now.

"Don't worry about them," Jorogumo said casually. "They are just very protective of me."

Erick smiled and nodded hesitantly.

"Come, let's sit and chat," Jorogumo said, walking to the middle of the room.

Erick followed behind and sat in a cobwebbed chair, while she sat on her throne. Erick noticed the larger spiders coming into view, who now blocked his escape, while keeping an eye on their queen. He would have to be very convincing if he wanted to live.

"So, answer me this question. Why would I do anything for you? Especially for a lowly human being like yourself," she asked, casually eating a fly.

Erick swallowed the lump in his throat, and tried to hide his fear of the massive spiders surrounding him.

"I want to get revenge on someone, but I cannot do it alone," he admitted.

"Which is it, love, power, or greed?" Jorogumo asked, amused.

"What does it matter?" Erick asked, casually.

"It matters to me," Jorogumo replied, sternly.

"All," Erick quickly said.

"All?" Jorogumo questioned, eyes raised.

"Yes, all three," Erick said, annoyed. "Is that a problem? Have I passed your test?"

Jorogumo laughed. "Answer me one more question before I decide."

"And what is that?" Erick asked, getting agitated.

"Explain to me the love, power and greed in your situation," Jorogumo said, amused.

Erick sighed annoyingly.

"The woman I want is in love with another man. I want power to prove I am better suited for her, and I want money to buy her anything she desires," Erick explained.

Jorogumo laughed and clapped her hands. "Oh, I love it, absolutely love it. You men think so little, when one should think of bigger goals."

"So, I guess that's a no then," Erick said bluntly.

"Oh, I didn't say I wouldn't help," Jorogumo said.

"Well, are you?" he asked.

"If I do decide to help you, what do I gain?" Jorogumo asked.

"What do you want?" Erick asked.

"Princess Iris's amethyst Gem," Jorogumo replied.

"Why? You have your spiders who listen to you," Erick said, confused.

"It's not for my spiders, but for the rest of the creatures out there. With the Gem, I could control them all," Jorogumo laughed.

Erick nodded in understanding. "I can get you the Gem."

"Excellent," she clapped her hands excitedly.

"Traitor," someone rasped from behind.

Erick and Jorogumo turned towards the prisoners who hadn't been cocooned yet. Amongst the prisoners were King Eros and Queen Athena of Kudzu.

"I'm guessing my daughter was right about the kidnapping?" King Eros barked.

"Yes," Erick sneered, smiling. "The plan went perfectly."

"How dare you," King Eros retorted.

Jorogumo laughed as King Eros tried to get free from his imprisonment.

"My spider's web is tough, so you won't be able to escape," Jorogumo said.

"Wait why can't you take the King or Queen's Gem?" Erick suddenly thought out loud. "All royals have them."

"Unfortunately, they both destroyed the Gems before I could take them," Jorogumo replied, annoyed.

"Clever, but also annoying," Erick said.

"What would your father think of you now, knowing you betrayed him and this kingdom?" King Eros asked.

"My father was an abusive drunk, who forced my mother to abandon me. Why do you think I left to train with the royal soldiers," Erick growled.

"He is still your father, and he still loves you I'm sure," King Eros assured.

"I highly doubt that," Erick spat, annoyed.

"It's true, my son," said another voice. "I'm sorry for all the hurt I caused you and your mother.”

“Dad!” Erick said with disgust and shock.

“Oh, how wonderful,” Jorogumo exclaimed, enjoying the drama.

“Help us please. You don’t want to cut a deal with the devil,” Erick’s father pleaded.

“Don’t tell me what I can and can’t do. You’ve never been a father to me. Why start now? Is it because you want to live,” Erick said, getting angrier.

“Son-,” Erick’s father began.

“Don’t call me that. I don’t care about you, and you have never cared for me. So don’t pretend,” Erick spat with rage.

“How about I calm this situation down,” Jorogumo said, clicking her fingers.

One of her massive spiders came over and shot a web at Erick’s father, causing him to stumble towards the ground with his legs bound. The gigantic spider then began to drag his father closer to it, while Erick’s father screamed.

“Erick, I’m sorry. Please forgive me,” Erick’s father pleaded, as he was being dragged closer to the spider’s mouth.

“Too late,” Erick said, watching his father’s demise without remorse.

King Eros and Queen Athena looked away in horror, as the massive spider devoured Erick’s father, silencing his screams.

“Well, now that’s over, let’s get to business, shall we,” Jorogumo said, walking away.

Erick glared at King Eros and Queen Athena, before following after Jorogumo.

CHAPTER THIRTY-ONE

"Similarly, encourage the young men to be self-controlled.
In everything set them an example by doing what is good.
In your teaching show integrity, seriousness and soundness
of speech that cannot be condemned, so that those who
oppose you may be ashamed because they have
nothing bad to say about us."

Titus 2:6-8

Prince Omari walked down the palace hallway to his father's office. He knocked twice before hearing his father's voice to enter. He walked into his father's office and bowed in front of him.

"Son, is everything alright?" King Jabari asked, looking up from his paperwork.

"Father, I wish to travel to the Kingdom of Zolatta," Omari stated.

"Why?" his father asked.

"I heard rumors-," Omari began.

"Rumors, what rumors?" his father asked.

"The King of Zolatta has a similar curse to me. Maybe he can teach me how to control it, or maybe he knows of a way to break free from it," Omari explained. "I'm sick of living in isolation. You wouldn't even let me help you when the cyclops attacked our kingdom. I feel useless."

King Jabari sighed and sat back in his chair, looking at his son.

"Dad, I want to live a normal life. To fall in love, to be a good father and husband," Omari said sadly.

King Jabari sighed.

"I understand. You may go on two conditions," King Jabari ordered.

"Anything, father," Omari sighed with relief.

"Say goodbye to your mother; she deserves to know, and come back home safe, please," King Jabari said.

Prince Omari went and hugged his father.

"I promise to come home safe," Omari said.

"Good luck, son. I'll be praying for you," King Jabari said.

"Thanks, Dad," Omari said, bowing before leaving the room.

Prince Omari left his father's office and went to the library, where his mother spent the evenings reading to the young kids of the village.

He entered the library and walked over to his mother, who had finished reading to the kids earlier than usual.

"Omari," Queen Nala said, hugging her son.

"Mother, I have decided to go to the Kingdom of Zolatta. I want to seek the King's help in breaking this curse, or be taught how to control it," Omari explained.

Queen Nala looked at her son for a moment, before nodding sadly.

"I'm proud of you," Queen Nala said. "Does your father know?"

Omari nodded. "Yes, I've just come from speaking with him."

"I love you, Omari. Stay safe and come home soon," Queen

Nala cried, hugging her son.

"I promise, Mother," Omari said, hugging her before leaving the library.

"God of Light, keep my son safe, please," Queen Nala prayed, as she watched her son walk out of the library.

Omari left the library and went to the kitchen, to grab a few things before his journey. The kitchen hand gave him some dried fruits, nuts, bread, and a couple of water flasks, then wished him well.

Walking out of the palace in broad daylight for the first time in years, was overwhelming for Prince Omari. His father had only let him outside at night, when no one was around to see his curse. People smiled and waved at Prince Omari as they walked by, and he returned the gestures. His kingdom's people were very friendly to him, but that was because they didn't know of the curse he carried.

Walking past different shops, Prince Omari took in the wonders of his kingdom. It took him a little extra time to get out of the kingdom, because of all the new things he had explored before heading out.

Once he entered the forest, he transformed into a large brown and yellow griffin.

This was the curse that the Prince of Darkness gave him as a child. Which is why his father isolated him for years out of fear and panic. Prince Omari felt a sense of peace and freedom, as he flew in broad daylight with no one around. It wouldn't take him long to get to the Kingdom of Zolatta with his wings. He just hoped that he could return home a changed man and curse-free.

CHAPTER THIRTY-TWO

"To him all the prophets bear witness that everyone who believes in him receives forgiveness of sins through his name."

Acts 10:43

Deep in the cave of Akuma, the Prince of Darkness fumed in anger over his creatures, that were being defeated by mere human beings. Even the people he had experimented on, and who were given abilities, were defeated.

He opened the Book of Darkness again and called forth another minotaur. The creature appeared before him with a gigantic, spiked axe, growling with hunger for its next victim.

"Go to the Kingdom of Zolatta with your brothers. Mildred will be heading there, no doubt. She must not live. Understood," the Prince of Darkness demanded.

The minotaur growled while tightening its hand over the axe.

"It will be done, Master," the minotaur growled viciously.

The minotaur turned away from its master and left the cave.

The Prince of Darkness smirked to himself as he watched the minotaur walk away. Minotaur's were vicious creatures, killing in a single blow with its axe. It was a creature of strength, and would be difficult to defeat. The Prince of Darkness thought about Mildred's betrayal, and how she would pay the price for it.

"Claud," the Prince of Darkness bellowed.

"Yes, Master," Claud said, bowing before him.

"Go to the Kingdom of Kudzu and bring me back Jorogumo's captured victims," the Prince of Darkness ordered.

"Of course, Master," Claud replied.

Claud bowed once more before leaving the cave of Akuma. Once outside, he transformed into a giant wolf, making it easier for him to run faster. He would not fail this mission. He had to succeed; otherwise, there would be consequences.

◆ ◆ ◆ ◆ ◆

"We're here," Malachi told Mildred.

Mildred stared at the Kingdom of Zolatta with dread, fear, and doubt. She wasn't ready to face the King and Queen, and reveal the truth to them about her. But she had to. No matter how painful it would be. She hoped she would feel better once it was done. She gripped the reins tighter as Amisha trotted down the path towards the kingdom.

The villagers stopped and stared at the new party arriving. Mildred wasn't sure if they were staring at Malachi, who was dressed in white and sat on a beautiful white stallion. Or Mildred, with her bright red hair, riding Amisha the alicorn. Or all of them combined.

Mildred followed Malachi as he led them to the front of the palace. Two guards stood outside the palace doors, watching them with suspicion.

"What business do you have here?" one of the guards asked.

"We wish to have an audience with the King and Queen of

Zolatta?" Malachi asked.

"I will go and inquire," said one of the guards.

"Thank you," Malachi said.

"Are you ok?" Malachi asked turning to Mildred.

Mildred nodded.

"In the Tanakh, it says, 'Trust in God with all your heart, and lean not on your own understanding.' Trust that he will look out for you, Mildred."

"Thank you," Mildred said, feeling a lot calmer.

After a short while, the guard returned to them at the front of the palace.

"I'm sorry, but the King and Queen cannot see you now. You can come back tomorrow when they hear the townspeople's petition," the guard explained.

"Thank you. Do you, by any chance, know of a good inn we could stay at for the night?" Malachi asked.

"There's the Crowned Fox, which I hear is good," the guard replied. "It's only about a mile from here."

"Thank you again," Malachi said.

Malachi and Mildred mounted their horses again, and trotted back down to the village. Women and children continued to stare at them with curiosity. Mildred tried her best to smile and wave, and felt happy when some returned the gestures. Others looked at her with fear, and interest at the unknown horse before them.

As they passed, Mildred looked at all the different shops until they came across the Crowned Fox Inn. She now understood why they called it the Crowned Fox Inn. It looked exactly like the King in his fox spirit form. Mildred felt her throat tighten; she was the reason the King had been cursed in the first place. By order of the Prince of Darkness. Something else she would have to reveal to the King tomorrow.

"I can tell you are feeling very upset and scared now. Would you like to sleep? We have had quite a long journey," Malachi asked.

"I don't think I can sleep," Mildred replied, feeling overwhelmed.

"I have some valerian that can help calm you," Malachi offered.

"Thank you, I'll take you up on that offer," Mildred said, relieved.

"Let's see if we can find two rooms first," Malachi said, tying up his horse.

Malachi and Mildred dismounted their horses and entered the Crowned Fox Inn. The atmosphere was homely and friendly. Musicians were playing on stage, while a few people danced, enjoying the music. It wasn't a big inn, but it wasn't a small one either. The smell of roast beef, potatoes and vegetables filled the air, and it immediately made Mildred hungry. After being on the road for so long, it was good to finally eat a cooked meal and sleep in a comfortable bed.

"Good evening, folks, my name is Nell. How may I help you?" Nell greeted in a cheery voice.

"Do you have two rooms available for the night?" Malachi asked.

"Of course, follow me," Nell said, heading towards the stairs.

Mildred and Malachi followed Nell up the stairs that led to the first floor.

"Room one," Nell said, showing the inside.

"You take this room, Mildred," Malachi offered.

"Thank you," Mildred said to both Malachi and Nell.

"Your very welcome," Nell said. "Your room will be next door. Is there anything else I can help you with?"

"Our horses are out the front. Could they be tended to please? Also, could we please have two hot meals sent to our rooms, along with some tea? We've had a long journey. Thank you," Malachi explained.

"You're welcome. I shall bring the meals up, and our stable boy will tend to your horses," Nell said, bowing before she left.

After Nell descended the stairs, Malachi took a pouch from his pocket.

"The valerian herb. Just put some in your tea, and it will help you sleep," Malachi explained.

"Thank you," Mildred said, taking the pouch.

"Until tomorrow," Malachi said. "Goodnight."

"Night," Mildred said, watching Malachi go into his room.

Mildred looked at the pouch and entered her room, closing the door behind her. She opened the bag and found a valerian root inside.

"Wait for the tea and eat first, Mildred," she told herself. "Otherwise, you'll go to bed on an empty stomach."

She put her bag onto the bed and went into the bathroom to wash up before eating. Looking at herself in the mirror, she was glad the King and Queen were busy today. Her face was dirty, and her hair was tangled and messy. She quickly had a wash before her food arrived.

A few minutes later, she heard a knock at the door, so she promptly dressed and answered it.

"I've brought your food and tea, dear," Nell said, handing Mildred the tray.

"Thank you so much for your kindness," Mildred said.

"My pleasure. Can I ask you a quick question?" Nell asked. "I hope I'm not being rude."

"Not at all," Mildred replied.

"Your horse-," Nell began.

Mildred smiled and nodded. "Her name is Amisha; she's an alicorn. A horse with wings and a horn. It's a gift to the King and

Queen of Zolatta. I'm seeing them tomorrow."

"Oh, how lovely. The King and Queen will be so grateful. How thoughtful of you," Nell said. "I won't keep you. Enjoy your meal."

"Thanks again," Mildred said, taking the tray into her room.

Mildred sat the tray on a nearby table, and retrieved the pouch of valerian root Malachi had given to her. Once she finished putting some valerian into her tea to simmer, she thanked the God of Light, then ate her dinner. The food was delicious, filling, and just what she needed. Drinking her tea, she thought about what she would say tomorrow. She decided not to think about it because she trusted in the God of Light. Feeling the effects of the valerian tea, she laid her head on the pillow and drifted off into a peaceful sleep.

When Mildred woke up the next day, she felt relaxed and refreshed. She got dressed and went down to the inn's common area. Malachi was already seated at a table, drinking tea, and having breakfast.

"Morning, how did you sleep?" Malachi asked, as Mildred made her way over.

"Very well. Thank you for the valerian, it really helped," Mildred said, sitting at the table.

"Well, look at you, all refreshed after a good night's sleep," Nell said, coming up to the table.

Nell placed a cup and a plate filled with toast, egg, and bacon on the table for Mildred, then began to pour some tea.

"Would you like some more tea, sir?" Nell asked.

"Yes, thank you," Malachi replied, giving his cup to her.

"There you go," Nell said. "Let me know if you need anything else."

"Thanks," Mildred said.

"Thank you," Malachi said smiling.

Mildred ate breakfast and drank her tea, while the other patrons went to start their day. Feeling full and satisfied after a good night's sleep and food, she also felt ready to start her day.

"Ready to see the King and Queen?" Malachi asked.

"Yes," Mildred said, standing up.

"You head to the stable while I pay Nell," Malachi suggested.

"Ok, thanks," Mildred said.

Mildred picked up her bag and headed to the stables. The stable boy was cleaning out one of the stalls, when Mildred came up behind him.

"Excuse me," Mildred said, getting the boy's attention.

The stable boy turned and smiled. "How can I help you miss?"

"Just wondering if you can prepare the white stallion and the alicorn for departure, please?" Mildred asked.

"Of course," he replied.

The stable boy put aside his rake and began to saddle their horses up. Malachi met Mildred outside once the stable boy was finished.

"This one is for you," the stable boy said, giving Amisha's reins to Mildred.

"And the stallion for you," the boy said, giving the reins to Malachi.

"Thank you for looking after them," Malachi said, giving the stable boy some money.

"Awesome, thanks," he beamed.

After mounting her horse, Mildred followed Malachi to the palace to see the King and Queen.

When they arrived, the guards directed them to leave their horses in the stable, and follow them to the throne room. Once the doors opened to the throne room, Mildred was overwhelmed by how many people wanted to see their King and Queen. Many thanked them for their kind and caring rule, after the hardship they suffered from the late King. While watching King Nikolai among his people, Mildred saw how much he had grown. Not just in appearance, but in knowledge and ruling. She was amazed at his Queen's beauty, grace, and kindness towards everyone, including her staff. Mildred and Malachi stood in line behind some people and waited for their turn to speak.

A man walked up with his daughter beside him, and both bowed to the King and Queen.

"How can we help you today?" Nikolai asked.

"My daughter wishes to work in the palace. I was wondering if you had any positions available?" the man asked.

"I'm not sure we-" Nikolai began, but was stopped when Queen Juliet touched his arm.

"I believe we'll require another cleaner, as one of our current staff is about to go on maternity leave," Juliet said.

The young women beamed.

"What is your name?" Nikolai asked.

"Helen," she replied, bowing again.

"I will inform our head of cleaning, and have her contact you regarding a position. Please give your details to Theo, and you should hear back in a few days," Nikolai instructed.

"Thank you, my King, my Queen," the man said, bowing, as they left the throne room full of hope.

Time went by, and people came and went after thanking the King and Queen for their help with different cases. Some needed better working conditions, others, justice for something done wrong. The line was getting shorter and shorter, and Mildred was starting to feel the pressure of speaking to the King and Queen. Eventually, her turn came up. She looked around the throne room to see only the staff, guards, Theo and the King and Queen present. All the other villagers who had come in with issues and problems, had left with solutions. Mildred walked forward nervously, with

Malachi beside her. After bowing, she stood up to face the King and Queen of Zolatta. Mildred's heart pounded in her chest, and her hands were getting sweaty. She felt like she was going to faint. She felt like she needed to run. Before she could think about moving, the king spoke to her, interrupting her thoughts.

"What can we do for you today?" Nikolai asked.

Mildred stared at him for a moment before clearing her throat.

"My name is Mildred, and I've come to make amends for the pain I have caused you. I have come to ask you for your forgiveness, share my knowledge about your current threat, and turn myself in," Mildred finished with a shaky voice.

Silence filled the throne room, as the King and Queen processed Mildred's words.

"What sin have you committed, Mildred?" Nikolai asked.

Mildred swallowed before speaking again.

"I'm the one who killed your father," Mildred replied with dread.

CHAPTER THIRTY-THREE

"Do not judge, or you too will be judged."

Matthew 7:1

Nikolai stared in shock at the woman standing in front of him. She fit the description the footman had described to him and Theo. But never in a million years did he think she would stand before him now, asking for forgiveness and turning herself in.

"Nikolai," he heard his wife's soft voice.

Nikolai turned to his wife with tears in his eyes.

"I need a minute," Nikolai's voice croaked.

Nikolai stood up without saying anything and left the throne room.

"Give us a moment, please," Juliet said, walking after her husband.

Nikolai swiftly made his way towards his office to compose himself. Once he closed the door behind him, he collapsed in his chair and rubbed his tired eyes. Juliet came in not long after and put a comforting hand on his shoulder.

"Talk to me," Juliet whispered.

"I never thought she would turn herself in, and ask for forgiveness," Nikolai began. "What am I to do?"

"Remember what you told me, about what your mother said to you in the trial," Juliet reminded him.

"Don't judge someone without hearing both sides to the story, and give people a second chance. It's what makes a good king," Nikolai recited, remembering his mother's words.

"Forgiveness is not easy, but it's a necessary part of healing a broken heart," Juliet said.

"Thank you," Nikolai said taking his wife's hand.

Juliet leaned in and kissed his cheek.

"You ready to go back out, or do you need another minute?" Juliet asked.

Nikolai let out a huge sigh. "I'm ready."

"I am with you," Juliet said, taking his hand. Nikolai stood up and took a deep breath.

"Thank you," Nikolai said kissing his wife.

Together, they left Nikolai's office and returned to the throne room. After opening the door and stepping in, Nikolai was a little shocked to see that Mildred hadn't fled yet. He sat down on his throne with his wife by his side, still hand in hand and breathed.

"Let us hear your story," Nikolai said.

Mildred sighed in relief.

"Thank you," Mildred began. "Firstly, I wish to apologize. I was a follower of the Prince of Darkness, doing whatever he ordered without question. No matter what he ordered. I have recently seen what a huge mistake it was. I have been trying to leave for some time now, so that I can tell someone what the Prince of Darkness has been planning. I have only just left recently, with the help of Malachi."

Mildred gestured towards Malachi.

"Malachi, like the angel?" Nikolai asked, bewildered.

"In the flesh," Malachi said smiling, standing beside Mildred. "The God of Light has given Mildred a mission to help you."

Nikolai turned his attention back to Mildred, to hear the rest of her story.

"The Prince of Darkness needs people's souls, in order to break free from his entrapment. One of his followers is already in the Kingdom of Kudzu, bringing him victims. If he breaks free, he will start a war with his creatures of darkness, causing fear, destruction, and slavery," Mildred finished.

Nikolai thought for a moment about what Mildred had just shared with him. A few things she said, were the same things his father had told him not too long ago. This made everything else she said most likely accurate. Also, the fact that Malachi, the God of Light's angel, was standing in his courtroom, spoke volume.

"That explains why we haven't heard from the King or Queen of Kudzu," Juliet explained.

"That's true," Nikolai said. "Do you know which of the Prince of Darkness's followers are in the Kingdom of Kudzu, Malachi?"

Malachi sighed and nodded.

"Judging by your expression, they're dangerous," Nikolai guessed.

"Yes, King Nikolai. This follower is the Prince of Darkness's second in charge. She is known as Jorogumo."

"Oh no!" Juliet said worriedly, patting Nix's head, who sat near her.

"You've heard of her, Queen Juliet?" Malachi asked, surprisingly.

"Yes. I did some research a while ago because we had some reports of creature sightings. We wanted to know more about what we were dealing with. Jorogumo was also in the book. I'd hoped we wouldn't be facing her, but it turns out the Prince of Darkness really does focus on people's fears," Juliet explained.

"Yes, he does," Malachi replied sadly.

"Who is Jorogumo, and how bad is she?" Theo asked.

"Jorogumo is a spider demon who has three different forms. Form one is fully human. This gives her the ability to blend in with other people, and act completely normal. Except for her reflection, which will show her true form. Form two is half human, half spider. Her top half is human, and her bottom half is a spider, which is quite scary when you look at her. Form three is fully spider. When she has fully transformed into this form, she's not like your everyday spider that you see crawling around the house. She is massive. Almost as big as a horse and carriage combined," Juliet explained.

"Oh dam," Theo said nervously.

"It gets worse," Mildred said.

"What could be worse than that?" Theo asked.

"She can control other spiders, who shoot super strong cobwebs to trap its victims," Malachi explained.

"I had to open my big mouth," Theo sighed.

Nikolai and Juliet smiled at Theo.

"I have another question. Does the Prince of Darkness have any weaknesses?" Nikolai asked.

"Yes, the crystal Gem. It has the power of light," Mildred said.

"The crystal Gem?" Nikolai questioned. "I thought it was just a myth."

"So did I. But the Prince of Darkness fears it. He's got his followers searching for it, so they can destroy it once it is found," Mildred said.

Nikolai sat back and thought for a moment. Finding something that was supposed to be a myth, would be difficult.

"Any ideas on where to look?" Nikolai asked Mildred.

"No, I do not know," Mildred said. "Sorry."

"No need to apologize for something you do not know,"

Nikolai reassured her.

Malachi bowed, then spoke.

"To start you on your journey in finding the crystal Gem, the God of Light has given you an alicorn," Malachi said.

"An alicorn?" Nikolai asked, bewildered.

"A horse with both a unicorn's horn, and pegasus wings," Juliet said, amazed.

"Yes, my Queen. She sits in your stable as we speak," Malachi said.

"I don't mean to be rude, Malachi. Is there a reason why the God of Light can't just tell us where the cystal Gem is?" Nikolai asked.

"The God of Light has a reason for everything he does and doesn't do. He does not reveal everything at once. Sometimes lessons need to be learned, or one must have their faith tested, or you may meet someone on this journey that could help you in the future war, or may need your help in return," Malachi explained.

"I understand what you mean," Nikolai said. "But how will this alicorn help us?"

"The alicorn species is known for their knowledge about the crystal Gem's whereabouts," Malachi explained. "You just have to ask her."

"Ask her?" Nikolai said confused.

"Yes, that's right," Malachi said, smiling. "You must ask her."

"Yes, but how can-," Nikolai began, but stopped and thought for a moment, then suddenly realized how stupid he sounded, then laughed.

Malachi smiled and nodded.

"I don't get it," Theo said dumbfounded.

"The Kingdom of Kudzu holds the amethyst Gem. Their power is to communicate with all types of animals. They can also take on the forms of different animals, and use their abilities,"

Juliet explained, smiling at her husband.

"Oh, wow," Theo said. "Wait, if Jorogumo has taken over the Kingdom of Kudzu, then we might not be able to get the person that holds the amethyst Gem. What then?" Theo asked.

"Trust in the God of Light. Find out for certain what has become of the Kingdom of Kudzu, then go from there," Malachi advised.

"I sense an adventure," Juliet said happily.

Both Theo and Nikolai laughed.

"An adventure it will be, but I must warn you. There are dangerous people who work for the Prince of Darkness, and will do anything to set him free. Be careful, and if you are unsure of anything, pray," Malachi told them.

"So, there are two reasons we need to go to the Kingdom of Kudzu. One is to help defeat this spider demon named Jorogumo, and the second is to ask a royal if they can translate what the alicorn says," Theo thought out loud.

"Yes, that sounds about right," Nikolai said.

A sudden rush of knocks sounded at the door, and a guard ran in breathless as if he had just run a mile.

"What's wrong?" Nikolai asked, seeing the guard in distress.

"A minotaur has just been sighted within the kingdom," the guard gasped.

"A minotaur?" Nikolai asked, shocked.

"A bunch of minotaur's, to be precise," the guard said with dread.

"The Prince of Darkness," Mildred whispered.

"What did you say?" Nikolai asked Mildred.

"I saw the Prince of Darkness summon one," Mildred said. "Back at the cave."

Nikolai turned to Theo.

"Get Captain Oberon and meet me in the conference room,"

Nikolai ordered, then he turned back to Malachi and Mildred. "Will you accompany me and Juliet to the conference room? We could use your knowledge and help."

"Yes, I'd be happy to assist," Mildred said.

"Of course," Malachi replied bowing.

Nikolai stood up, took his wife's hand, and walked out of the throne room with Nix following behind them. As they headed down the corridor to the conference room, the palace staff rushed around in panic at the news.Fear and panic coursed through Nikolai, as he was concerned for Juliet's safety, and the safety of his people.

Once they entered the conference room, Nikolai took a seat at the head of the table, while Juliet sat beside him with Nix at her feet. Malachi and Mildred choose seats across from the table. Theo rushed in with Captain Oberon behind him, along with a few of his soldiers, and they all took a seat.

"Report?" Nikolai asked Oberon.

"The people that have their homes on the outskirts of the kingdom, have fled into the village. The minotaur's have been seen there currently eating the livestock, and destroying houses," Captain Oberon stated.

"At least they're occupied for the time being," Theo said.

"Juliet, could you please share what you have discovered about minotaur's," Nikolai asked her.

"Of course. A minotaur has a man's body, and a bull's head and tail. It's a vicious beast and cannibal. The book says it also fights with a gigantic axe. A minotaur can be killed with its own horn, when stabbed in the chest or neck area," Juliet explained.

"This is going to be tough," Captain Oberon thought aloud. "Considering there are a few of them."

"I agree. Your thoughts?" Nikolai asked.

"A group of five soldiers to one minotaur, I reckon," Captain

Oberon suggested. "Because we will need enough soldiers for all the minotaur's, and protection for the villagers and Your Highnesses."

"Forget me. Focus on Juliet and the other's," Nikolai ordered. "Evacuate the villagers to the palace if needed. I can take on one of the minotaur's with my fox form."

"I can help you, Your Highness," Captain Oberon suggested.

"No need," Nikolai replied.

Juliet placed her hand on her husband's arm and looked at him with worry. He sighed in defeat.

"I would appreciate your help, Captain," Nikolai said, hoping Juliet was less worried.

"Will you and your maids tend to the wounded?" Nikolai asked Juliet.

"Of course," Juliet nodded.

"Any other questions?" Nikolai asked, looking around the room.

No one answered.

"Ok. Soldiers, form your teams and defeat the minotaur's within the kingdom. Theo, Mildred, and Malachi help evacuate the villagers to the palace. Juliet focus on healing the wounded," Nikolai ordered, standing up.

The others rushed out of the room to their assigned posts, leaving Nikolai and Juliet behind. Nikolai turned to his wife and took her hands in his.

"Promise me you'll be careful," Juliet whispered.

"I promise," Nikolai replied, leaning in to kiss her.

She kissed him back.

"Call me if you need me," Nikolai told her, then looked to the ground. "Nix, please keep her safe."

Nix barked his approval.

"Your Highness, sorry to interrupt," Ruth and Grace entered

the room. "We met Theo in the hall, and he explained we were needed."

Juliet wiped her eyes and nodded.

"Follow me," Juliet said, leaving the room with her maid's and Nix following behind.

Nikolai started the painful transformation into his fox form. Bones adjusted as his body and bones morphed into a fox. Once the transformation was complete, Nikolai ran out of the palace to find the first minotaur.

People were running and screaming as one of the minotaur's within the kingdom, ran amuck smashing houses and buildings. It stopped its destruction once it saw Nikolai and growled. Running towards him with its spiked axe in hand, Nikolai dodged the first attack that was meant for his shoulder. Coming up from behind the minotaur, Nikolai grabbed a hold of its legs, torso, arms, and neck with his many tails.

Nikolai saw Captain Oberon running up towards him and the minotaur with his sword drawn. Nikolai used one of his tails that wasn't being used, as a step for Oberon to reach the minotaur's horn. The minotaur roared angrily at being bounded up, and tried to break free.

Oberon used his sword and strength to slice one of the minotaur's horns clean off. The minotaur howled in pain and shook Nikolai and Oberon off. Oberon and Nikolai fell to the ground, but quickly regained their footing to continue the fight. They stood side by side, panting with exhaustion from holding on to the minotaur. Oberon held firmly onto the severed horn as the minotaur roared with anger.

"We need another plan. The minotaur won't let us bound it again," Captain Oberon said.

"I'll be the distraction," Nikolai growled.

Nikolai took off before Oberon could disagree with him.

Running up to the minotaur, Nikolai slammed his shoulder into its stomach, causing it to collide into a nearby building. Nikolai restrained both the minotaur's hands so Oberon could have clear access to the minotaur's chest. Hearing the Captain close behind him, Nikolai moved his body aside as Oberon plunged the horn into the beast's chest. The minotaur roared in pain, then collapsed to the ground, dead.

Nikolai suddenly heard a villager scream from behind him. Turning around, he saw that the building the minotaur had attacked was collapsing. He quickly ran over and held onto the building, just before it came down onto the villager.

"Come now, don't be afraid. Your king is holding onto the building," Captain Oberon said to the frightened villager. "Let's get you to the palace, your king cannot hold it up much longer."

The villager looked up to see Nikolai in his fox form, holding up the building to prevent it from collapsing. The villager managed to get out with Oberon's help unharmed. Once they were out, Nikolai slowly lowered the damaged building to the ground.

"Go to Juliet and get yourself healed," Nikolai growled to the villager.

"Thank you, my King," the villager replied, before running off.

"How many more minotaur's are in the kingdom?" Nikolai growled to Captain Oberon.

"Two, Your Highness," he replied. "Follow me."

Nikolai ran behind Oberon as he led the way to the other beasts attacking his kingdom. This minotaur had managed to make its way to the palace steps. Fighting three soldiers, the minotaur was getting closer to the palace doors, where Juliet and the villagers were hiding inside.

Nikolai ran up to the minotaur and grabbed its torso, while his many tails clasped around its legs, arms, and neck, preventing it from moving. Nikolai used the same strategy he used with the previous minotaur. He let Oberon use one of his tails to reach the minotaur's head, slicing off the horn, then quickly stabbed the beast in the chest. Once Nikolai let go, the minotaur collapsed to the ground.

"Get yourself healed by Juliet," Nikolai growled to the three injured men.

"We can still fight with you, Your Highness," one of the soldiers said.

"Get yourself healed first. I can't have you passing out during a battle from blood loss," Nikolai growled.

The soldier looked down at his wounded knee, then looked back at the King, embarrassed.

"Of course, King Nikolai," the soldier replied, leaving to get healed.

"Is it me or does this attack on the kingdom seem too easy?" Captain Oberon asked. "If the Prince of Darkness wanted to, he could have sent more minotaur's to destroy the kingdom. But he didn't; why is that? We're missing something."

"You're right, it does seem too easy," Nikolai growled in agreement, looking around suspiciously.

"Surely, the Prince of Darkness knew of your fox form, and knew you could have easily defeated these minotaur's by yourself. So why did he send them in the first place?" Captain Oberon asked.

Nikolai looked around at the destruction the minotaur's had caused around his kingdom. Buildings and homes had been destroyed. No casualties from what he could see, and all the minotaur's were trying to get into the palace.

"Do you reckon he's after the Queen?" Captain Oberon asked.

"No, I don't think so. He's had plenty of opportunities to attack her. Why would he choose today," Nikolai growled, thinking.

Nikolai's heart stopped.

"Oh no," Nikolai growled.

"What is it, Your Highness?" Captain Oberon asked.

"The Prince of Darkness didn't send the minotaur after me or Juliet. He must have spies who told him about Mildred's betrayal," Nikolai growled.

"That does make sense," Captain Oberon said. "Where is Mildred now?"

"With Juliet in the palace," Nikolai growled with worry.

Captain Oberon and Nikolai ran up the stairs to the palace, and headed straight for the hallway that led to the ballroom. They hoped the villagers, Juliet and Mildred were hiding and safe. Nikolai hoped that the last minotaur hadn't found any of them, and if it had, he prayed he wasn't too late.

The hallway was busy with staff coming and going from tending to the cares of the wounded, that Captain Oberon and Nikolai found it challenging to get through. Nikolai saw Malachi rushing down the hallway towards the kitchen with an empty bowl, and stopped him.

"Malachi, where is Juliet and Mildred?" Nikolai growled in a panicked voice.

"Tending to the wounded in the palace gardens," he replied, rushing to the kitchen.

Captain Oberon whistled for the staff's attention.

"Step aside, please, make way for the King," he yelled.

Staff stepped aside quickly as Nikolai ran down the hallway with Oberon behind him, towards the palace gardens in fear. When Nikolai and Oberon entered the palace gardens, they could see many of the villagers huddled with loved ones and friends. There was fear and panic in the air, while the rest of the villagers and soldiers lay on makeshift beds, unconscious from being injured.

Nikolai looked around the garden and spotted Juliet with

Nix and Mildred. They were all confronting the last minotaur. Mildred with her Gem's earth power, Juliet with one of the wounded soldier's swords, and Nix scratching and biting at the minotaur. Nikolai's heart stopped. Juliet was in arm's reach of the minotaur's next attack, and there was no way he could reach her in time.

"Noooooooooo," Nikolai roared, racing towards his wife.

CHAPTER THIRTY-FOUR

*"Blessed is the one who perseveres under trial because,
having stood the test, that person will receive the crown of life
that the Lord has promised to those who love him."*

James 1:12

Juliet held a sword and defended herself and the villagers against the minotaur's attack. As Queen, it was her duty to protect her kingdom, and she will do that to the best of her abilities, no matter what.

Nix whined beside Juliet as she braced for another attack from the minotaur. She tightened her grip around the sword's hilt, prepared to defend herself, the villagers, Mildred, and Nix.

The minotaur pushed Mildred aside, causing her to stumble and fall to the ground. The vines that she conjured up with her Gem, broke away from the minotaur, making it free to attack. The minotaur turned its attention towards Juliet, holding onto its spiked axe, growling at her. Juliet held up the sword to defend herself and braced for the next attack.

Nix barked, then attacked the minotaur by biting into its leg, causing it to stumble. The minotaur grabbed the wolf and threw him against the wall.

"Nix," Juliet cried.

Nix tried to get up but then collapsed to the ground, injured.

Juliet turned back to face the minotaur. It held the axe above its head, preparing for another strike. Juliet trembled but held the sword firmly.Juliet heard Nikolai yelling her name, just before the axe came down on her. Fearing death, Juliet closed her eyes. Suddenly she felt something heavy crash into her side, and she collapsed onto the ground.

Still alive, Juliet opened her eyes to find Mildred where she was supposed to be. The minotaur's axe was deeply embedded into her neck and shoulder. The minotaur roared triumphantly, then forced Mildred to the ground, striking her again in the stomach. Nikolai and Oberon ran and intercepted the minotaur before it attacked again. Nikolai bounded the minotaur with his fox tails, while Oberon sliced the beast's horn off. Oberon then plunged the horn into the minotaur's chest, causing it to stumble and collapse. Juliet stood up and ran over to where Mildred lay, in a pool of blood, gasping for air. Kneeling beside her, Juliet began to heal her wounds.

"No, don't," Mildred choked, grabbing Juliet's hand.

"Let me heal your wounds," Juliet cried.

"No," Mildred wheezed, as she began to cough up blood.

"Why?" Juliet whispered.

"I am alone here, and I wish to be with the God of Light," Mildred croaked.

"You are not alone; you have me, Malachi and Nikolai," Juliet said, attempting to heal her wounds again.

Mildred took the Queen's hand in her own and smiled.

"Thank you for your kindness, Your Highness. But I want to live with the God of Light," she coughed again. "The alicorn will help you find the crystal Gem. Trust in the God of Light, and thank you.”

“Thank you for saving me,” Juliet cried.

Mildred smiled.

“When I’m gone, Nikolai will be free from his curse, the fox spirit. Tell him I’m sorry,” Mildred cried.

“I will. Thank you for your help and sacrifice,” Juliet cried.

“One more thing, there is another person out there like the King,” Mildred coughed, struggling to breathe.

“It’s ok,” Juliet whispered. “Don’t speak.”

Mildred smiled once more at the Queen, as the light in her eyes disappeared. She breathed her last breath, but not before whispering one final word.

“Serpentina.”

Juliet sat there with tears running down her face. She opened her hand to see what Mildred had given her just before passing. She had Mildred’s emerald Gem, which has the power to control earth. Juliet looked over at Mildred and quietly thanked her.

“What’s happening to me?” Juliet heard her husband say from behind her.

Juliet turned to see her husband surrounded by light, while transforming back into a human. She quickly grabbed a nearby towel and covered him up as the light faded.

“Mildred said that when she’s gone, your curse will be too. She also said that she’s sorry,” Juliet explained.

Nikolai hugged his wife tightly.

“Are you ok?” Juliet whispered.

“Yes, are you?” Nikolai asked.

“I am,” Juliet said, hugging her husband back.

Nikolai stood up with his wife by his side, and wrapped the towel properly around the lower half of his body, while Captain Oberon offered his jacket for the upper half.

“Thanks, Captain,” Nikolai said, taking the jacket.

Captain Oberon nodded.

Malachi entered the palace garden and knelt beside Mildred.

"She said she didn't want to be healed. She wanted to be with the God of Light instead," Juliet explained.

"I had a feeling she was planning this all along," Malachi said.

"Why didn't you say anything? Why didn't you change her mind," Juliet cried.

"It was her choice, and I respected that. Plus, this is not a goodbye," Malachi said.

"What do you mean?" Juliet asked.

"When your time on earth is finished, you'll see her in heaven," Malachi explained.

"How do you know she's gone to heaven? She did some pretty horrible things in her life?" Captain Oberon asked.

"For God so loved the world that he gave his only Son, that whoever believes in him shall not perish but have eternal life. John chapter 3 verse 16. Mildred gave her heart to the God of Light and repented. She believed in him, so she will be in heaven," Malachi explained.

"I'm glad she had a change of heart," Juliet said.

"Me too," Nikolai agreed.

"Um, no offence, but what's happening to you?" Captain Oberon asked Malachi.

Malachi was covered from head to toe in a bright golden light. Enormous white wings erupted from his back, and he smiled.

"My time here is done," Malachi said.

"Thank you for all your help, Malachi," Nikolai said.

"Thank you," Juliet whispered.

Captain Oberon nodded at Malachi.

"I will see you all in the future. Goodbye friends, and remember, trust in the God of Light, and good luck in your travels," Malachi said, before flying up into the sky.

CHAPTER THIRTY-FIVE

"The righteous perish, and no one takes it to heart;
the devout are taken away, and no one understands
that the righteous are taken away to be spared from evil."

Isaiah 57: 1-2

The following day, Mildred was laid to rest in a beautiful coffin. The only people who were at her funeral, were the ones who knew the truth about her and her change in allegiance. Nikolai and Juliet were glad that Mildred came to their side. They both said a little prayer of thanks, for all the help and knowledge Mildred had shared, and for her sacrifice.

The kingdom then got into fixing all the broken houses, that had fallen in the recent attack. Many villagers came to help one another. Offering food or water, and opening their homes to people without housing until their houses were finished. Captain Oberon doubled the patrols in fear that there would be another attack. To everyone's relief, there were no more sightings of any creatures of darkness, after searching the whole kingdom.

Nikolai received word that Finnick and Jarreth were a day's

ride away, and that their mission was a success. This made things seem a bit easier, considering the recent attack, and the kingdoms being cut off from one another for so long. After hearing the news that they have now got allies from both kingdoms, it meant that they could start preparing for the coming war.

Juliet was happy to have received a letter from her mother, about her upcoming wedding to Captain Issac. Having a wedding seemed odd at first, considering all that they've been through, and what they will have to endure in the future. But after all the hardships they've been through, it's nice to know they can still see the good in life.

Nikolai and Juliet walked hand in hand to the palace stables, to see the alicorn Mildred and Malachi had brought to them. They both walked up to the stall and saw Amisha for the first time. She was a white mare with white wings, with a golden horn that sat atop her forehead. Her mane and tail were white with bits of gold throughout.

She was stunning.

"Hello, Amisha," Juliet greeted, patting the alicorn's head. "She's stunning, Nikolai."

"She is. You're a fortunate Queen," he said, smiling while leaning on the stall.

"Amisha belongs to the both of us," Juliet stated.

"I already have Nix. I want Amisha to be yours," Nikolai said, smiling at his wife.

Juliet smiled at her husband as she walked up towards him. She wrapped her hands around his neck and kissed him. His hands came around her waist as he pulled her closer to him.

"I love you," Juliet whispered between kisses.

"I love you too," Nikolai replied.

"I'm sorry to interrupt you at all the wrong times, it seems," Theo said, feeling guilty.

Juliet and Nikolai laughed.

"What is it, Theo?" Nikolai asked.

"I hate to interrupt you, but my brother Fitzwilliam is here to see you. Also, Finnick and Jarreth are back from their mission. Both are waiting for you in the conference room for a debrief," Theo explained.

"Shall we?" Nikolai said, offering his arm to his wife.

Juliet smiled and took her husband's offered arm.

"You coming, Theo?" Nikolai called after him.

"Yes, I'm coming," Theo replied, walking beside his friend.

Once Theo, Juliet and Nikolai entered the conference room, they sat down around the table.

"I'm sorry, Your Highness, we're just waiting on Captain Oberon," Finnick said.

"No need to apologize. He's been busy with the kingdom's security lately," Nikolai said.

"I heard about the attack from one of our friends," Finnick said. "No casualties?"

"No casualties," Nikolai reassured.

"Have you heard from my father?" Finnick asked.

"He and his people are fine too. The minotaur wasn't interested in them. It was sent here to kill someone else," Nikolai said with sadness.

"Oh, anyone we know?" Finnick asked.

"No," Juliet said sadly, "but she gave up her life for us."

Nikolai took his wife's hand and smiled.

"She was a follower of the Prince of Darkness, but changed her allegiance to the God of Light. She gave us some valuable information, which I'll share once Captain Oberon arrives," Nikolai explained.

"Here. Sorry, Your Highness," Captain Oberon said, walking into the room and taking a seat.

"Ok, let me start by telling you what Mildred shared with us," Nikolai began. "The Prince of Darkness has one of his followers already in the Kingdom of Kudzu. Her name is Jorogumo, and she is known as the spider demon. It's why we haven't been able to get through to them. Mildred said that the Prince of Darkness is summoning the creatures of darkness to aid him in this war. Also, to break free, he needs to consume many souls from humans. I know it all seems bad, but the Prince of Darkness has a weakness. The crystal Gem, which has the power of light."

"Isn't the crystal Gem a myth?" Finnick asked.

"No, it is very much real," Fitzwilliam replied. "The God of Light gave it to us to use when we needed it most. It was hidden with a mythical species, to protect it from people who would use it for evil."

"The alicorn race," Juliet said.

"The what?" Fitzwilliam asked.

"Mildred and Malachi brought us the key to finding the crystal Gem. Her name is Amisha, and she's an alicorn. Half unicorn, half pegasus," Juliet explained.

"No way," Finnick said excitedly. "I need to see this."

"In time, you will," Nikolai laughed.

"Excuse me, Your Highness, but we have a letter for you from Princess Iris," Finnick said, taking out the letter.

Nikolai opened the letter and read the contents inside, while everybody anxiously waited.

"Princess Iris has asked for our assistance in defeating Jorogumo. She has also agreed to an alliance with us," Nikolai said.

"That's a relief, knowing a royal is still alive," Theo said. "But it doesn't explain what happened to the King and Queen."

"Jorogumo most likely killed them," Finnick said with concern.

"So, what is our next move?" Captain Oberon asked.

"Travel to the Kingdom of Kudzu, and see if we can help rid the kingdom of Jorogumo. After, we ask a royal if they can interpret what Amisha says, about the whereabouts of the crystal Gem," Nikolai explained to everyone.

"I think that's a good idea," Captain Oberon agreed. "You have my support and the support of my men."

"Agreed," Finnick said excitedly.

"*Agreed*," Jarreth signed.

"Thank you," Nikolai replied.

"I can help, too," Theo said.

"I need your help here, within the kingdom, to help run things while I'm away. I'll ask Lord Hain to act as Captain while Oberon is with us," Nikolai explained.

"Oh, thank goodness. I wanted to be supportive, but I can't fight to save myself. I'm happy to stay and look after the kingdom," Theo said, relieved.

There was laughter amongst the group.

"What do you need me to do?" Fitzwilliam asked.

"Collect information and send it to Theo or myself. Make sure our weapons are ready before we depart for our mission. Also help Theo in any way while I'm away," Nikolai said.

"Done," Fitzwilliam replied.

"Ok, we leave in two days. Make sure you're all ready by then," Nikolai told the group.

They all stood up and left the conference room, leaving Nikolai and Juliet to themselves.

"If I wanted to come along, would you allow it?" Juliet asked.

"Yes, of course. We will need your healing powers, and the power of your emerald Gem once you have mastered it," Nikolai said.

"Thank you. I would hate to be stuck at home constantly

worrying about you," Juliet said, relieved.

"Having you close by my side puts me at ease," Nikolai said, kissing his wife's hand.

Juliet smiled at her husband. "I'm glad you think so too."

CHAPTER THIRTY-SIX

*"If we confess our sins, he is faithful and just
and will forgive us our sins and purify us
from all unrighteousness."*

1 John 1:9

Anna slithered her way into the cave of Akuma. She was excited to tell her Master what had happened to Mildred, and knew he would be pleased with the news.

Before she stood before the Master, Anna transformed into her human form. She braided her long black hair to keep it out of her face, and dressed in all-black clothing, before presenting herself to the Master.

"What news do you bring?" the Prince of Darkness growled impatiently.

"Mildred is dead," Anna replied.

The Prince of Darkness laughed aloud.

"Finally, something good," he laughed again.

"What is our next move, Master?" Anna asked.

"I need you to find the crystal Gem and bring it to me," the

Prince of Darkness ordered. "Kill anyone who gets in your way."

Anna nodded then left. On her way out, she spotted another dark follower.

"Claud," Anna hissed.

"Anna," Claud growled.

Claud went straight into the cave of Akuma, to present two full wagons of people bounded by Jorogumo, to the Prince of Darkness. Claud returned to his human self and bowed before his Master.

"Jorogumo has done well," the Prince of Darkness smirked. "Claud, bring one close to me."

Claud picked up one of the humans bound in cobwebs, and carried them over to the Prince of Darkness, placing them in front of him. Claud quickly stood back and watched his Master devour the human soul. Claud watched in disgust and fear, as his Master consumed soul after soul. The screams of the humans echoed throughout the cave of Akuma, causing Claud to shiver with fear.

"Aren't they supposed to be dead," Claud asked.

"Oh, no, they have to still be alive, but only just, for our Master to consume their soul," Serpentina explained.

Serpentina looked at Claud with a smirk on her face. She was beautiful. She had dark blue eyes that shined with the night sky, and long blonde hair that hung loosely around her petite figure. Claud couldn't help but stare at the Master's most trusted person. Serpentina was one of the Prince of Darkness's first experiments. He made it so she could transform into a basilisk, and Serpentina was close to her Master.

Serpentina grew up loved by everyone around her. She was the most beautiful person in her village, and she took advantage of that fact. Serpentina grew up with a cold heart, and would manipulate people in her town, causing them to quarrel amongst each other. When Serpentina came of age, nobody wanted to marry her, even though she had grown up to be quite beautiful. They all feared her because of her cold heart, and manipulative ways. Feeling angry and hurt, Serpentina left her small village and came across the Prince of Darkness, who preyed on her vulnerability. Promising her power and adoration, she agreed to serve the Prince of Darkness, and help him in any way possible. She spent years serving the Prince of Darkness by doing his dirty work. She lured people to the cave for him to devour, amongst other tasks. But Serpentina started to get impatience and wanted power. The Prince of Darkness took advantage of her and experimented on her, making her able to transform into a basilisk. After experimenting with her new abilities, Serpentina returned to her home village to get revenge on all who wronged her.

Now standing before him in the cave of Akuma, Serpentina stared in awe at her Master.

"Isn't this exciting? After thousands of years, our Master will finally be free," Serpentina said happily.

"Yes, it is," Claud said, looking at Serpentina.

"Why did you join up with our Master in the first place?" Serpentina asked Claud.

Claud looked at Serpentina with skepticism.

"What, I'm curious," Serpentina said, bumping his shoulder and smiling.

"I met Selina when she started to serve our Master. But she ended up getting killed, so I wanted revenge, and to kill whoever killed her," Claud explained.

"And do you know who killed her?" Serpentina asked.

"Captain Issac from the Kingdom of Elaxon," Claud said, angrily.

"A little birdie told me he's soon to be King Issac," Serpentina giggled.

"Not before I get to him," Claud snarled.

Serpentina giggled again. "Oh, men with their little goals. You must think bigger."

The Prince of Darkness wiped his mouth with his hands and laughed. Shriveled-up dead bodies lay at his feet. Claud had to hold down his last meal, as he felt sick at the sight of it.

"Bring me more," the Prince of Darkness laughed.

Claud went over and started moving the dead bodies back onto the first wagon. He was a little annoyed at Serpentina for not helping him, but didn't dare question or insult the Master's most trusted person. The consequences would most certainly mean death, as he saw now. Once the task was completed, he moved the first wagon away and brought the second one over. He repeated the same thing he had done before. He placed the bounded humans at his Master's feet for him to devour.

"Good boy," Serpentina teased.

Claud ignored her comment and went to dispose of the first wagon. Pushing the wagon outside, he walked a mile before stopping. He went around the area and began picking up sticks for a fire. Once he completed this task, he began to burn the bodies. Smoke filled the area as Claud lifted the bodies into the bonfire individually. He stood back after discarding the last body, and covered his mouth due to the stench. He sighed, wishing this task were given to another. After the bodies were gone, Claud started making his way back to the cave of Akuma, to wait for his Master to finish his next meal.

Upon arrival, the Prince of Darkness finished his last person, and Claud could hear people laughing around the cave. The Prince of Darkness closed his eyes, focusing on his power of darkness. Black dust surrounded him as he continued to chant words. The dust began to cover the chains that bound him up, and eventually they broke, freeing the Prince of Darkness.

"Finally," he yelled triumphantly.

The Prince of Darkness began to stand up, but collapsed back to the ground. Serpentina rushed to his side and helped him stand up, keeping her hands around him for support.

The Prince of Darkness growled.

"That spell took all my energy," he fumed. "I'll need more souls to get stronger."

The Prince of Darkness looked up at Claud.

"Go back to Jorogumo and bring me back some more humans," the Prince of Darkness demanded.

"Understood," Claud said, bowing to his Master before leaving.

"Sit down, Master; you need to rest," Serpentina encouraged.

The Prince of Darkness was about to get angry at Serpentina, but then remembered that he still needed her, until he regained his strength. He sat back down with the help of Serpentina, to his disgust. He hated being weak. When his energy was restored, he would show the world what would happen if they refuse him.

Chapter Thirty-Seven

*"In him we have redemption through his blood, the forgiveness
of sins, in accordance with the riches of God's grace."*

Ephesians 1:7

Prince Omari had flown for hours before landing to have
something to eat and rest. Transforming back to human, he got
out the food the kitchen hand had given him. Looking around the
forest, he was amazed at the beauty of it all. Being isolated in the
palace had made this journey a bit difficult. He wasn't sure which
plants were poisonous or edible, so he had to ration what he had.
He was also unsure which animals were dangerous and which
ones weren't. He just hoped to make friends who understood him
and didn't judge.

Being isolated all his life, King Jabari hired a teacher to teach
Prince Omari the basics of math, english, and how to rule when his
father passed. But on the special occasion when he had finished
studying the other subjects, his teacher would teach him about
the outside world through books. But that wasn't very often, so
Prince Omari's knowledge of the outside world was limited.

Packing his food away, he took out his water flask and drank. He scanned the area and found a river with a waterfall. Remembering what his teacher had taught him about fresh water, he filled both flasks.

Omari then heard a rustle behind him in the bushes. Turning around, he saw nothing and continued filling up his flask. He heard the bushes behind him rustle again, along with a hissing sound this time. Turning around, he found himself face-to-face with a giant snake. Luckily for Prince Omari, his teacher had taught him about this particular creature.

It was known as an anaconda.

This anaconda was green with black spots covering its body. It slithered out of the bushes and revealed its size. It looked to be about 4.5 meters long, meaning it was female. Prince Omari backed away from the incoming anaconda. He tried to think of a way to flee without it coming after him or attacking him. He couldn't transform because he would be vulnerable for too long while changing, and he couldn't go into the water because the anacondas were much faster in the water than on land. The only option left was to use his kingdom's Gem abilities. Prince Omari still had doubts because even though he'd been training all his life with the Gem, he's never used it in a real fight before.

"Right, I can do this," Omari told himself.

His kingdom's Gem was a ruby Gem, which gave him the power of strength. The ruby Gem was embedded into his gauntlets, which were on both of his arms. Every generation could choose where to have them, and that's where Omari decided to have his.

Bumping his fists together, he prepared for the incoming attack.

"Well, well, well, what do we have here? The Master will be thrilled with you," Anna hissed.

"The Master?" Omari asked, confused.

Then he suddenly realized who the Master she spoke of was. The Prince of Darkness. He had overheard his father talking about him to his soldiers, just before the attack on the kingdom. Also, his teacher had taught him about all the horrible things the Prince of Darkness had done, before his imprisonment. Prince Omari had both fists raised, ready for the attack.

Anna slithered closer to Omari and raised her head to strike him. Jumping out of the way, Omari found his footing, ran up to Anna and punched her, causing her to smash into a tree. Omari took this chance and started to run away, but was tripped over by Anna's long snake body. Falling to the ground, he turned onto his back, shielding his face with his arms as she attacked again. Blocking and protecting himself from the multiple attacks by Anna, Omari tried to find an opening to launch an attack.

Just before Anna struck again, Omari grabbed her snake body and stood up. Using his strength, he threw her into a tree with such force, that she collapsed in a bundle on the ground. Omari waited to see if Anna would get up again, but she was too beaten up to move her body. Wiping the blood from his face, Omari turned and fled toward the Kingdom of Zolatta, but not before he heard Anna say something.

"Next time, prince, next time," she hissed.

Omari hoped he would never come across her again, but the Prince of Darkness had other plans. Transforming back into his griffin form, Omari took flight and was relieved to see the Kingdom of Zolatta within view. Flying over the houses on the outskirts of the kingdom, Omari could hear screams from the villagers below. He was a little shocked, considering he heard from his teacher that the King of Zolatta could transform into a fox spirit.

He continued to fly over them and straight to the palace. Coming over the village, he heard arrows coming from below.

Dodging the arrows that were coming for him, he tried to land to transform back to human, but his attackers wouldn't let him. Pain pierced through his thigh, and he turned to see that an arrow had made its mark.

He began to descend to the ground at a fast pace. Once he hit the ground, guards surrounded him with their weapons raised. Fearing death, he used his wings to cover his face and waited for the incoming strike.

"I'm sorry, mother, father," Omari whispered.

"Stop," Nikolai yelled. "Weapon's down."

Omari peeked through a tiny gap in his wings, to see the King of Zolatta running up to him. Nikolai slowed and stopped a few steps away from Omari in his griffin form.

"I'm not going to hurt you," Nikolai reassured.

Omari unshielded his wings that covered his face and looked up at King Nikolai.

"Juliet," Nikolai said, never taking his eyes off the griffin. "Get me a towel, please."

"Yes, of course," Juliet said, rushing back inside the palace.

"Your Highness, this may be a creature sent by the Prince of Darkness," Oberon voiced.

"If he were sent here by the Prince of Darkness, he would have killed some people already. But he didn't. He's scared. Look, he's shielding himself from us," Nikolai explained.

"Nikolai," Juliet called, handing the towel to her husband.

"We're not going to hurt you," Nikolai told the griffin.

Prince Omari started transforming into his human self. Once done, Nikolai gave Omari the towel to cover himself.

"Are you okay?" Nikolai asked.

"Yes, Your Highness, thank you," Omari replied, relieved.

"Come inside the palace. My wife can heal your wounds," Nikolai said, gesturing for him to follow.

Omari followed the King and Queen back inside the palace, and into one of the bedrooms, where a manservant got him some clothes to dress. Once dressed, Omari followed the manservant to a seating area, where the King, Queen and Captain Oberon waited. Prince Omari bowed before them.

"Please take a seat," Nikolai said, gesturing to the couch.

"Thank you," Omari said.

"This is my wife, Juliet. She'll heal your wound," Nikolai said.

Juliet approached Omari, lifting his leg onto the couch, and started healing him.

"What brings you to my kingdom?" Nikolai asked.

"My name is Prince Omari. My father is King Jabari from the Kingdom of Neylon. I've come to ask for your help, and to help you in return," he explained.

"I didn't know King Jabari had a son," Captain Oberon said.

"Not many people do. I have been isolated most of my life because of my curse. My ability to turn into a griffin," Omari explained.

"How can we help?" Nikolai asked.

"Well, your people accept you as their King despite your curse. I was hoping you would teach me how to control it, or better yet, to break free from it," Omari explained.

"Do you know who cursed you in the first place?" Nikolai asked.

"The Prince of Darkness," Omari replied.

"The Prince of Darkness would've made the curse, but who put it on you?" Nikolai asked.

Omari stared blankly at Nikolai.

"It's okay if you don't know; I didn't either for a while," Nikolai said.

"The Prince of Darkness made the curse, but since he's been

trapped for thousands of years, someone else would have placed the curse for him," Juliet explained, sitting back beside her husband. "The only way to rid yourself of the curse is to find out who did it, and end their life. Only then will you be free from the curse that you have."

"Oh," Omari said sadly.

"Wait a minute," Juliet thought aloud. "Just before Mildred passed, she said there was another person out there like you, Nikolai."

She turned towards her husband.

"Did she say a name?" Omari asked.

"Serpentina," Juliet replied. "Does that ring a bell?"

Everyone in the room shook their head.

"Well, until the time comes when we find Serpentina, I would like to offer my assistance and learn how to control my curse properly," Omari offered.

"We're about to travel to the Kingdom of Kudzu, to assist in defeating one of the Prince of Darkness's followers. You are welcome to join us. We can work on your control, and update you on how we can defeat the Prince of Darkness," Nikolai explained.

"Thank you. I will assist in any way I can," Omari said.

"Great, get plenty of rest because we leave tomorrow morning," Nikolai said.

CHAPTER THIRTY-EIGHT

"For I know the plans I have for you," declares the Lord,
"plans to prosper you and not to harm you,
plans to give you hope and a future."

Jeremiah 29:11

Erick walked back to the campsite, where Princess Iris and the villagers called home for the time being. Thinking about his deal with Jorogumo, he smirked to himself. He would finally get his way soon with Princess Iris and Jarreth. He just had to decide on a plan first. A plan that ensured Jarreth would come back to Kudzu, to save Iris.

Erick walked back through the forest with ease, knowing that Jorogumo's minions wouldn't attack him anymore. He came through the same way he had left, noticing a new guard standing at his guard post. He panicked a little, trying to think of a good enough excuse, to explain his absence for the past couple of hours.

"Captain Erick," the guard said, seeing his Captain approach him.

"What is it, Chase?" Erick asked, annoyed.

"Tom wasn't at his assigned post when I came to relieve him of his duty," Chase said.

"I relieved him of his duty. I just heard a noise from the forest, thought it was the enemy, so I went to check it out. I didn't think I'd been gone for so long. I might have gotten lost since it was so dark," Erick acted dumbly. "You know how it is."

"Oh, that's okay. Sorry, I didn't mean to question you, Captain. You are not the first to get lost in these woods," Chase admitted.

"It is easy to get lost," Erick said, returning to camp. "Good night, solider."

"Night, Captain," Chase replied, returning to his duties.

Chase watched his Captain walk back to his tent with curiosity. He would have to mention this situation to the Princess in the morning.

Princess Iris first came to Chase after the kidnapping incident. As her father's most trusted soldier, Chase agreed to spy on Erick. He never liked his new Captain very much. Using fear and bribery to get his way in life, was despicable. Chase never agreed with him, but had to act like he did, so he could report back to the King and now the Princess.

Watching his Captain enter his tent, he suspected Erick was up to something, but didn't know what.

The Prince of Darkness sat in the cave of Akuma, fuming that he didn't have the strength to do the things he wanted to do. And that was to rule the four kingdoms, and to cause fear and panic. He needed the sapphire healing Gem from the Kingdom of Elaxon to heal himself, but Selina had failed at getting it for him. The Prince of Darkness had underestimated these people, and that angered him even more.

He looked around the cave at all his followers. There was Serpentina, his first experiment, who could transform into a basilisk. Claud who could transform into a massive wolf. Anna, who was currently out trying to find the crystal Gem, could transform into a big anaconda. Jorogumo who was collecting victims for him in the Kingdom of Kudzu, was a spider demon who could turn into a giant spider, and could control other spiders to do her bidding.

He needed more people to join his side, but that meant giving up more of his power to them, for them to join him. He opened his Book of Darkness once again and looked through its pages, thinking to himself. Planning.

CHAPTER THIRTY-NINE

"Do not forsake your friend or a friend of your family,
and do not go to your relative's house when disaster strikes you
- better a neighbor nearby than a relative far away."

Proverbs 27:10

After a couple of hours of travelling, Nikolai thought it was best to stop for a rest. While Juliet, Omari, Jarreth and Finnick rested, Nikolai and Captain Oberon continued to train. Nikolai wanted to master his Gem, so he and his allies could have the upper hand in the coming threat, that was waiting for them in the Kingdom of Kudzu. Juliet sat on the grass underneath a tall tree with Nix by her side, while watching Captain Oberon teach her husband how to use the Sword of the Kings. The sword was powerful and belonged to the Kingdom of Zolatta and its generation of rulers. Having the kingdom's Gem inside the hilt of the sword, enabled the blade to light into flames whilst in combat.

While Nikolai learned how to use the sword, Juliet was teaching herself how to use the emerald Gem that Mildred had given to her, just before her passing. She placed her hand just above the grass and concentrated on willing it to move. A vine sprouted from the ground, rising a few centimeters, before turning into a beautiful yellow daisy. Juliet smiled to herself; she was beginning to get the hang of it. Jarreth knelt beside Juliet with a plate full of fruit, nuts, and cheese.

"*Hungry, Queen Juliet?*" Jarreth signed.

"Thank you, Jarreth," Juliet said, taking an apple and a few grapes.

Jarreth went over to Finnick who stood near the outside of the camp on patrol, and showed him the plate filled with fruits, nuts, and cheese.

"Thanks Jarreth," Finnick said, grabbing a few of each. "Hey, want to hear a cheesy joke?" Finnick held up the cheese he was holding and laughed.

Jarreth shook his head at his friend's bad joke. Standing beside him, they both watched their Captain and King fight.

Juliet smiled at Finnick's joke, then stood up and walked over to Amisha, her alicorn, which Mildred and Malachi had given to her only a week ago.

"Hey girl," Juliet said to Amisha.

Amisha lowered her head for a pat, which made Juliet smile, as she patted her head. Nix then came up behind Juliet and sniffed at Amisha's face, then licked it.

Juliet laughed, patting Nix on the head. "Good boy Nix."

"You hungry?" Juliet asked her alicorn.

Amisha lowered her head and sniffed at Juliet's hand, to find the source of the food. Juliet smiled and gave Amisha an apple, which she devoured in one bite. She gave another apple to Amisha, then patted her head, while eating some grapes herself.

"She's a beautiful alicorn," Finnick said coming up. "Have you experienced her flying yet?"

"Not yet. I'm just getting used to her, while she's getting used to me," Juliet replied, smiling at Amisha sniffing her hand.

"Fair enough," Finnick said.

"What is she?" Omari asked, coming up to Juliet and Amisha.

"She's an alicorn. A horse that has a unicorn horn and pegasus wings," Juliet explained, patting Amisha.

"It's amazing to see what creatures the God of Light has created," Omari said amazed. "Still learning about them of course."

"Don't worry, you'll get there. We'll help you," Finnick said, patting his back.

"Thank you, Lieutenant," Omari replied.

"Prince Omari, you can call me Finnick. Everyone else does," Finnick said annoyed.

"Sorry, still not used to these things," Omari said embarrassed.

"Don't stress, you'll get there," Finnick said.

"What's your kingdom like?" Juliet asked Omari.

"Our kingdom is known for how big our quarry is. So, less trees and more stone, sand, and rocks."

"Does the majority of the people in your kingdom work in the quarry?" Juliet asked.

"Yes, it's a good job. It never runs out of work," Omari replied nodding.

"What does one dig up at a quarry?" Finnick asked.

"Stone, rocks, sand, gravel, just to name a few," Omari explained. "It's actually where my ancestors found the first Gem."

"Really, in your quarry?" Finnick asked.

"Yes," Omari replied.

"What stops any person from coming in and stealing one. I thought the Gems were only given to royalty?" Juliet asked.

"They are. Once a royal reaches their tenth birthday, they go down into the deepest part of the quarry. The Gem is actually embedded into the stone, and only a royal can remove it. Once removed, the royal can choose where they want to wear it. I chose a gauntlet," Omari explained, showing them his weapon.

"So, what power does your Gem have?" Finnick asked.

"Strength," Omari said, holding up his arms. "It's why I chose to have the ruby Gem embedded within my gauntlets."

"That's awesome," Finnick said amazed.

"Finnick," Captain Oberon called.

"Yes Captain," Finnick said, walking over to him.

"I need a break. You duel with the King," Captain Oberon panted.

"Yes sir," Finnick replied, grabbing his Captain's sword.

Jarreth went over to his Captain and gave him some food and water, before going back and watching Finnick duel with the King.

"Thanks, Jarreth," Oberon said, taking the food and water.

"You are very nice and respectful to your men," Juliet said, coming up to Oberon.

"Thanks, Your Highness," Oberon said, taking a drink of water. "We're like a family, always looking out for one another."

"I think it's amazing how you and Finnick learnt sign language, just so you could communicate with Jarreth," Juliet said in admiration.

"He's a good lad. Just had a troubled past," Oberon replied.

Juliet walked over with Omari and watched the match between Finnick and Nikolai. After clashing swords for a few minutes, Nikolai ended up being able to activate his topaz Gem. This made Finnick put his hands up in defeat.

"Wait, I'd rather not be burnt and unrecognizable to the ladies," Finnick blurted out.

Jarreth sighed with embarrassment, covering his face with his hand. Captain Oberon rolled his eyes. Juliet, Nikolai, and Omari laughed. Juliet then walked up to her husband with some water and food.

"That was amazing. You can now use the Gem in your sword in future battles," Juliet exclaimed.

"All the training Captain Oberon put me through for the past couple of days was worth it," Nikolai said, drinking his water. "How's your training going?"

"Good, as you can see with all the flowers blooming around us," Juliet said looking around.

"I'm glad," Nikolai laughed.

"Do you need any healing?" Juliet asked.

"Yes please, if you don't mind," Nikolai replied.

"I don't mind," Juliet said smiling.

It was dusk when they finally stopped for the night. They only stopped once during the day, as they wanted to reach their destination quickly. Juliet, who was feeling the effects, was eager to stretch her legs. Once she dismounted her horse, she let Amisha roam free to eat and drink, while she walked around. She was glad she had brought suitable riding clothes and boots. Her husband came up to her and gave her something to drink.

"Thank you, Nikolai," she said. "How are you doing?"

"Good, now that I know I can use my kingdom's topaz Gem. But I'll feel better once we reach the Kingdom of Kudzu," Nikolai replied.

"Me too," she said, as Nix came up to them.

"Hey Nix," Nikolai said, patting the white wolf. "I bet he's enjoying all the running."

"I bet he is," Juliet said patting his head. "Does he hunt for his own food?"

"Yes, don't worry about him," Nikolai said. "He prefers his

meals somewhat fresh."

Omari walked past them and looked to the forest ahead of them. The darkness made the forest all the more eerie and scary. Omari shivered in his jacket then turned to Finnick.

"Why can't we go any further?" Omari asked.

"Jorogumo's minions hide in the forest a mile up ahead. Unless you want to get eaten by a massive spider, I suggest you sleep here for tonight," Finnick explained.

"Right. Damn I hate spiders," Omari said with disgust.

"Me too. But they're not your average-size spiders, they're so much bigger," Jarreth signed.

"You're joking right," Omari asked. "Right?"

Jarreth shook his head.

Omari swallowed the lump in his throat, and looked towards the dark eerie forest that lay ahead. "God of Light, please protect us from anything that wasn't sent by you."

Once camp was set up, they all sat around the fire to keep themselves warm. But little did they know that something was waiting and watching them through the edge of the forest. Something so small you couldn't see it in the darkness, unless you got too close.

Even then it would be too late.

CHAPTER FORTY

"I can do all things through Christ who gives me strength."

Philippians 4:13

Iris was full of hope when a soldier came to tell her, that the King and Queen of Zolatta was within view of their camp. She was happy and relieved for their help, and was also excited to see Jarreth again. Walking out of her tent, she made her way over to greet her guests.

"Princess Iris," Lucas called, running up to her.

"Hey Lucas, are you ok?" she asked.

"Can I come with you to see Finnick and Jarreth?" Lucas pleaded.

"Of course. I bet they'll be happy to see you too," Iris said smiling.

Together, Lucas and Iris walked up to greet the King and Queen of Zolatta, and their companions.

"Welcome, Your Highness," Iris greeted. "I'm Princess Iris. Thank you for replying to my letter and for your aid."

"It's nice to meet you," Nikolai said, dismounting his horse.

"My name is Nikolai, and this is my wife, Juliet."

"It's so nice to meet you, Princess Iris," Juliet greeted with a bow.

"And you, Queen Juliet," Iris replied, returning the gesture.

"This is Captain Oberon," Nikolai introduced, to which Oberon just nodded.

"This here is Prince Omari from the Kingdom of Neylon. He will be joining us on our quest," Nikolai said, gesturing to Omari.

"Hi," Omari greeted, with a wave and a smile.

"And you remember Lieutenant Finnick and Lieutenant Jarreth," Nikolai said, gesturing to the two soldiers.

"Yes they were very helpful last time," Iris replied with a smile.

"It's good to see you again Princess Iris," Finnick said. "Jarreth couldn't wait to see you again, after finding out we were coming back here."

Iris smiled and blushed.

"*I'm happy to see you again,*" Jarreth signed.

"*Me too,*" Iris signed to him privately.

"Hey Lucas, I hope you have been practicing your knife throwing," Finnick said.

"I have. Every day since you left," Lucas replied.

"Ok buddy, let's see. Are you coming too, Jarreth?" Finnick said, walking off with Lucas.

Jarreth smiled at Iris, then bowed before following Lucas and Finnick.

"Come this way and I'll explain my situation to you," Iris said, leading the way back to her tent.

Nikolai, Juliet, Omari, and Oberon followed Iris back through the camp, and to her tent. Along the way they saw many people, young and old, who fled their homes because of Jorogumo and her minions. A lot of them greeted Nikolai and his companions, and thanked them for their kindness. Nix followed behind Nikolai and Juliet, sniffing the villager's hands for food. A few of them gladly gave him food and a good pat, before Nix ran back to join the group. Iris held her tent open while her guests gathered inside. Once inside they all gathered around the table, while Edith prepared the refreshments, and Iris explained her current situation.

"I have asked you here to help me reclaim my kingdom. Jorogumo, a spider demon working for the Prince of Darkness, came into my kingdom and captured and killed many of my people, including my parents," Iris explained.

"How did such a big spider get past your guards?" Captain Oberon asked confused.

"Jorogumo has three forms. Human, spider, and half of each," Iris said. "She deceived us all in her human form."

"When she's disguised as human, you can only see her true form by mirror or reflection," Juliet told the group. "At least that's what I read in the book."

"You are correct, Your Highness," Iris said. "That's why the casualty number was so high. Some of us managed to flee, but others weren't so lucky."

"Do you know where Jorogumo's hideout is?" Nikolai asked.

"The dungeons of my kingdom," Iris replied. "Jarreth found it, when he was trying to find survivors."

"Do you have a plan, Princess Iris?" Oberon asked.

"Sort of. It's half a plan," Iris said guilty. "Jorogumo hasn't attacked anyone yet. It's only been her minions, which are her medium size spiders. Her guards on the other hand, are humungous. They will be a problem. I thought we could start by luring them out, and eliminating them first, before entering the dungeons. I haven't thought about it much after that."

"It's a good start, Princess Iris. Don't stress. You've had to step up a lot since the attack," Captain Oberon said with sympathy. "Who is your Captain, and can I speak to him about a battle plan?"

Princess Iris sighed and hesitated.

"His name is Erick. I don't trust him, due to circumstances of the past. But my father had to agree with the previous Captain when he was appointed, due to no evidence regarding the actions of his past. He's also been very suspicious lately," Iris explained. "I have someone watching him at the moment."

"You think he's changed sides?" Nikolai asked.

"Yes I do," Iris said plainly.

"Which soldiers do you trust?" Captain Oberon asked.

"Chase. He's the one who has been spying on Erick for me," Iris explained.

Captain Oberon nodded. "I'll need a word with him when he's free."

"Of course Captain," Iris replied.

"Well, all we can do now is wait till I talk with Chase, and come up with a plan. Then we can go from there," Oberon said standing up. "I'll go find him now."

Erick smiled as he walked through the camp with confidence. He walked up to Princess Iris's tent, but stopped short as soon as he heard his name mentioned. He stopped, and slowly moved closer to the tent, to hear more of the conversation. After hearing that Princess Iris has doubts about him, he walked away angry and a bit panicked. If Princess Iris had her suspicions about him, how was he supposed to take her Gem. He had to think of a different plan and fast. Seeing the Captain from Zolatta exiting the tent, Erick walked up to him and introduced himself.

"Captain Erick, nice to meet you," Erick said playing nice.

"Captain Oberon, nice to meet you to," Oberon greeted, eyeing Erick suspiciously.

"Thank you for coming to assist in taking back our home," Erick lied.

"Glad we can help," Oberon said, starting to walk off. "Excuse me, I need to be somewhere."

"Don't you need help in preparing a plan of attack. I am the Captain of the Royal Guard of Kudzu after all," Erick voiced.

Oberon stared at Erick suspiciously, wondering what he was playing at. Then he thought it was best to keep his enemies close, so he nodded.

"Do you know where I can find Chase?" Oberon asked.

"He should be on a break now, maybe the food tent. Follow me, I'll show you," Erick said, walking in the direction of the food tent.

Oberon followed Erick through the camp and towards the food tent, where so many others were having their lunch.

"Chase," Erick called, walking up to the solider.

"Captain, what can I do for you?" Chase asked, standing up.

"This here is Captain Oberon from Zolatta. We are going to discuss a plan to take back the kingdom," Erick said triumphantly.

"And you need me why?" Chase asked Erick.

"The Princess request's that you join us in making a battle plan," Captain Oberon said, eyeing Chase.

"Of course, anything to help the Princess," Chase replied, clearly getting the hint.

"Take a seat." Chase said to both men.

✦ ✦ ✦ ✦ ✦

"That was awesome Lucas," Finnick praised.

"Thanks, I've been practicing since you and Jarreth left,"

Lucas told both Lieutenants.

"*You've done well,*" Jarreth sighed, then clapped.

"Thanks Jarreth," Lucas said, understanding his sign language, with a big grin plastered across his face.

Jarreth and Finnick both stared at Lucas shocked.

"Princess Iris taught me sign language while you were away," Lucas explained.

"*You have a great teacher,*" Jarreth signed, testing Lucas again.

"She is a great teacher," Lucas laughed.

Jarreth smiled at Princess Iris's and Lucas's kindness.

"That's amazing Lucas," Finnick said grinning.

"What are you going to teach me next?" Lucas asked with enthusiasm.

"*What do you want to learn?*" Jarreth signed.

"Hmmm," Lucas thought. "Archery."

"*I can help with that,*" Jarreth signed, taking out his bow and arrow.

Jarreth readied his bow and arrow, aiming it at the tree they had used for knife throwing. He took a deep breath then released the arrow, hitting it straight into the tree trunk.

"Wow," Lucas exclaimed.

"*Now you try,*" Jarreth signed, showing Lucas how to hold the bow and arrow.

Lucas held the bow like Jarreth had shown him, and concentrated on his intended target.

The tree.

He took the arrow Jarreth had given him, and placed it into his bow. Lucas then took a deep breath, and released the arrow. The arrow shot through the air, hitting the bottom of the tree.

"Yes it hit," Lucas said happily.

"Well done," Finnick said clapping.

"*Great job. Now…*," Jarreth signed, walking towards the tree and marking it. "*Try and aim at the target.*"

"Jarreth, Finnick, a word," Captain Oberon called, coming up to them.

"Sure, hold on Lucas," Finnick said, as he and Jarreth went over to their Captain.

"Battle meeting in ten minutes in the food tent," Captain Oberon said. "And be careful of Captain Erick. Princess Iris doesn't trust him and neither do I. There's something about him that doesn't seem right."

"Yes sir," Finnick replied.

Jarreth nodded.

Captain Oberon nodded before walking away.

"*This Erick fellow must be bad, if the Captain doesn't even trust him*," Jarreth signed.

"Yeah, he must be, for the Captain to warn us like that," Finnick said worriedly.

"I heard from one of the soldiers, that he's been sneaking out at night and going back to the kingdom," Lucas said, coming up to them.

"Really?" Finnick said in disbelief.

"*Why would he go back home when Jorogumo is there, unless he's switched sides*," Jarreth sighed.

"That makes sense," Finnick thought out loud. "Sorry Lucas we need to go. We'll train later."

"Ok, I'll see you later," Lucas said, feeling sad that his training was cut short.

Jarreth and Finnick made their way over to the food tent, meeting up with Nikolai, Juliet, and Omari along the way. When they arrived at the food tent, they all went inside and sat down at the tables provided.

"Evening everyone. This is Chase, and Captain Erick," Oberon introduced. "Chase, Captain Erick, this is King Nikolai, Queen Juliet, and Prince Omari. And you already know Finnick, Jarreth and Princess Iris."

Oberon sat down at the table with the others.

"Now that introductions are out of the way, let's speak of the battle plan," Oberon voiced. "We will start by going in the back way to the kingdom. Stealth is our strength. We must not let Jorogumo know we are there until the last minute. Once we are at the palace doors, we go in slowly and carefully, then attack. Queen Juliet and Chase, your job is to find any survivors and get them out. Jarreth, Princess Iris, Prince Omari and Finnick, your job is to fight Jorogumo's big guard spiders. You need to get them distracted while King Nikolai, myself, and Captain Erick takes on Jorogumo herself. The rest of the soldier's will attack anything that moves that is not human."

Once Oberon had finished explaining, everyone nodded at their assigned roles, to let Oberon know they had understood the assignment.

"Any questions?" Oberon asked the group. "No. Good, we go at dawn tomorrow."

Then Captain Oberon dismissed everyone. Erick was the first to leave the group while the others stayed behind and chatted. Now that he knew the battle plan, he intended to go and tell Jorogumo herself. Back over at the table, Jarreth looked up to find Iris waving for his attention.

"*Do you want to go for a walk?*" Iris asked him.

"*I'd love to,*" Jarreth signed.

They both got up and headed outside. Jarreth followed as Iris lead him to a secluded spot, then sat down on the grass. Jarreth sat down next to her.

"*Is everything ok?*" Jarreth signed, seeing her distress.

"*No. I don't trust Erick. So, Captain Oberon and I came up with a plan, to check if my suspicions are correct,"* Iris signed to Jarreth.

"Ok," Jarreth nodded. *"What's the plan?"*

"The plan is that we come in from the front of the palace, and drop in smoke bombs to draw out Jorogumo's big guard spiders. We'll need Juliet's and your long-distance abilities, to attack and weaken the spiders. Nikolai, Omari, and Juliet will take down one of the spiders, while Captain Oberon, myself, and you will take down another. Finnick will oversee my men, and they will kill the smaller spiders that emerge. Once Jorogumo's big guard spiders are defeated, we all go down into the dungeons, and take out Jorogumo herself, along with any smaller spiders that emerge. We'll then rescue the remaining survivors," Iris explained in sign language.

"Sounds good," Jarreth nodded, signing.

"I need you to tell Finnick the plan, while I tell Juliet. She'll then tell Nikolai. Captain Oberon will tell Omari in private. I've already told Chase as he's currently trailing Erick as we speak," Iris signed.

"I will let Finnick know," Jarreth signed, smiling as he took Iris's hand. *"Try not to stress too much about it."*

Iris smiled, leaning her head on Jarreth's shoulder while holding his hand. "I'll try."

Chapter Forty-One

*"And while they were eating, he said, truly I tell you,
one of you will betray me."*

Matthew 26:21

Erick left the tent quickly and walked out of the campsite. He had to inform Jorogumo about the plan Princess Iris and the other's had plotted against her. He ran through the forest, not caring if Jorogumo's spiders jumped out or not. He had to use this plan to his advantage, to try and steal Princess Iris's Gem for Jorogumo.

Once he entered the kingdom, he continued to run until he got to the palace doors. Only then did he stop to catch his breath.

Chase, who had been following Erick since he left the food tent, watched as Erick went into the palace. Chase continued to follow him. He slowly and quietly followed, opening the palace doors, and standing at the entrance of the dungeons. He hid, not wanting to give away his position, and listened.

Walking down the dungeon steps carefully but quickly, Erick came across one of Jorogumo's big guard spiders. It hissed at him, showing its fangs.

"Woah," he said, holding his hands up. "Just need to speak with your queen."

"Let him through," Erick heard Jorogumo's voice.

The massive spider moved out of the way and back into the corner to hide, while still watching out for its queen. Erick walked down the steps and into the dungeon's main area. Looking around, he saw that King Eros and Queen Athena were still alive. He frowned at them while walking up to Jorogumo, who was talking with a young man.

"Erick, how nice to see you again. What news do you bring?" Jorogumo's cold voice rang.

"Princess Iris has requested help from the King and Queen of Zolatta. They have arrived and have made plans to attack tomorrow at dawn. They plan to come in from the back entrance, then down here to attack," Erick said proudly.

"Well done," Jorogumo said smiling. "We will ambush them once they come into my dungeons."

"No," Queen Athena cried.

"You will never get away with this Erick," King Eros warned.

"I already have," Erick proclaimed.

"My daughter has the God of Light on her side. I have faith in him and my daughter," King Eros said proudly.

"Whatever," Erick replied casually. "What do you want me to do, Jorogumo?"

"Stay the good Captain for now. Tomorrow in the heat of the ambush, steal Princess Iris's Gem for me, and I will end the person called Jarreth," Jorogumo laughed.

"Deal," Erick said, walking out of the dungeons smirking to himself.

✦ ✦ ✦ ✦ ✦

Chase ran out of the palace as soon as he heard footsteps coming from the dungeon steps. He fled into the forest and made his way back to the camp. Anger coursed through him, after finding out what Erick had been up to.

It was treason. And he would pay dearly for it.

Chase started to slow down once he saw the camp within view. Upon arrival he saw Princess Iris and Jarreth walking hand in hand. He waved to them both indicating he had news to share. While waiting for them to arrive, he stood to catch his breath.

"What did you find?" Iris asked concerned.

"Erick has made a deal with Jorogumo," Chase said, catching his breath.

"What!" Iris exclaimed.

"He's made a deal to steal your Gem, Princess. In exchange Jorogumo will kill Jarreth," Chase explained.

Iris squeezed Jarreth's hand in worry and anger. Tears began to run down her cheek, and Jarreth, noticing them, wiped them away.

"First my parents, now you," Iris said, looking up at Jarreth. "Why?"

"*I'm not going anywhere. We have the upper hand in the battle remember,*" Jarreth signed, reminding Iris.

Princess Iris sniffed then nodded. "We do."

"Princess, what do you want us to do about Erick?" Chase asked.

"Do you know which soldiers are loyal to him?" Iris asked.

"I only know of a few men, but there might be more," Chase replied.

"That makes things harder," Iris said. "I don't want us watching our backs during the battle."

"If I may speak freely, Your Highness?" Chase asked.

Princess Iris nodded.

"The men are afraid of Jorogumo. I have heard them talking during meals and training. I don't think they will risk treason, and side with Erick in this situation. I don't think they'll follow him after finding out what he's done," Chase explained.

Iris nodded. "I hope you are right."

"I am," Chase replied.

"Perfect, I'll let the others know of the update," Iris said.

Chase nodded then walked off to prepare for tomorrow's battle.

"I'll go and tell Finnick the update. Make sure someone is always with you," Jarreth signed.

"Thank you," Iris replied.

Jarreth squeezed her hand once more before going to find Finnick, while Iris went to find Juliet.

"Queen Juliet," Iris said, finding the Queen still in the food tent with her husband. "Can I have a word with you privately?"

"Of course. I'll be back," Juliet told her husband, before following Iris out of the tent.

Juliet followed Iris as she led her to her tent. Once inside she sat at the table with Iris, where food was already prepared for them.

"Is everything ok?" Juliet asked.

Iris shook her head and began to explain the update Chase had shared with her, and to tell her of Erick's treason.

✦ ✦ ✦ ✦ ✦

The next morning at the food tent, Princess Iris stood up and announced to her people, the plan of reclaiming their home.

"Today with the help of the King and Queen of Zolatta and their friends, we will take back our kingdom from Jorogumo and her minions," Iris declared.

The whole food tent erupted into cheers, as her people clapped and cried with happiness, feeling relieved to be able to go back home. Lucas went up to Jarreth and sat down next to him.

"Can I fight as well?" Lucas asked.

"That's up to Princess Iris to decide," Jarreth signed. *"Your knife throwing is really good. But can you do it in battle, when you must make quick decisions. Plus, your still learning archery."*

"I guess I'm not ready after all," Lucas said pouting.

"We'll start with an easy mission, not war," Jarreth promised.

"Deal," Lucas said feeling better.

"You ready Jarreth?" Finnick asked.

Jarreth nodded, then stood up to follow after Finnick. They walked to the edge of the camp, just before the forest started, in the direction of the kingdom. Soldiers who were loyal to the crown stood with their weapons ready. Jarreth saw Captain Oberon talking with Nikolai, Juliet, Omari, and Iris. After he finished speaking to them, he turned to address the crowd.

"Today we fight for your home. To take it back from Jorogumo and her minions. I know many of you have lost loved ones, family, and friends. So today we fight for them, and for the people back at camp. Some of you may not make it back today. But you will fight with honor for your home, and for the crown," Captain Oberon yelled, striking the air with a clenched fist.

"For the crown," Captain Erick yelled to his men.

"For the crown," they all yelled back.

Oberon then turned around and began leading the army into the forest. Jarreth and Finnick ran up to their Captain, and ran beside him while they talked.

"Finnick, eyes on Jarreth and Princess Iris. You know they're both targets now," Oberon whispered, so only his lieutenants heard.

"Yes sir," Finnick replied seriously.

They all continued to run through the forest, while being on the lookout for Jorogumo's minions that lurked within. The closer they got to the Kingdom of Kudzu, the more they saw and heard soldiers eliminating Jorogumo's small to medium sized spiders. Finnick heard a yelp behind him and turned to find a medium sized spider attached to a soldier's face. He grabbed it off, and threw it to the ground. He then brought his axe down on top of the creature, killing it instantly.

"Thanks," the soldier said shaking.

"Eye's on the enemy," Finnick reminded him, before running off to help another soldier.

"Keep moving," Oberon yelled to the men.

They pushed on until they reached the outskirts of the Kingdom of Kudzu. Only then did they stop to rest, and regroup after the small attack.

Thankfully no one was missing.

Captain Oberon continued towards the kingdom, with the soldiers from Kudzu following behind. After seeing the kingdom up close, Oberon heard a few gasps and murmurs from the men. This would be the first time they saw their home in ruins, after fleeing from it a few months back.

Oberon slowed to a walk just as they entered the kingdom, and unsheathed his broadsword. Everyone kept on the lookout for the enemy.

"Excuse me, Captain Oberon," Erick said, running up to walk beside Oberon.

"What is it?" Oberon asked, keeping a lookout, as they slowly made their way closer to the palace.

"I thought the plan was to come in from the back?" Erick said, with a note of panic in his voice.

"Change of plans. Didn't anyone tell you?" Captain Oberon said casually.

"No, they did not. I'm the Captain, and this is unacceptable," Erick continued. "We should really stick with the previous plan and enter from the back."

"Not happening," Oberon said, coming to a stop and turning around.

"Finnick," Oberon called.

"Here Captain," Finnick replied, running up to him.

"Remember the plan," Oberon said, giving his Lieutenant the smoke bomb.

"Yes sir," Finnick replied nodding.

Finnick ran ahead to the palace doors and slowly opened them. He crept inside quickly and quietly.

"That's not right," Finnick expressed with disgust, seeing the multiple sizes of spiders that hung casually on the palace walls.

He cautiously walked past them and stood at the opening to the dungeons, holding onto the smoke bomb. He heard movement down below. Quickly he undid the cap to the smoke bomb, and threw it down into the dungeons, running back outside quickly. The minute he got outside, he heard the smoke bomb go off inside the dungeons.

"Look alive men," Oberon announced, seeing smoke seep out of the palace doors.

Nikolai, who stood behind Oberon, unsheathed his sword, and readied himself. Juliet, who had Nix by her side, was ready to summon the earth around her. Omari who wore his gauntlets, stood ready, waiting for the attack to start. Oberon had his broadsword out as he moved over to join Jarreth, who had his bow and arrow ready, while standing next to Iris who had taken on the abilities of a tiger. Finnick came up with his axe in hand, as he stood in front of Princess Iris's men, ready to lead them.

There were sounds of screeching and heavy movements coming from the palace. Then a massive spider crawled out and came to a stop not far from them, with its two front legs in the air ready to attack. It hissed at the men, showing its sharp fangs.

"Group one, ready?" Captain Oberon yelled.

"Ready," Nikolai yelled, leading his team.

Nikolai, Juliet, Nix and Omari ran up and intersected the spider, before it crawled back inside the palace.

"Group two, ready?" Captain Oberon yelled.

"Ready," Iris yelled with Jarreth nodding beside her.

"I'll leave the rest to you Finnick," Captain Oberon said, running after his group.

"Yes sir," Finnick replied, turning back to the men of Kudzu. "Your job is to eliminate any of the smaller spiders. You leave the big ones for the others. Understood."

"Yes sir," the men replied, with their weapons raised.

Juliet used her emerald Gem to summon vines that wrapped around the spider's legs, preventing it from escaping. Omari came from the side and used his strength to punch the massive spider, smashing it into a wall. Nikolai then ran up to the spider, with his sword flaming, and stabbed the massive spider multiple times.

"I don't think you stabbed it enough," Omari joked, as he and Juliet came and stood next to Nikolai.

"Nah I don't think so either," Nikolai replied, grinning at Omari's joke.

The three of them stood watching the massive spider, as its legs curled up around its body and died.

Nix barked from behind them.

"Watch out guys," Juliet said, looking behind them.

"Oh great," Omari said. "There's more of them."

Another massive spider came thundering out of the palace.

Juliet used her vines to capture and drag it towards her group, and away from Finnick's group, who were fighting the much smaller spiders. Nix, seeing the much smaller spiders over near

Finnick and the solders, ran over and helped disposed of them.

"Ready?" Nikolai asked.

"Ready," Omari answered, bumping his fist together.

Juliet bounded the spider with her vines, causing it to collapse onto the ground. Omari came up and punched the spider into the ground, causing an indentation from the impact. Nikolai saw his chance and came up, piercing his sword into the creature's stomach, killing it instantly.

"How many do you think are down there?" Omari asked, wiping the cobwebs off his body.

"Who knows," Nikolai puffed with exhaustion.

There was a scream behind them, and Nikolai and Omari turned to see that one of the soldiers had multiple spiders on him, as he tried to swat them off. Running over to help, Omari and Nikolai swatted the spiders off and killed them one by one, until the solider was eventually free.

"Are you ok?" Nikolai asked the soldier.

"It bit me," he said, showing Nikolai the bite mark.

The soldier suddenly collapsed to the ground and started violently shaking, while white froth came from his mouth.

"Juliet," Nikolai called.

Juliet came running over and knelt beside the wounded soldier, and began healing him immediately.

"What's wrong with him?" Omari asked confused.

"Turns out the spiders are poisonous. You need to warn everyone," Juliet instructed, looking at both men. "Now."

"Stay and protect your wife. I'll let everyone know," Omari said running off.

On the other side of the battlefield, Jarreth used his bow and arrows to shoot at the incoming spider, while avoiding the webs that were being shot his way. Iris, using her tiger-like abilities, used her speed and sharp claws to weaken the spider, by cutting off its long legs one by one. When the spider finally collapsed, Oberon used his broadsword to pierce it, causing it to die instantly.

"Captain," Omari called, running up to him.

"What's wrong?" Captain Oberon asked.

"Queen Juliet said the spiders are poisonous, so be careful," Omari explained.

"Thanks for the heads up," Iris called out after him.

Omari nodded then ran off to let the others know.

"*Look*," Jarreth signed, pointing behind Captain Oberon.

Oberon, Iris, and Jarreth watched as Erick killed the spiders that came after him, all the while moving closer towards the palace. Erick turned around once the spiders were gone, and smirked at them while saluting them. He was about to head into the dungeons, when Jorogumo emerged from the palace, enraged at the chaos and dead corpses of her kind.

Jorogumo turned and glared at Erick "Traitor."

"No, I-," Erick began, but was cut off when Jorogumo used one of her spider legs to stab Erick in the stomach, lifting him up closer to her face.

"They tricked me," Erick insisted, coughing up blood.

"You should have been a better spy," she hissed, before throwing him to the ground to bleed out.

"How dare you hurt my babies," Jorogumo screamed.

The battlefield went quiet for a moment, as everyone gazed in horror at Jorogumo in her half human-half spider form, for the first time. Many of the men backed away in fear and panic. Jorogumo screamed again, as she shot webs out in all different directions, hitting multiple soldiers at a time.

"How dare you," she screeched, as her big spider legs thundered towards them.

"Change of plans," Captain Oberon said to his team.

Oberon turned his attention to Jorogumo with his weapon

ready. The others came and stood by his side, ready to face the Prince of Darkness's second in command.

Jorogumo raced towards them with such speed, that dust collected behind her. They all scattered around her, cutting off her escape route. Juliet tried to use her vines to hold Jorogumo down, but Jorogumo sliced through her vines using her long fingernails. She turned around and hissed at Jarreth, as he continued to shoot arrows from afar, while the others thought of another plan.

"Any chance you can create a hole for her to fall into?" Finnick joked.

Oberon looked at Finnick seriously, as a plan started to form.

"Sorry sir, bad time for a joke," Finnick apologized.

"No, you may be onto something here," Oberon stated.

"We can create one in the dungeons," Iris suggested. "Then use Prince Omari's strength to put a ton of stone on her, sealing her inside."

"Great idea. Do you know where in the dungeons you want to trap her?" Oberon asked.

"I'll have to look inside first. Since her take over, I'm not sure what she's done to the dungeons," Iris explained.

"We'll keep her distracted here while you and Prince Omari scout the dungeons," Oberon instructed, running up to Jorogumo.

"Ok," Iris and Omari replied, running towards the palace doors.

Nikolai blocked Jorogumo's incoming attack with his sword. Focusing on his topaz Gem, his sword's blade erupted into flames causing Jorogumo to scream and back away. She looked at her burnt hands, anger coursing through her. From the corner of her eye, she saw Iris and Omari running into the palace. Smiling to herself she turned her attention to them.

"Over here," Oberon yelled.

But Jorogumo didn't listen, as her next victims were heading down into the dungeons. Jarreth ran up to Jorogumo and jumped onto her back, plunging his dagger into her shoulder. Jorogumo screamed in pain as she tried to shake off her attacker.

But Jarreth held on.

Jorogumo ran after Iris and Omari while smashing into surrounding walls, trying to shake off Jarreth, but Jarreth wouldn't budge. Coming down into the dungeons, Jorogumo climbed up onto the wall and walked along the ceiling. Jarreth, who couldn't hold on any longer, fell to the ground. Holding onto his bruised arm, Jarreth quickly got up and avoided Jorogumo's spider leg, which attempted to impale him. Both Jorogumo and Jarreth heard a whistle and looked around for the source. Iris and Omari were standing at the back of the dungeons trying to get Jorogumo's attention.

"Over here Jorogumo," Iris called, waving.

Jorogumo ran towards them while shooting her webs at them, missing each time. Jorogumo got angrier and angrier as she continued to chase after Iris. Iris used her tiger speed to dodge Jorogumo, while trying to get the spider demon to turn her back towards the wall, where herself and Omari had laid their trap. Jorogumo shot out her webs and managed to hit Iris, making her fall to the ground, bounded by the cobwebs. Jorogumo ran over to Iris and stood over her, hissing at her captured prey.

"I'll be taking that Gem of yours," Jorogumo snarled, standing over Iris.

Jorogumo reached towards the Gem that was in Iris's crown, on her forehead. Before she could take it, Jarreth came up and sliced Jorogumo's hand clean off. Jorogumo recoiled, screeching in pain.

While Jorogumo was distracted, Omari used his strength to punch her, causing Jorogumo to smash into the wall, and fall into the pit that he and Iris had made beforehand. Jorogumo screeched as she fell into the pit below, her body being impaled on the steel dungeon doors, that Omari had broken off and planted below.

Silence filled the dungeons as Omari sighed with relief.

Turning around Omari noticed prisoners who were still alive, and went over to help them. Jarreth used his dagger to cut the web that was bounding Iris. Once free they both embraced.

"Thank you," Iris said, shivering with fear.

Jarreth broke the hug and looked at Iris with concern, while caressing her face.

"I'm ok," she assured, smiling at him.

Jarreth smiled and nodded.

"Uh guys. There are more spiders coming out of the walls," Omari mentioned, smashing them with his fists.

Iris felt Jarreth suddenly tense and was just about to ask him what was wrong, when he was suddenly thrusted backward. Jorogumo's web was attached to his foot, and he was being dragged backwards into the deep hole where Jorogumo lay dying. Iris ran after Jarreth as he tried to use his dagger, to stop himself from moving any further.

"Jarreth," Iris cried, trying to reach him.

Iris dove towards the ground, just managing to reach Jarreth's hand before he fell into the hole.

"Hold on Jarreth," Iris said, trying to pull him up herself.

Jarreth looked down at the web that was still covering his foot and sighed sadly.

"Prince Omari, a little help here," Iris cried out.

"Hang on, I'm surrounded at the moment," Omari replied, smashing the spiders one by one.

Jarreth looked at Iris sadly, and was about to silently say something to her.

"No, don't," Iris choked, holding back tears.

Iris slid a bit closer to the pit. She reached out behind her to try and find something to hold onto, but there was nothing there.

"Help anyone," Iris cried.

"Hang on, I'm coming," Omari called. "Ouch, it bit me."

Iris looked back toward Jarreth. "Help is coming, just hold on Jarreth."

Jarreth smiled up at her then shook his head sadly, loosening his hold on her.

"Don't Jarreth," Iris cried. "Please, I care about you."

"*I care about you too*," Jarreth mouthed.

Jarreth loosened the grip he had on Iris, and fell into the pit below.

"Nooooooooo," Iris screamed.

CHAPTER FORTY-TWO

*"But if we walk in the light, as he is in the light,
we have fellowship with one another, and the blood of Jesus,
his Son, purifies us from all sin."*

1 John 1:7

Oberon, Nikolai, Juliet, Finnick,and the army from Kudzu, ran down into the dungeons to find Iris sitting on her knees, hugging herself as she cried. Omari was a few feet away laying on the floor shaking, while clutching his arm, as white froth foamed from his mouth. Nix went off and killed the remaining smaller spiders that were still within the dungeons, making sure that none had escaped.

"Your Highness, Omari has been bitten," Captain Oberon informed.

"On it," Juliet replied, rushing to Omari.

"Kill the spiders," Captain Oberon shouted to the men of Kudzu. "Finnick, King Nikolai, cut the survivors down from the wall."

Finnick and Nikolai ran over to help the remaining survivors.

"Princess Iris," Oberon said, kneeling in front of her.

Iris continued to cry.

"Where's Jarreth?" Oberon asked, looking around the room.

Iris pointed to the pit that she and Omari had made for Jorogumo, while she continued to cry. Oberon looked to the Princess, then to the pit with concern. He stood up and walked to the edge of the pit, that was meant for Jorogumo, and looked down. It was too dark to see anything, so he went back to the Princess.

"What happened?" Oberon asked.

"We backed Jorogumo far enough so that when Prince Omari punched her, she would fall into the pit. And it worked, but she took Jarreth with her, using her web. I couldn't save him," Iris cried harder. "I couldn't save him."

Oberon was about to say something when an older women came up to them, kneeling in front of Iris and embraced her.

"Iris my child, I saw the whole thing. It wasn't your fault," the women reassured.

Iris looked up at the women who was hugging her.

"Mother," she cried, hugging her tighter.

"It's ok," Queen Athena soothed. "It's ok."

"Captain," Chase said, coming up to Oberon.

Oberon walked away to give the women their privacy, and went over to Chase.

"Report," Oberon said.

"All the big and medium spiders are all dead or have fled. We are currently opening the cocooned pile to see who's alive. So far, I cannot find King Eros," Chase replied.

"My husband didn't make it," Queen Athena whispered, looking up at the men with tears in her eyes.

"What!" Iris choked, looking at her mother.

Queen Athena nodded while trying to hold back her tears, but they still ran down her cheeks.

"Yesterday after Erick left, Jorogumo poisoned him," Athena's voice broke.

Iris hugged her mother again, as she cried for her father and for Jarreth.

"I'm sorry for your loss," Oberon said to Queen Athena.

"Thank you for coming to help my daughter, and my people, to reclaim our home," Athena cried.

Oberon nodded, then walked away with Chase beside him.

"How's Prince Omari doing?" Oberon asked Juliet.

"The poison has been extracted. He just needs to rest," Juliet advised standing up. "Has anyone else been poisoned and need healing?"

Chase looked at Juliet then Oberon.

"What's wrong?" Juliet asked.

"King Eros was poisoned, but that happened yesterday. Is there any chance he can be saved?" Chase asked.

"I can try, but I can't promise you anything," Juliet said, following Chase to the body.

"Here," Chase said, pointing to the man lying on the ground.

Juliet knelt to the ground and began healing King Eros. After about five minutes of healing, there was still no sign of a heartbeat.

"I'm sorry, but there's nothing else I can do," Juliet said standing up.

"I'm grateful you tried. Thank you, Queen Juliet," Chase replied, turning back towards Queen Athena and Princess Iris.

"Hey," Nikolai said, hugging his wife. "Are you ok?"

"I'm fine now," Juliet replied, embracing her husband.

"Your Highnesses," Oberon said clearing his throat.

Juliet and Nikolai looked at Captain Oberon.

"Jarreth," Oberon sighed heavily. "He didn't make it."

"No," Juliet said sadly "I'm so sorry."

"How are you, Captain? He was your friend and lieutenant,"

Nikolai asked with sympathy.

"He was like a son to me, but I will mourn for him later. Right now, we must help the survivors back to camp," Oberon advised, walking off before Nikolai could say anything else.

Oberon ordered some of the soldiers to take as many survivors as they could, back to camp, while others stayed back to find life amongst the cocooned victims. With each victim they freed from the cocooned webs, the more death they found.

None of them had survived.

But they still brought the bodies back, so the people could give them a proper burial, and closure to their families and friends. The walk back to camp was a slow progress. Soldiers carried the wounded from battle, and people mourned in silence. Others were still on their guard, just in case any spiders who had fled attacked. Juliet and Nikolai walked side by side with Nix trailing behind them. Juliet looked at Princess Iris with worry and sympathy. Jarreth and Iris had gotten close since they came here to help reclaim Iris's kingdom. Losing Jarreth like that, broke everyone who knew him.

"How are you doing Prince Omari?" Juliet asked, as Omari walked up to them.

"I'm ok. I didn't really know Jarreth, but from the short time I did, he was a good friend," Omari replied sadly.

"He was a good soldier to," Nikolai said, sighing as he remembered memories.

"He will be missed by all," Juliet said sympathetically.

Once they all got back to the camp, the villagers clapped and cheered at their victory. Some ran up to soldiers and hugged them, while others looked around at their missing family, friend, or spouse. Queen Athena walked to the front of the crowd and whistled for everyone's attention.

"Can we please get the wounded to the medical tent please, so

Queen Juliet can heal their wounds. All nurses who are available please report to her Highness for instructions, thank you," Queen Athena ordered.

Juliet followed the wounded soldiers to the medical tent, and got straight into healing the most critical. She directed the nurses to attend to all the wounded who had minor injuries, and asked to be notified of the direst ones.

"Your Highness," a nurse said, coming up to Juliet. "There's another soldier who needs your healing."

"Where are they?" Juliet asked.

"Bed three," the nurse replied.

"Of course, I'll be with them in a minute," Juliet replied nodding.

Once Juliet finished healing her current patient, she moved over to bed three. The soldier who was lying on the bed, had spider bite's all over her body.

"Is she going to be ok?" the gentleman asked, holding the soldier's hand.

"I'll do my best," Juliet promised.

Juliet got to work healing the women's multiple spider bites. After using her healing abilities on the women for half an hour, Juliet managed to extract all the poison from her body. Juliet leaned back on the vacant bed behind her, wiping the sweat from her forehead, and sighed.

"Is she ok?" the gentleman asked.

"Yes, all the poison has been extracted. She just needs to rest now," Juliet puffed.

"Thank you, Your Highness," the gentlemen replied.

Juliet smiled. "You're welcome."

Nikolai came up to his wife and put his hand around her waist to support her.

"You need rest," Nikolai said, helping her out of the tent.

Together they walked out of the medical tent and straight over to the food tent, sitting down at the same table as Omari, Oberon and Finnick.

"You ok, Your Highness?" Oberon asked.

"Just a little tired," Juliet replied.

"Healing other people drains her energy," Nikolai explained.

"Strong women," Oberon said, raising his glass at Nikolai.

Nikolai smiled while holding Juliet's hand.

"Here you go Your Highnesses," Dottie said, placing two hot plates of food in front of them. "Thank you for all you've done for us."

"Thank you," Juliet replied.

"Thank you," Nikolai replied.

Queen Athena stood up and tapped her glass gently to get everybody's attention.

"In honour of our fallen friends, family, and spouses, I'd like to make a toast for their sacrifice and bravery in reclaiming our home. They will be missed and loved by all. We pray for the family, friends and spouses who are grieving. I would also like to give my thanks to the King and Queen of Zolatta, and their companions for coming to our aid," Queen Athena declared. "It will be a slow process of recovery for our kingdom, but by working together we can achieve it."

There were cheers, clapping and the clanking of glasses, as the people celebrated their victory.

"I would also like to appoint Chase, as our new Captain of the Royal Guard," Queen Athena declared.

A round of applause erupted amongst the crowd, as Chase held up his glass and smiled. Lucas walked over to the table where Finnick was sitting at with his friends.

"Can I sit with you?" Lucas asked sadly.

"Of course you can, buddy," Finnick replied, moving over to

make room.

"I heard about-," Lucas began, swallowing the lump in his throat, and trying not to cry.

"I know buddy, I know," Finnick replied, patting Lucas on the head.

They all ate their dinner in silence, while listening to the crowd chatter about their victory, and fights against the spiders. Once they had finished eating, the group was so exhausted from the battle and recovery mission, that they all had an early night.

While Juliet lay in her husband's arms, she thought about Iris and her losses.

"Are you ok?" Nikolai asked, kissing his wife's forehead.

"Just thinking about Iris. She's the only one with the amethyst Gem, and I'm not keen on asking her to speak to Amisha while she's mourning. But we also don't know how long we have until the Prince of Darkness starts his war. What do we do?" Juliet asked.

"Pray about it, and we'll think about it in the morning," Nikolai yawned. "It's all we can do now."

Juliet smiled at him, wrapping her arms around him in an embrace, and eventually drifting off to sleep.

✦ ✦ ✦ ✦ ✦

The next day when Juliet woke up, she was surprised to see that Nikolai was already awake smiling at her.

"Morning beautiful," Nikolai greeted.

"Morning. Did you sleep?" Juliet asked.

"I did. Only woke up about half an hour ago," Nikolai replied.

"Are you ready for breakfast?" Juliet asked.

"I am," Nikolai said.

After having a quick wash and getting dressed, Nikolai and

Juliet walked out of their tent, and headed for the food tent. Upon arriving they saw Omari and Captain Oberon standing in the breakfast line. Juliet and Nikolai went to stand in line behind them.

"Morning Captain, morning Prince Omari," Nikolai greeted. "How are you both feeling today?"

"Ok," Oberon replied nodding. "And you?"

"We're ok," Nikolai replied.

"Bit sore, but fine," Omari yawned.

"Did you get healed by Juliet?" Nikolai asked.

"Yes, thank you," Omari replied.

Finnick came up behind Juliet and Nikolai, yawning.

"Captain. Your Highnesses," Finnick greeted groggily.

"How are you feeling, Finnick?" Juliet asked worried.

"Yeh, ok," Finnick replied, shrugging his shoulders.

"I'm sorry, Finnick," Juliet said sympathetically.

"Thanks, Your Highness," Finnick replied sadly.

"Next please," Dottie called, from behind the food table.

Nikolai and Juliet walked up and took a plate to Dottie.

"Your Highness, I'm sorry for your loss. Jarreth was a great young fellow," Dottie expressed.

"Thank you, he was," Nikolai said.

"Thank you," Juliet said, as Dottie filled their plates up.

Nikolai and Juliet walked over and sat at one of the tables. There were lots of talk amongst the soldiers and villagers, about the battle yesterday. Stories were being told and acted out, as villagers and soldiers laughed amongst each other. Juliet looked around the room for Iris and her mother. She saw Queen Athena seated at a table, talking with the elders and Chase, but Iris was nowhere to be found.

"Are you ok?" Nikolai asked his wife.

"I can't see Princess Iris anywhere. I'm worried about her,"

Juliet replied looking around.

"Dottie said she was eating her breakfast in her tent," Finnick notified, overhearing their conversation.

He sat down next to Nikolai and sighed.

"Can I sit here please?" Lucas asked.

"Sure, take a seat anywhere," Nikolai said smiling.

Lucas took a seat next to Finnick and dug into his food.

"So, what's our next plan?" Oberon asked Nikolai, sitting down.

Nikolai sighed.

"I think it would be best to ask Queen Athena to speak to Amisha, as time is of the essence. We don't know when the Prince of Darkness will attack," Nikolai instructed.

"I think that is wise," Oberon replied nodding.

"Queen Athena doesn't have her amethyst Gem anymore," Lucas chimed into the conversation.

"What happened to it?" Juliet asked.

Lucas shrugged. "I just noticed this morning that she wasn't wearing it, and the royals always wear it."

"We'll have to ask her after breakfast," Nikolai said. "Then we'll have to continue on with our quest."

After breakfast Nikolai, Juliet, Oberon, Omari and Finnick went over to Queen Athena, hoping to speak with her.

"Queen Athena, can we have a word with you please?" Nikolai asked.

"Of course," Queen Athena replied, gesturing for them to sit at her table. "What can I do for you?"

"We are on a quest to find the crystal Gem. It's known to be the Prince of Darkness's weakness, but only Amisha, our alicorn knows it's location. We were hoping you could ask her for the location." Nikolai explained.

"It's good to know that the Prince of Darkness has a weakness, but I'm sorry I cannot help you. When my husband and I were captured by Jorogumo, we destroyed our Gem's, to prevent Jorogumo from using them for evil," Queen Athena replied sadly.

"No need to apologize. You did what you had to do," Juliet said with sympathy.

"Have you asked my daughter?" Queen Athena asked.

"No. We weren't sure if she would be up to the task, after losing both her father and Jarreth," Nikolai said.

Queen Athena nodded. "I'll talk to her."

"Thank you," Juliet replied with a smile.

While Queen Athena went to see her daughter, Juliet and the others went to prepare for their departure.

Amisha neighed at the sight of Juliet, lowering her head for a pat.

"Hey Amisha," Juliet greeted with a smile, patting her head.

Amisha sniffed at Juliet's hand, trying to find the source of the food.

"Here you go," Juliet laughed, giving her a carrot.

She stroked Amisha's mane and smiled.

"She's gorgeous," Iris exclaimed.

Juliet turned around to see Iris standing behind her, looking tired and worn down, but smiling anyways.

Juliet went up and hugged Iris.

"I'm so sorry," Juliet whispered.

Iris broke down in tears and hugged Juliet back. "Thanks."

Oberon, Finnick, Omari and Nikolai watched with sympathy and sadness.

"I didn't even get to tell him how much I cared for him," Iris cried.

"He knew," Finnick said, his voice breaking.

"What?" Iris asked.

"Jarreth was so happy after he met you. He wasn't very

talkative even through sign language, but you could tell he was happy," Finnick said wiping his eyes.

"Really?" Iris said hopeful.

"What the lad says is true. I've never seen Jarreth as happy as he was, until he met you," Oberon explained. "He knew."

"Thank you. I really needed to hear that," Iris sniffled. "My mother said you needed my help with Amisha. Something about the location of the crystal Gem."

"Yes please, it would be a great help," Juliet said.

"Hi Amisha, my name is Iris," she greeted the alicorn.

Amisha neighed at Iris.

Iris chuckled. "Before she tells me the location, she wants Juliet to know that she loves you, and you are a great owner."

"Awe, I love you to," Juliet said, patting Amisha's head.

Amisha neighed again as Iris listened.

"In the sun mountain you will find,
a mythical race of my kind.
Across the bridge is a waterfall,
don't look down as it's quite a fall.
Behind the fall is a door of thorns,
the only way to remove it, is with a horn.
Once inside find a door with fauna,
there you will find the Cave of Lumina," Iris interpreted.

"Any ideas?" Nikolai asked everyone.

Juliet thought for a minute as she pondered over the riddle.

"I think the riddle refers to Mount Solana, as the sun mountain," Juliet responded. "Because Solana mean sun."

"Mount Solana is only a day's ride from here," Iris advised, pointing towards its direction.

"Thank the God of Light," Omari said embarrassed. "I'm still not used to being on a horse for so long."

"You know you don't have to ride if you don't want to," Nikolai pointed out.

"I can't exactly keep up on foot," Omari replied confused.

"I wasn't referring to you walking," Nikolai hinted.

Omari thought for a second, then looked at Nikolai in shock.

"I don't want to frighten anyone, so I'll stick to riding," Omari said sheepishly.

"I highly doubt you can frighten me," Finnick said with confidence.

"If you feel more comfortable flying, then fly," Oberon said shrugging.

"I've been in my Fox spirit form in front of Juliet many times, and she was never scared," Nikolai said smiling at his wife.

"Am I missing something here?" Iris asked confused.

"Nikolai was cursed as a child by the Prince of Darkness, which enabled him to transform into a fox spirit," Juliet explained. "But he found out who cursed him. She eventually changed sides and helped us. In the end she sacrificed herself to save me, resulting in Nikolai being free from his curse."

"But before she passed, she told us of another person out there just like me. Turns out it was Prince Omari, who can transform into a griffin," Nikolai explained.

"That's so cool," Iris said interested. "Imagine the abilities I could get from a griffin, alicorn or even Nix, by using my Gem's ability."

"That would be awesome," Juliet said smiling at Iris.

"Well, if you're all ok with my griffin form, then I'll fly. It's much easier than riding anyways," Omari said pleased.

"Great, we'll leave first thing in the morning," Nikolai announced to the group. "To Mount Solana, to find the Prince of Darkness's weakness. We managed to have victory over Jorogumo and her minions, but the biggest threat is yet to come."

✦ ✦ ✦ ✦ ✦

It was dark and dusty, deep in the dungeons below the Kingdom of Kudzu, and something stirred from the pit below. A light shone within the dungeons and glided into the pit, revealing Jorogumo's dead body. The light stayed near the spider's body, to check to see if there were any signs of life. When the light couldn't see any, it moved over to the next victim.

A body lay still on the ground a few meters away. The light went over to the body and checked for a pulse. It was there, but only just. The light began to change into a person, then immediately began healing the young man. The young man opened his eyes and stared into the light.

"Don't worry Jarreth, you're going to be fine. My name is Malachi, and I'm here to help you," the angel whispered smiling.

Character Index

King Nikolai - King of Zolatta. Wife is Juliet. Wields a sword which holds the topaz Gem. Sword can wield fire with Gem in hilt.

Queen Juliet - Queen of Zolatta. Husband is Nikolai. Holds the sapphire Gem which enables her to heal. Mother is Queen Julia.

Queen Julia - Queen of Elaxon. Daughter is Juliet.

Captain Issac - Captain of the Royal Guard from the Kingdom of Elaxon.

Theo - King's adviser and friend. Brother to Fitzwilliam. Lives in the Kingdom of Zolatta.

Fitzwilliam - Work's as a blacksmith and spy for the King. Theo's brother who lives in the Kingdom of Zolatta.

Priest Phil - Priest of the church from the Kingdom of Zolatta.

Grace - Queen Juliet's maid.

Ruth - Queen Juliet's maid.

Oberon - Captain of the Royal Guard from the Kingdom of Zolatta.

Finnick - 1st Lieutenant from the Kingdom of Zolatta, son to Lord Hain.

Lord Hain - Lord of Silverwood, father to Finnick.

Jarreth - 2nd Lieutenant from the Kingdom of Zolatta. Is Mute.

Princess Iris - Princess of Kudzu. Holds the amethyst Gem. Can understand animals, and use their abilities because of her Gem.

Prince Omari - Prince of Neylon. Holds the ruby Gem. Father is King Jabari and Mother Queen Nala.

King Jabari - King of Neylon. Wife is Nala and Son is Omari.

Queen Nala - Husband is Jabari. Son is Omari.

Nix - White wolf that Nikolai saves.
Nix becomes loyal to Nikolai and Juliet.

Prince of Darkness - Evil being that was imprisoned by the God of Light. Manipulates and experiments on his followers. Also known as the Dark One, or Dark Master.

The God of Light - Good being that spreads love and peace. Protects from the evil one.

Matthew - Blacksmith from the Kingdom of Elaxon, cousin to Theo and Fitzwilliam who resides in Zolatta.

King Harold - King of Zolatta. Nikolai's father.

Priest John - Priest from the Kingdom of Elaxon.

Selina - Serves the Dark One. Can shapeshift into a wolf.

Harkin - Serves the Dark One. Has bat wings and other abilities of a bat. Dark One experimented on him.

Tanakh - Hebrew word meaning Bible.

Jorogumo - Serves the Dark One. Is a spider demon. Takes over the Kingdom of Kudzu.

Erick - Captain of the Royal Guard from the Kingdom of Kudzu. Betrays Princess Iris.

Lucas - Young boy from Kingdom of Kudzu, that Jarreth trains to fight.

Kirsten - Captain of the Royal Guard for the Kingdom of Neylon.

Ethan - 1st Lieutenant from the Kingdom of Neylon.

Claud - Serves the Dark One. Can transform into a wolf.

Amisha - Alicorn. Half pegasus and half unicorn. Belongs to Juliet. White mare, with white wings and a golden horn. Mane and tail is white with bits of gold.

Dottie - Elderly women from Kudzu. Is like an aunt to Lucas after his parents passed.

Akuma - Cave where the Prince of Darkness and his followers reside.

Nell - Owner of the Crowned Fox inn. Resides in the Kingdom of Zolatta.

Lord Blackstone - Lord of Ashmore. A noble in the Kingdom of Zolatta. Loyal to the King.

Lacy - Juliet's childhood friend who lives and owns a bakery, in the Kingdom of Elaxon.

Levi - Nikolai's man servant/valet.

King Eros - King of the Kingdom of Kudzu. Wife is Queen Athena. Daughter is Princess Iris.

Queen Athena - Queen of the Kingdom of Kudzu. Husband is King Eros. Daughter is Princess Iris.

Edith - Princess Iris's maid.

Serpentina - A follower of the Prince of Darkness. Can transform into a basilisk.

Chase - A solider from the Kingdom of Kudzu. Is a spy for Princess Iris.

Anna - A follower of the Prince of Darkness. Can transform into an anaconda.

About the Author

My name is Lucy. I started writing when I was in high school and loved it. I haven't chosen a particular genre that I like to write about, as I'm still new at writing. But I would love to explore all genres in the future.

I also love to read books in my spare time. I can go from reading Disney one day, to horror the next, so I'm keen to give almost any book a go.

I live on the Sunshine Coast in Australia and love it. I love going for walks along the beach, and rainforest walks. This gives me time to think of good book ideas, and to be with my family and friends at the same time.

I'm a Christian who loves God, and goes to church. What I love about my church is that the people there are all so kind and welcoming. We also love to help our community. I also work part-time as a carer in aged care, as I love to help people.

Author's Notes & Acknowledgements

Hi everyone. Thank you for taking the time to read my novel. I am so happy that I was able to publish this book.

The Gems of Destiny is a work of fiction. Any names of places mentioned in this book are all fictional.

I would like to acknowledge my sister Larissa, for giving me advice for my book, editing, and proofreading it for me. For also helping me along the way during the editing, proofreading, and publishing journey.

I would like to acknowledge Kelly, a good friend of mine. She helped me with choosing some of the creatures that are mentioned in my book. Thank you for lending me your books on mythological creatures.

I would like to acknowledge Isis, another friend of mine. She was the person who named King Nikolai and Mildred. She also created the characters, Captain Oberon, Finnick and Jarreth, their personalities, and their weapons. I'm glad she did, as I had so much fun writing about these three characters, and their strong bond that they have.

I would also like to acknowledge Jendy and Pastor Phil, who serve at Hope Community Church on the Sunshine Coast. Thank you for all the biblical references, ideas, and advice throughout the book process. Thank you for the constant prayer. God knows I needed it.

I would like to acknowledge my other sister Luana, for giving me some good names for my characters, and for also being supportive of my book writing process.

I would like to acknowledge a friend from church, Eli. All the dad jokes and Finnick's humour were inspired by him. Thanks for making us laugh with all your jokes.

I would like to thank The Book Studio in Bli Bli, for helping me throughout my publishing journey.

For those of you who loved this book and would like to see more of this universe, and its characters, let me know on Instagram or Facebook. I can happily say this will be a small series.